BURNING STONES

BURNING STONES

STEVEN MILLS

COSMOS BOOKS

BURNING STONES

Cosmos Books
www.cosmos-books.com

CHAPTER 1

The Perseids meteor shower belonged to Alex Gauthier and his daughter, Gemma. Ever since Gemma was eight years old Alex made sure they were camped out under the stars for at least one night of momentous meteor viewing every August. And he wasn't going to let this year be any goddamn different.

He climbed the hill to the dried-up hay field where they'd set up the fire camp. At the top of the hill high above the Slocan River a bench of land spread away from him to the north. Tents and old trucks and all the detritus of a makeshift camp—boards for tables, rounds of wood for chairs, rickety-walled outhouses on the perimeter—were scattered over the dust and dried humps of grass. Dirt and ash buffeted him. This wind, this bastard child of the forest fire that ate up the valley behind him, blew hot and furious, as the fire pulled in fresh oxygen. He shielded his eyes with his arm and rummaged around the camp until he found Mickey Evdikimoff, Winlaw's fire chief, crouching down in the lee of his pickup, drawing in the dust with a screwdriver.

Mickey looked up as Alex approached, mopped his face with a shirtsleeve. "We got half-a-dozen new fires, serious fires, last night with the lightning storm," he said as he pointed at several circles he'd drawn on the ground. "If this one here comes up this watershed"—he jabbed at the ground with the screwdriver—"it'll end up behind the firebreak. We'll have to pull back and start all over again."

"That's just great," Alex said, annoyance flashing through his fatigue. A week of camping out in an old industrial ambulance with his sleep fractured by nightmares, a week of firefighting, of tending the blisters and burns and heat exhaustion of those able-bodied enough to still firefight had incinerated what little patience Alex had left.

He glanced over his shoulder. The valley was narrow, running mostly north-south, and was walled in with steep treed ridges. The skinny valley bottom was mostly wasting river paralleled by a dilapidated two-lane highway and dotted with houses and small farms that sometimes clotted together into communities. Most of the houses had been abandoned. The fire, like a virus that leaps from person to person, household to household, had eaten up the south end of the valley, devouring this barn, then that house, this copse of trees, then flashed up that slope to those houses. Now it was making its way along the mountain slopes on both sides of the river, leaping from tree to tree to tree, all the while hurling smoke into the air and pouring a bone-colored ash down on them as if consecrating their bodies for the hereafter.

Alex crouched as if to study Mickey's dirt map. His thighs stabbed with pain in protest. Fighting fires was a young person's game—way too hard on a guy staring down the barrel of fifty—but the dearth of people hadn't left the rest of them much choice. He looked at Mickey. "I say we cut our losses, retreat up the valley and backburn. Fight fire with fire."

Mickey grunted. "Backburning's tricky business, Al. Especially with things this dry. Wind turns at the wrong moment . . . "

"Yeah, yeah. I know. I'm just fed up." He licked his lips, tasted ash. "I need to go home, Mick. Promised Gemma I'd be back by now."

Mickey didn't even take his eyes off the ground. "You can take my truck. I'm sure Willow'll cover for you."

Alex squinted at the fire chief, who normally would have put up at least a half-assed fight. Mickey's gray hair flopped and twisted in the hot wind.

"I need someone to go north, anyway," Mickey added, which explained why he hadn't made a fuss. "To New Denver, maybe further. We need a fallback position, somewhere to evacuate to if we can't get this bitch contained. I've already got the folks half-way to Winlaw on twenty-four-hour evacuation notice."

"Can't you find someone else?"

"I need someone who still has all his smarts, someone who knows what we'll need when the shit hits the fan."

"When? Not if?"

Mickey coughed, spat into the dust. "Take my brother with you. Get him out of my hair for a while. He's pissing too many people off."

"Ah, jeez, Mick, I just want to go home. Spend some time with Gemma. Maybe . . . " Alex's voice skidded to a standstill. "Christ. All right. Jesus, if it's not one thing, it's another."

Mickey shrugged with one shoulder, jutted his jaw in the direction of the fire. "Shit, Al, everybody's getting tired. We all got better things to do, especially with winter coming, but if we don't beat this fire . . . We got no choppers, no water bombers, and no RAP attack crew dropping out of the sky at the eleventh hour to save our asses—hell, we barely got enough fuel to keep the equipment we do have running."

"We're not going to win this one, are we?"

"I don't think so. Not without rain in biblical proportions." Mickey straightened up, pushed his glasses up on his nose. "Keys are in the ignition." He slapped dust off his jeans with a hand. "You'll take Yuri?"

Alex nodded even though he wasn't the least bit interested in babysitting Mickey's alcoholic kid brother. Maybe he could find someone else to join them, kind of water down Yuri's personality. It'd probably just be for a few days anyway.

He'd barely see Gemma, though. They'd have one night, maybe two, to lie out on the deck in their sleeping bags and watch for tiny stones burning through the atmosphere. *Fireworks*, she used to call them: the Perseids meteor shower, the burning tears of St. Lawrence.

There would probably be too much damn smoke so see anything anyway.

Gemma was twenty-one years old already, and it seemed as though her life was flashing before his eyes, arcing brightly across the night sky, too soon gone, only the retinal afterimage of her lingering until that too vanished, filled in with the night's darkness.

Alex took a deep breath, straightened with a groan, and climbed into the driver's seat of Mickey's four-door pickup. "Thanks, Mick. I'll grab my stuff then round up Yuri."

"Don't stay away too long."

After handing Mickey his pack and some locked-open e-scroll maps he let rattle around in the back seat, Alex fired up the motor and headed off between the sundry tents toward the highway. In the rearview mirror he saw Mickey pull something from his shirt pocket and hold it up to his mouth. His Nitro. Alex shook his head. *You stubborn ass,* he thought, *you were having chest pain the whole time you were talking to me, weren't you?*

He bounced the pickup south along the highway, the frost heaves and potholes rattling the dust and ash off the truck. Spotted knapweed, plantain and dandelion invaded the cracks in the asphalt. A couple of years without maintenance took its toll on a low priority highway like this one. Alex pulled up beside the ambulance, which sat in the driveway of an abandoned farmhouse where the rag-tag fire crews mustered and checked their equipment every morning. Willow was reluctant about being the only paramedic left at the fire, but agreed to hold down the fort until he got back or sent a replacement. Mickey had put Yuri in charge of tool maintenance to keep him away from the other crews so Alex had no trouble finding him out behind the farmhouse overhauling a chainsaw.

"But who's going to look after the equipment?" Yuri argued, his face flaring red. Alex was used to Yuri's petulance and self-importance, and tried not to be irritated. Yuri rubbed grease off his hands with a rag.

"He just told me to take you with me to New Denver."

"That's bullshit, there's way too much to be done here."

Alex shrugged noncommittally. "I'm just telling you what he said."

"We'll see."

"Take his truck," Alex said, and threw him the keys.

Yuri gunned the engine and the truck shot away, spewing stones and dust back at Alex. "Asshole," Alex muttered as he turned and headed back to the ambulance.

Yuri drove them north from the fire camp toward Winlaw, pounding the pickup over the disintegrating highway, passing abandoned, weatherworn homes, eerily dark, their dirty blinds rattling in protest through broken windows. Alex sat in the passenger seat, firmly strapped in with the four-point. He'd wanted to scribble in his journal, a beaten-up lined notebook he carried with him everywhere, but the ride was so rough there was no point.

"Slow down, for Christ's sake," he said finally.

Yuri simply grunted, but eased back on the accelerator anyway. Alex felt himself slowly unclench. Hot air blasted in through the open windows, wicking the life right out of him.

"Pack of lucies at two o'clock," Yuri said, pointing through the cracked windshield.

Alex stuffed his notebook in his pack. "Slow right down, Yuri," he said. "I want to get a good look."

"What for? You seen one, you seen 'em all."

Half-a-dozen small brown shapes crouched in a thicket of overgrown raspberries in an abandoned yard by the highway watching the truck with wide eyes. Short legs, body hair, and that particular attitude of the head, sitting on elongated cervical vertebrae, making the face jut forward.

Alex pulled a small DV camera out of his pack as Yuri eased the truck to a standstill. The oldest, an end-stage adolescent female, sixteen or seventeen years old, looking to be six or seven months pregnant, stood and sniffed at the air, a large hand hooded over her eyes. She made motions with her other hand and the younger ones crept deeper into the rows of raspberries. Alex panned the camera over the ones disappearing, zooming quickly, looking for telltale clothing, jewelry, scars—anything that might identify them. Four boys, two girls, from five to a dozen years old, all end-stage. He turned the camera back on the adolescent female. She was naked save for a purple fleece jacket, which she wore around her hips like a skirt, sleeves knotted up underneath her round belly. Alex guessed her height at about a meter and a half. Rust-brown hair covered most of her bare chest and arms. Her head-hair, a darker brown, was pulled back into a matted ponytail and tied with a green twist-tie. Dust-brown eyes, closely set. Her nostrils, like two cave openings, flared as she sniffed the smoky air. She bared her teeth and jutted her jaw in the direction of the truck.

Alex braced his elbows on the door, shot her carefully. He didn't recognize her, but she wore earrings, small amber studs with silver settings. She backed away, turned and vanished amongst the raspberry canes.

"Why do you bother with this bullshit?" Yuri said. "We can't do anything for them. It's better we don't know who they are. When they're that far gone, they're hard to tell apart anyway. And shit, that jacket she was wearing probably isn't even hers. Probably found it in one of the abandoned houses. Just let them be." Yuri shrugged for effect, then dropped back into his seat as if bored, elbow hanging out the open window.

When he got to Winlaw, Alex would download the DV onto the e-scroll at the school, post a close-up in hardcopy with all the other ones on the bulletin board. "Somebody might recognize those earrings," he said, not willing to let it go.

"So what if they do," Yuri muttered. "They're as good as dead anyway."

"But her parents might not be." Alex was unable to keep the snide edge off his voice. "And maybe they'd like to know she's okay." He couldn't help but think, *Unlike you, Yuri.*

"If you can call being like that 'okay,'" Yuri shot back.

"It's going to happen to all of us, even you, Yuri."

"Uh-uh," Yuri said. He pointed an index finger at his temple, pulled an invisible trigger, jerked his head.

Alex jumped, his heart stuttering. "Oh, for crying out loud."

"If that's what it comes down to, yeah. I'm not turning into a fucking monkey. Bad enough it's happening to my kid; it's not going to happen to me."

Alex lolled his head back. "You're not going to shoot yourself, Yuri. Jesus God Almighty."

"And you're just going to let yourself turn into one of those?" Yuri said. "So you can run around the woods bare-ass naked and eat goddamn caterpillars and grubs?"

"They'll find a cure," Alex said, although he didn't believe it himself, had never believed it.

"Bull-fucking-shit they will. They can't even fix the bloody highway. Or make the goddamn phones work. And you still think there's someone sitting in a lab somewhere busily whipping up a cure? And even if they did find a cure, it'd never get to *us*."

Alex panned the camera over the raspberry canes again. One of the brown shapes hadn't moved, wasn't moving. He slipped the camera into his pack and opened the truck door.

"What are you doing?"

"There's one on the ground. I think it's injured."

"Injured?"

Alex scrabbled down the bank and up the other side of the dusty ditch. The brown shape still hadn't moved. He couldn't tell from here if it was breathing or not.

Yuri came up behind him. "What are you going to kill it with?"

"Jesus, Yuri."

"Well?"

Alex pushed through the prickly overgrown canes until he crouched beside the bloating body. A boy, maybe six years old, naked with thick hair covering his arms and legs, heavy jawed with a prominent brow ridge. There were no signs of trauma. He'd been coughing up rusty looking phlegm just before he'd died. Probably pneumonia, which was no surprise. Sometimes, out of the blue, the alveoli in the lungs would just start to lose their elasticity—pretty common complication. Probably died early that morning.

Alex backed out of the raspberry thicket, canes breaking under his boots like hollow bones.

They climbed back into the truck. Yuri kicked off the brake and the truck leapt forward.Alex felt suddenly cold despite the furnace air whipping in the open windows. His heart chattered like an automatic weapon. No matter how hard he tried, he couldn't escape it: that little brown shape, bloated with death in a row of forgotten raspberry canes, was the future. He cared nothing for his own future, it was Gemma's he feared.

CHAPTER 2

The sky was a jabber of stars. Alex pulled his sleeping bag up over his arms. It was well after midnight and the August night air already had the bite of Fall to it. Gemma lay on her thermarest beside him, with Coyote, her elderly Husky-Shepherd cross, snuggled against her, and her feet—her "hobbit feet" as she called them, the toes long and thin, the tops "disgustingly hairy"—dutifully pointed northeast, the primo direction for optimal meteor viewing. The valleys in the Selkirk Mountains of southeastern British Columbia were long and narrow, however, and therefore not the best venues for meteor viewing, especially if one was hoping to see a lot of Earthgrazers, the especially bright meteors that zipped across the sky just above the horizon. Usually, Alex and Gemma would hike to the top of the ridge behind their house or camp up in the mountains to get a wider view of the sky, but Alex was simply too tired and stiff to bother making the trek.

Alex nodded up at the sky. "See," he said, "I told you it would clear up just for us."

"The universe doesn't work that way, Dad, in case you haven't noticed."

This was the time when there were to be no walls between them: what needed to be said was to be said. That was the deal they'd made when Gemma was eight years old, the summer she'd come to live with him full-time, when his ex-wife's ovarian cancer started to eat her alive. Somehow, in the dark under the sweep of stars, it seemed easier to talk. They'd exchange gossip, Gemma would announce her dreams, her new career paths, and sometimes, at least when she was younger, her latest crushes. He'd try to answer all her questions with as much honesty as he could muster. *Why did you and mom get divorced? How come we can't cure cancer yet? Will I get cancer, too, like Mom? Are you going to die?*

"It's cleared up every single year for us," he insisted.

She was shaking her head. "I'm positive we missed one year, Dad, 'cause of rain," she said.

"When? *I'm* positive we haven't missed a single year."

"Well, when we hiked to the top of Mt. Lucifer, remember? It rained buckets."

He vaguely recalled an onslaught against the tent fly as they half-heartedly discussed whether they'd brave one more day in the sodden, socked-in mountains of Valhalla Provincial Park to maybe catch the tail end of the meteor shower.

"Okay, so we missed it once. You're right."

"Don't sound so surprised. Of course I'm right."

He snorted.

He'd been startled at the sight of his daughter this afternoon when she met him at the top of the long gravel driveway to their house. He'd been away only a week, yet her lower jaw seemed larger, squarer, and her brow ridge protruded even further, hooding her eyes, dropping them deeper into her skull, while her upper chest seemed substantially narrower. And he swore that the weakness on her left side was more pronounced. Maybe she'd had another small stroke while he'd been gone and simply hasn't said anything. It had been three months since her last stroke, her third, so it was unlikely she would regain full use of her arm and leg despite regular physiotherapy treatments with Marika. He had struggled to hide his alarm, and she seemed to be doing the same—he knew he'd lost more weight—by grinning at him and throwing herself in his arms while Coyote barked at them.

Gemma coughed, startling him. She had picked up a respiratory tract infection—all the smoke hadn't helped—while he'd been away. She'd done the right thing, though, gone over to the elementary school across the river where they'd set up the makeshift hospital, and gotten antibiotics. The amoxicillin seemed to be doing the trick.

"Why can't you ever say no, Dad?" she said. "You could barely walk when you got home today you were so tired. And then you hobbled around the house like you were eighty years old. Why can't someone else go?"

He didn't have the heart to tell her what Mickey had said, that Alex needed to go because he still had his smarts. *Unlike a lot of other people*, Mickey had implied. But he was still kicking himself for agreeing.

"It's not that I'm complaining about doing all the damn work around here," Gemma said with a toss of her head that he assumed encompassed the house and the garden and the chicken coop, "but I *am* doing all the damn work around here. And there's a lot to do before winter comes. And besides"—she gave him a sidelong look, her face strangely pale in the starlight—"saying no once in a while wouldn't kill you, you know. It might force someone else to step up and pitch in for a change."

They'd had this argument a hundred times before. "I already said I'd go. It'll only be for a few days."

She huffed.

Irritation flared in him, kindling a sudden, fierce anger. That dismissive huffing sound, like the grunt of a bear finding a garbage can empty, always annoyed him. He clamped his mouth shut, barricading the anger inside.

His job, not only as a paramedic but also as the Unit Chief of the ambulance service in Winlaw, took up plenty of his time, and yet everywhere he looked he saw more work that needed to be done, more people who needed help, so it never took much convincing to get him to take on additional responsibilities. As a result he hadn't been keeping up with his end of the duties at home. He knew that. Nor had he been spending the time he should with Gemma. He knew that, too.

Lately, though, when he was with Gemma, his emotions seemed too close to the surface, too thinly hidden, like a smoldering hotspot under the duff that could, at any moment, whip up into a fiery maelstrom of grief and despair. It was this fear of losing himself in despair that made him want to wrap his work around himself, made him want to protect himself with busyness, with other people's emergencies and crises, just so that he could be saved from his own. From Gemma's.

A third of the people in the valley had died over the past four years. Another third had fled, overwhelmed by loss, by the threat of summer fires, hoping to track down missing loved ones in the cities, searching for non-existent jobs, for medical care beyond the first aid they could be given here, or simply because they couldn't face yet another sodden, gray winter in this skinny rat-tail of a valley. The pool of human resources simply leaked away. And while the Lucy Syndrome chewed up more and more of the people who remained, the forest fires burned up the rest of their resources, human and otherwise. Sweeping thunderstorms, promising rain but delivering only lightning and fire, had filled most of June and July. Made it seem like the whole world was on fire.

He turned toward Gemma, who was lying on her back, the stars turning her skin deathly white. Alex tried to scatter the dark fear that smothered his weakening hope. "What do you think of staying at Marika and Bill's while I'm gone?" he said.

She rolled onto her side to face him, head propped up on an elbow. "Jeez, Dad, I'm twenty-one. I don't need babysitters."

"Well, Marika's coming with me for a break from Darlene, and Bill was saying he could really use a hand. He says Darlene's so strong now he can't really handle her alone. I talked to him down at the school a bit when I got back."

"What about the chickens and the fruit trees and the garden? Without me and Coyote here, the bears or the packs will just come on in and strip the place clean."

"I get worried about you being here alone so much," he said but regretted it the moment the words were past his teeth.

She simply stared at him.

He tried a different avenue: "Have the packs been coming around much lately?"

"Actually, no."

"Maybe they've moved on."

"Maybe—until word gets out that no one is living here." She lay back down. "And what about getting ready to evacuate? Who's going to pack things up if I'm not here?"

"We can do some of that tomorrow. Mickey said he'd try to give us plenty of warning—if it even comes to that. And besides, you're only going to be a few klicks up the road."

She let out a long breath, clearly deciding not to argue. "Poor Darlene," she said instead.

Alex was glad of the change in topic. "She still seems healthy enough, Bill says. No complications yet."

"Marika says she can hardly talk anymore." The bitterness in her voice chilled him.

"You know what I mean."

"Yeah." A long, sad breath, like wind through broken trees, escaped her. He guessed at the memory rushing into her mind: Marika and Bill's three-year-old son, Colin, drowning as his lungs filled with fluid, while his heart, irreparably damaged from the Lucy Syndrome's misfiring changes, struggled to fight the preload. They'd buried him a year ago May. (Yuri and Mickey had spent a week earlier that spring clearing a hectare of land beside the original cemetery to make more room.) It just wasn't right.

"Seems that Darlene and Bill haven't been getting along too well lately," Alex said, trying to shake the memory out of his head. "He thinks you might be able to deal with her a little better. You know how much she likes you."

"Bill's not the most patient guy in the world," Gemma said. "Well, I could ride my bike down to look after the garden. And Coyote could use the exercise, going back and forth." Coyote, hearing her name, rested her head on Gemma's belly. "You could use some exercise, couldn't you, girl?" Gemma said to her.

"I can see if the truck will start. You could use that, as long as there's gas in the tank."

They were quiet for quite a while, staring up at the sky.

"I remember the first time you took me camping," Gemma said, her voice unusually soft. "It was up in Kokanee Glacier Park and we laid in our sleeping bags on that big rock over by the Alpine Club's cabin on Kaslo Lake. I used to call them 'fireworks,' remember?"

"Uh-huh."

"And you explained to me how they were actually small stones, dust really, the largest ones only as big as marbles, from the Swift-Tuttle comet, stones burning up when they hit the atmosphere, making streaks of light. Like fireworks, but without the explosions. I remember being amazed that something as hard as a stone could be burned up by the air." She was silent for a moment. "Tell me the story of St. Lawrence."

Alex let the stars smudge into flakes of light as the story seeped into his mind. "Lawrence had been a deacon in the Roman Catholic Church, and he was in charge of the church's property and money. One day he was ordered to give over all the property and money to the Roman Emperor for the upkeep of the armies. 'Give me three days,' he told the Emperor. But in those three days he sold all the property and all the church's gold and silver, and gave all the money he got for it to the people who were poor, or sick, or disabled, to the widows and the orphans, and anyone else in need. The Roman Emperor was so mad when he found out Lawrence had tricked him that he had him killed."

In the back of his mind Alex could hear Gemma's eight-year-old voice, tight with incredulity: "He killed him! Just for helping poor people? That's stupid." That summer night seemed like such a very long time ago.

"Dad?" Gemma turned toward him in the dark. Two meteors arced through the sky dead above Alex. "Dad, I don't want to end up like Darlene," she said. "Or like Colin. If I get so that I can't talk anymore, or think anymore—so that I'm not *me* anymore—I want you to kill me. Okay? Grampa's old gun is still in the basement, and there are bullets for it. I checked." She started to cry a little. "I've thought about this a lot. It'd be quick, right? They say your body's so shocked you don't feel anything really, right?"

A low, long pain stretched through him and he pulled her closer. "It won't come to that, missy."

She pushed away, as if making a space for her words. "Dad, that's a lie and you know it."

Alex reached out to her, stroked her hair, her face. "What if you change your mind?" he said quietly. "What if you decide you don't want to die and you can't tell me?"

"What if you can't look after me anymore?" she threw back at him. "What if there are complications and I'm in so much pain, but I can't tell you, or we don't have medicine anymore? What if I start trying to hurt you to run away like the others? You'll have to lock me up, like Darlene—I don't want that, and I don't want to live in the bush like an animal either." She put her hand on his cheek, an intimacy that brought tears to his eyes. "You know it's going to come to that, don't you?"

He kissed her forehead. "Maybe being devolved isn't so bad," he said. "We don't really know what it's like. What if you still like living?"

She was quiet for a long time. "What if it's absolutely horrible," she said finally, "and I can't tell you how bad it is?" She took his face in her big hands, as if he were the child. "Dad, I want you to promise me you'll do it." A sob jumped out of her. "I'd rather be dead than live like that," she said. "Promise me."

They lay in silence, his arm curled behind her neck, her head on his shoulder.

He promised. He could feel her shaking, her whole body rocking lightly, and he knew she was crying. *He promised to kill his own daughter.* A wildfire of loss swirled through him, consuming him, while above, across the arch of heaven, stones burned in the air, flaring momentarily, then vanishing, seemingly witnessed in all the world by him alone.

CHAPTER 3

"Let's go, missy!" Alex called out as he lowered Gemma's mountain bike into the back of his small Mitsubishi pick-up. He opened the shed, picked the newest looking of several 12-volt batteries sitting on the floor, and hauled it out to the truck. He rested it on the radiator for a moment, letting the twinge in his back dissipate, before lowering it onto the tray. He slipped the cable clamps over the terminals, tightened the bolts with a small crescent wrench, then slammed the hood shut. At the other end of the truck, he dropped the tailgate and lifted the blue Coleman cooler into the box.

"We're taking the truck?" Gemma said, blinking in the sunlight as she stood at the back door, her pack slung over one shoulder.

"It might as well be over at Marika and Bill's. You can use it, then, if you want."

"I wish you would have told me. I thought we were riding our bikes over. I could have packed a ton more stuff."

"We talked about it yesterday, remember?" Alex let his irritation slide. She'd been having problems with recent memory since her last stroke. "Well, you can always just drive it back and get whatever you need." Alex slapped dirt from the battery off his T-shirt.

"Coyote!" Gemma called out as she hobbled down the steps.

"You look sore today."

"Yeah. Stupid legs ache, right in the bones. I feel like an old lady."

"You walk like one, too," he said, attempting a grin.

"You're one to talk."

"Yeah, yeah, yeah."

Coyote loped around the side of the shed, ducking her head as she padded over to Gemma. "Good girl. In the truck. Hup." Coyote leapt up onto the tailgate, settled herself in the back beside the cooler.

Alex slammed the tailgate shut. "Okay, let's see if it'll start."

Gemma swung her pack onto the bike and climbed into the cab. She fumbled with the seatbelt while Alex slid behind the wheel. "You in?" he asked. The seatbelt clicked and she gave him a thumbs-up.

Alex turned the key. Nothing. Easing the emergency brake off, he stuck out a leg and pushed. The truck creaked forward, started to roll. Alex slammed his door shut, pulled on his seatbelt. He let the truck pick up a bit of speed then popped the clutch. Tires bit gravel. He popped the clutch again. The motor fired, sputtered, caught. Gemma let out a whoop, and Alex grinned at her as the Mitsubishi shuddered and missed but kept running. He steered down the steep driveway and out onto the paved back road, shifting into third and heading north to Marika and Bill's place, bouncing and banging through the potholes and cracks in the pavement.

"Jesus, Dad, slow down," Gemma said, reaching for the handgrip above the door, "or you'll bounce Coyote right out of the back." Alex shifted down to second, stuck his elbow out the window, enjoying the cooler morning air by the river. Smoke hung low in the valley, a sheet of gray-blue haze muffling color, dampening down the sunlight.

It seemed to Alex that Gemma's voice sounded muddier, thicker, more throaty than it had a week ago. Maybe he was imagining it. Sometimes the omnipresent smoke in the air made him think everything in his life seemed less sharp, less distinct. He shouldn't be going away. Not now. She was changing, failing. When was he going to learn? *It'll only be a few days*, he tried to reassure himself.

But he could no longer deny that she was sliding closer and closer to the plunge into end-stage. His clinical skills as a paramedic droned the key features of the syndrome through his head against his will: voice degradation; cognitive and memory impairment (*but*, he argued, *that could simply be from the strokes*); rapid diminution with concurrent musculoskeletal reformation; immune system suppression (*the respiratory tract infection, remember?*); pain; and, of course, anger, irritability, depression, mood swings, *et cetera*. The Lucy virus was devolving her right before his very eyes.

But what if the devolving burned out her ability to speak while he was away? What if that infection returned and she developed pneumonia, or complications with her heart, or had another stroke? What if the devolution suddenly crippled her, running amok instead of following its genetically prescribed path?

Stop it, he told himself, *just stop it.*

"Dad?" Gemma said, startling him. *Had he said something out loud*? "Dad, you turn here."

Marika and Bill's gravel driveway appeared on the left. He braked hard, cranked the wheel, and bounced the truck up the washboard. In the rearview mirror, Coyote hugged the bottom of the pick-up bed, ears flattened.

Snugged in against the hillside, Marika and Bill's cedar-sided house, weathered gray, seemed tired. White paint peeled from the fascia and the window casings. The asphalt shingles curled at the edges, as if pained with arthritis. Knots and bellows of vibrant perennial gardens surrounded the house. Bill's Victorian Cottage garden, on the east side of the house, carried some local fame—once part of the garden tour in the valley every spring. A wide vegetable garden filled most of what had been the lower front lawn, which bordered the road. The poplar trees were gone, replaced by struggling apple and pear trees and two high-efficiency windmills.

"What the hell is that?" Gemma said, pointing.

"Bill said he'd built Darlene an outdoor play area, something secure, but I wasn't really sure what he meant." The play area, which ran down one side of the house, looked brutish and hard with its steel posts and wire mesh fencing. It even had a wire mesh ceiling.

"It looks like a cage in a goddamn zoo."

"Well, if it keeps her safe—"

"Don't even think about putting me in cage like that. Jesus. What's the world coming to?"

Backing in beside Bill's dead Jeep Cherokee, Alex parked with the nose of the Mitsubishi facing downhill. The *I ♥ LUCIES* bumper sticker on the back of Bill's jeep had faded in the sunlight.

Coyote leaped over the tailgate and bounded up to Bill, who was latching the door of the chicken coop. He leaned his rifle against the coop and tousled Coyote's fur, scratching her thick neck.

"What's the gun for?" Gemma asked as she climbed out of the truck.

Bill looked down at the gun. "A bear has been going through the property the last few days. Mostly looking for compost or garbage. Made a mess of one of the apple trees, though."

"You wouldn't shoot it, would you?"

He tipped his head, gave Coyote a final scratch. "Not if I don't have to."

Alex dropped the tailgate, slid the cooler out onto it. "Some tomatoes and a few other things we'd already picked from the garden—they're just going to go bad while I'm gone."

"Sure. No sense wasting them." Bill flipped open the lid, then looked at Alex and grinned, his forehead wrinkling high onto his bald scalp. "Beer doesn't go bad in a few days, Al," he said.

"Those in there are the last half-dozen of that batch Mickey and Yuri made up before the fire."

"Then we'll have a little celebration when you get back."

"You don't need to save them," Alex said as he lifted the cooler and followed Bill to the door. "I'm sure there's plenty more."

"I wouldn't hold your breath. That's Yuri we're talking about here."

"Gemma?" Alex called over his shoulder. "I brought a bag of books for Marika. They're behind the seat. Could you grab them for me?" He ignored her petulant growl.

Bill held the door for him. Alex set the cooler just inside on the concrete floor.

"There's been a pack of kids hanging around here the last few days," Bill said, his voice low. "Most of them end-stage, a few mid-stage, but a couple of the older ones are hardly changed at all. Could just be leading the others into a whack of trouble, stealing stuff, wrecking things just for the helluvit. One of the mid-stage kids is Yuri's, and he wasn't exactly a model citizen to begin with." Bill pulled the clip from his rifle. "Man, I hate guns," he said.

"You recognize any of the others?"

Bill shook his head. "It was near dusk, and the younger ones were getting pretty skittish being out in he open near dark like that, so they were keeping their distance." He led Alex up the stairs to the main floor where Marika was wiping down the kitchen table.

"Can I offer you some breakfast, Alex?" she said, tossing the cloth across the kitchen to the sink.

"No thanks, we ate." Alex dropped into a chair at the table.

The kitchen was tightly cluttered. A heavy wood-fired cookstove sat in front of the north wall, the table was jammed into a bay window that looked south down the valley, while the sink faced east, a bank of wood-frame windows above it, giving a good view of the main vegetable garden, and in the distance, the Slocan River.

"Bill," Marika said, "will you see to Darlene? She's been pretty quiet since breakfast, and she's supposed to be getting dressed. She might be needing some help."

Bill leaned the rifle in the corner by the door. "She probably went back to sleep. She was up most of the goddamn night 'cause of the pack coming around." Then he took a deep breath, looked from Marika to Alex and back to Marika. "Sure," he said, "I'll check." Bill ducked into the hallway, shoulders hunched forward.

Alex met Marika when he'd first arrived in the Slocan Valley thirteen years before. He'd hurt his back lifting a patient on a call and had limped into her walk-in-basement-slash-clinic for physiotherapy because she lived only a half-dozen kilometers north of him. She'd balled her red hair on top of her head to keep it out of her face while she worked on his locked muscles. These days, though, she wore her signature red hair cropped short. Only a few months ago, Darlene, in one of her fits of frustrated rage, had leapt on Marika, pounding her with her long arms, grabbing fistfuls of Marika's hair and wrenching it out of her scalp. Marika drove her back, hitting and slapping her, sending her scuttling to her closet hideout. Alex cut her hair for her in his kitchen, her dark curls skidding across the floor in the breeze from the open sliding-glass doors. Tears slopped onto her T-shirt as she told him about hitting Darlene, something she'd promised herself she'd never, ever, do, and about how she'd actually been afraid, reacting with gut-sickening fear, as if she were being attacked by an animal rather than by her own ten-year-old daughter. Alex had said little as he sheared away her hair, his own heart already whipped raw.

"So when is Yuri supposed to be here?" she said.

"Around five-thirty, six." He checked his watch. "Any time now."

"Darlene's so excited that Gemma's coming for a few days." She fussed at the stove. "Are you sure I can't fix you up some breakfast? You need some meat on that bone rack of yours."

"Unless you're offering a cheeseburger and fries with a kick-ass chocolate milkshake, I've had all the breakfast I can take, thanks."

She scowled at him. "Who pissed in your cornflakes this morning?"

Outside the bay window a flock of cedar waxwings rushed out of the birch tree as if on a mission. The green of the conifer trees on the property due south was already muted by smoke. Out the windows over the sink, the sun peeked over the ridge to the east, glowing like a single ember in the sheet-metal sky.

Marika settled into the chair across the table from Alex. "Thanks for dragging me along," she said. "It'll be nice to get away."

Alex shrugged. "Hey, it's you doing me the favor."

"How come you're the one going, anyway? It's not like you don't have enough to do already."

"It's the curse of not be able to say no."

"Why doesn't June go? It's not like she'd be missed."

"I need somebody to hold down the fort here."

"That's a pile of crap. You should be delegating this out."

"So, who pissed in *your* cornflakes this morning?" he said with a grin.

"Smart ass." She rubbed a hand through her hair. "But you know what I mean. You only have so much time, Alex. You know that." The corners of her mouth tightened, and Alex knew Marika would cry if she kept talking. It seemed that everyone's grief smoldered just below the surface these days.

The basement door crashed open. "Sorry!" Gemma called up the stairs.

Marika sniffed, leaned back in her chair and wiped her eyes with the back of her hand.

Excited hooting erupted from Darlene's bedroom down the hall, followed by delighted wall-thumping and what sounded like Darlene jumping on her bed. Marika ran her hand through her hair again and sighed.

"Thanks for taking in Gemma," Alex said quietly. "I really was getting worried about her staying alone at the house with me gone so much."

"Hey, she'll be a big help. Darlene loves her to death. And at least Gemma can handle her. That means a lot to me. And to Bill."

Alex gave her a wry grin. "Yeah, that extra strength comes in handy sometimes."

The pounding and howling stopped suddenly. Bill's voice murmured down the hall. Excited hooting erupted once again.

Gemma lurched into the kitchen, her pack on one shoulder and the cloth bag of books clutched in her good hand. She dropped her pack at the top of the stairs. "Hey, Marika," she said.

Marika got up and hugged her. "You want some tea?"

Gemma shook her head. "Nah. I'm fine." She shifted her weight from foot to foot, muscles bulging in her bowed legs. "I'm going to go see Darlene," she said to Alex. "I'll see you when you get back."

Alex, his throat suddenly tight and small, stood and wrapped Gemma in his arms. She'd shrunk so much these past few months that her head rested against his chest. He stroked her hair. "I love you, missy," he whispered, and as he held her he wondered what it would be like to never hug his daughter again, to never talk with her, to never lay on the deck with her under the stars watching 'fireworks.'

Gemma squeezed him and let go. Alex scrubbed at his eyes. *You're getting all mushy and sentimental in your old age,* Gemma had said to him some time back, and he didn't know if it was because he was pushing fifty, or because life had changed so much in the past four years that he simply couldn't hide how attached he was to what he still had.

"You can put your stuff in Colin's room, hon," Marika said to Gemma.

Gemma picked up her pack and headed down the hallway.

Alex sat back down in the chair, his throat tight and tense.

"Fire situation's not looking good," he said finally as he cleared his throat.

"Yeah, Bill told me. We've already made up our list of stuff we'll take if we're evacuated. Bill's going to do some packing while I'm gone. Any news from New Denver?"

He wiped at his eyes again as he shook his head. "June says nobody has come down the valley the last ten days, which seems strange after the steady stream of folks moving through here since the snow melted."

"Probably got their own fire troubles."

"Man, I hope not."

The rumble of a diesel motor invaded the kitchen. Alex could see Mickey's truck bouncing up the road, Yuri at the wheel.

"I don't know what Willow sees in that guy," Marika said.

"His charming personality?"

"So, when are you going to get yourself a little honey to shack up with?" she said, an old joke between them.

With a grunt that Alex thought encapsulated a decent enough response, he pushed himself up out of his chair and headed toward the stairs.

"You could at least find someone just to boink once every blue moon," she said. "Just for the helluvit."

A horn sounded below the kitchen's east-facing windows.

"Mind your own business, girl," he said as he creaked his way down the stairs, his thighs still aching, his lower back annoyingly stiff.

"Be there in a minute," Marika said, "just want to say goodbye."

Outside Mickey's pickup growled like an old dog. Yuri waved at him from the driver's seat. Alex retrieved his pack from his truck and threw it amongst all the cargo in the back of Mickey's pickup—extra diesel and a stack of solar panels and clamps, with a few truck parts and a toolbox; a chainsaw and its accoutrements; shovels, axes, mattocks and a single piss-can in case they ran into some hotspots; a basket stretcher and jump kit; several boxes jammed with odds and ends June thought they might be able to trade for things she needed for the hospital, including half a dozen cases of Mickey and Yuri's homemade beer and a case of elderberry wine.

"Hey, old man!"

Alex looked back and up to see Gemma waving to him from the barred window in Darlene's bedroom. He waved and blew her a kiss. She blew him a kiss back. Alex grabbed it out of the air and held on.

CHAPTER 4

The truck bumped north, crawling over the neglected pavement in second gear. Potholes pitted the road like craters from small artillery fire.

Marika had convinced Yuri to let her drive—some bullshit story, Alex was sure, about getting carsick in the back seat—and so Yuri rode shotgun and Alex got stuck in the back seat. Marika and Yuri argued the whole way to Slocan, mostly about why the government had gone belly up. Marika was pretty damn certain that the IMF's recall of a chunk of Canada's debt did it, which was nothing short of outright shit-and-abuse because the Americans believed the asshole who released the Lucy virus had come into the US from Canada. Yuri, on the other hand, believed it wasn't that complicated. He said that there just weren't enough people left to run the government properly, like when you run a business, you need a minimum number of workers or nothing gets done. So what if the IMF wants its money back? There's no one around to even write the bastards a cheque.

Finally, when it seemed that Marika was more stubborn than Yuri had anticipated, Yuri pulled his leather baseball cap low over his eyes and settled in for a nap. "Wake me when we get there," he said, crossing his arms over a T-shirt permanently stained with grease and motor oil. Yuri worked for Mickey whenever Mickey needed him at the garage next to the Mini-Mart, which wasn't much these days since the fuel trucks stopped coming up the valley just after the first snowfall last winter. And then the mudslide this spring south of Lebahdo Flats cut off any local highway traffic for almost a month while the community worked at building a road over the slide. These days Yuri mostly helped with whatever repair work the volunteer fire department needed doing. It seemed to Alex that Mickey just tried to keep Yuri busy. And out of trouble.

Yuri had been a regular customer for the ambulance service in Winlaw for several years after he lost his job when the pulp mill in Castlegar closed down. Pissed to the gills, he drove his pickup truck down a bank avoiding a deer, then climbed back up to the highway and lay on the side of the road until someone found him. Six months later he fell seven meters off an unfinished balcony in an unfamiliar house when he got up to take a piss after a party. Then he killed a thirteen-year-old boy after drinking all night with some friends. Alex attended that call, arriving on the scene to find that Yuri had hit two kids walking on the shoulder of the highway. One had been thrown twenty meters: he was dead at the scene, lying face-up with massive, open head injuries. (Alex remembered the ice-shiver of sickness he felt laying the yellow emergency blanket over the boy's pale face). The second boy suffered two broken femurs and a damaged spleen, and although he lived, he was never the same kid.

As for Mickey, he just shrugged the whole thing off, seemingly content to be needed by Yuri. He fixed up one of his kids' rooms for him when Yuri got out of prison after serving his time for killing the boy—Mickey's wife had left him and their five-bedroom bungalow, taking the kids and the dog, years earlier. Yuri had been sober for four or five years, but Alex had heard rumors this past winter that he'd started up again with Mickey's homemade beer and wine.

With Yuri napping in the front seat Marika seemed content to crawl the truck along in silence.

Alex scratched the date in his notebook. *13 August 2020*. He owned a meter-high stack of these blue-lined spiral-bound notebooks. He could easily have used his e-scroll, but he liked the carnal experience of scratching pen on paper, filling line after line, with no delete function. He didn't want to be able to delete his words, to take them back with the touch of a finger. He filled those notebooks with the detritus of his life: long descriptions of daily life with Gemma, sticky snarls of confusion, rants and rages, to-do lists, quotes from books he'd read, long ramblings about ugly ambulance calls that had kept him awake at night, facts he didn't want to forget. He kept a journal almost compulsively, as if doing so could somehow save him, sorting through the understory of his life, naming the dark green bits, the flowery parts, the dirt and the shit. The notebook had become his confidant, and his release.

And his access to the past, to when life was normal, the way it was supposed to be; his access to Gemma as a normal ten-year-old, the two of them canoeing on Slocan Lake to look at the petroglyphs; as a twelve-year-old charging down the driveway on her mountain bike; as a fourteen-year-old, bent over the kitchen table studying for a science test.

Lucy, Alex scrawled in his notebook. *LucyLucyLucy.* That one word, that name, had filled countless lines over the past few years. Because of that word life was no longer normal. Gemma was no longer normal. He knew in which notebook he'd written the explanation; in his mind's eye he could see the page, he's reread it so many times, his messy scrawl in blue pen: *Lucy: the small brown remains that paleoanthropologists Don Johanson and Tom Gray howled at and hugged each other over in the heat of the Ethiopian sun in 1974. A partial skeleton, named Lucy over beer and music*—"Lucy in the Sky with Diamonds"—*a female hominid who (not 'that,' but 'who') died 3.5 million years ago.* Australopithecus afarensis. *Lucy. Or, Hadar collection acquisition number: AL 288-1.* The script was branded into his memory.

LucyLucyLucyLucyLucyLucyLucyLucyLucy.

Gemma isn't a lucy, she's a person, Alex wrote. *We are people; we are not our disease. Devolving won't change that.*

He tugged on an ear, let out a long slow breath.

And yet, when I think of the ones who are end-stage and lost, like those I got on DV, like the dead boy in the raspberry canes, thinking of them as "lucies" makes it easier somehow to make-believe that Gemma is never going to become one of them. They're too different, too other—'different' doesn't mean non-human, though . . . Besides, we'll all become lucies, sooner than later, or die getting there. "Planet of the lucies," that's all that'll be left: a diaspora of variously devolving hominids, maybe to re-evolve so that millions of years from now we'll once again dominate the earth—and maybe do it a little smarter, I hope. Or maybe we'll just devolve all the way back into the four-legged Ramapithecus, *or, maybe we won't even stop there, maybe we'll just keep on devolving all the way back to* Eozostrodon, *that nocturnal mouse-sized critter which shared the planet with the dinosaurs. I can almost feel my nose twitching in anticipation.*

Or maybe—and more likely—the whole lot of us will die off before the devolving finishes its course. I just hope that Gemma rethinks—

"Ah, crap," Marika said.

Alex looked up through the cracked windshield. "Where are we?"

"Enterprise Creek." She eased the truck to a standstill. "Or, what used to be Enterprise Creek."

Yuri grunted and sat up.

The micro-hydroelectric plant that had been built on the creek to feed the valley additional power, and the road built over top of the plant, were gone. A chunk of the mountain had slipped away above the highway and had filled the drainage with rocks and dirt and splintered trees. A footpath had been worn across the face of the slide since it had come down, probably early in the spring. Several abandoned vehicles sat on the highway at the north end of the slide. The creek was nowhere in sight.

Alex leaned against the front seat. "I don't think we can get the truck across that."

"It doesn't look that bad," Yuri said. "We've got a saw and some tools, plus the winch on the front of the truck. Probably only a couple of spots where we might have to take the saw to some deadfall."

It took them the rest of the morning to cut a wide enough swath for the truck to crawl through. Mosquitoes and horse flies dogged them as they worked and sweated and growled at one another. While working on the very last deadfall, Yuri nicked his foot with the chainsaw, chewing a hole through his boot and chunking a dime-sized bite of meat out of his instep. Alex patched him up. Marika shook her head while she sharpened and refueled the saw on the tailgate of the truck.

"I told you we shouldn't have let him use the saw," she said to Alex, making a face.

"I'm right here, girl," Yuri said as he pulled his sock on. "I think I'm going to climb up into the basket stretcher and lie there in the back of the truck and keep my foot up. Maybe have a little nap. I was up late last night putting the alternator back in the truck so we could actually leave this morning."

"Now that he's injured," Marika said to Alex, "he's really not much good to us, is he? Maybe we should just, you know, leave him behind to fend for himself. One less mouth to feed, and all that."

Yuri was on his feet now, testing his injured foot.

"I say we set him adrift on an ice flow," Alex chimed in. "'One less mouth to feed, and all that.'" Marika laughed.

"It's a slippery slope though," Alex continued. "Casting the injured and the elderly aside. Next thing you know, the fascists are in power."

"What would you know about fascists?" Yuri snapped, his face suddenly red and splotchy. "My family had to leave Russia because of the goddamn fascists."

"Actually, Yuri," Marika said, "Tsar Nicholas was an autocrat."

"Well, smart-ass, he acted just like a goddamn fascist, killing and exiling the Doukhobours just because they were pacifists."

Marika bungeed the saw into place beside the gas can, pulling on the hooks to make sure they held. "It was over a hundred years ago, Yuri. Don't get your shirt all in a twist."

"Are you guys going to stand here and argue all day?" Alex said, tossing his jumpkit in the back of the truck.

Yuri ignored him. "History is important. No matter what happens, we should never forget it." He hauled himself up onto the load in the back of the truck.

Marika slammed the tailgate shut. "There isn't going to be anybody left to remember it," she said.

"That's why Mickey's putting it all in a book," Yuri said from the basket stretcher on top of the load in the back of the truck.

Alex arched his back, stretching, then twisted until he felt a satisfying crack. "Mickey's writing a book?"

"Yeah, a book. About our family. About where we came from. What happened to us. Then, some time, way in the future, somebody will find his book and read it, and they'll know all about the Evdikimoffs. We won't be forgotten."

"That's actually not a bad idea," Marika said. "If anybody *is* left to read it. You know, *everybody* should write a book. Then, at the least, there'd be a great collage of stories documenting the lives of the last survivors and their families."

Marika fired up the motor. Alex couldn't decide whether she was making fun of Yuri, or not. Probably.

"You make it sound like we're heroes or something," Yuri hollered from the back as Marika eased the truck off the last few feet off the slide and back onto the rutted pavement.

"Well, we are heroes," she called out. "Ordinary people promoted to heroic heights by the unfeeling circumstances of history."

"You are so full of crap, Marika, it isn't even funny," Yuri called back.

Alex laughed.

He rode up front with Marika in a comfortable silence, his notebook open on his lap. They had passed the parking lot for the lookout over Slocan Lake, which had been built back in 1957 when the highway was first paved, and had begun the long, winding descent that would eventually land them in Silverton, about three kilometers south of New Denver. Last time Alex had been this way—for Tom Rilkoff's funeral, the husband of New Denver's ambulance unit chief—was over a year ago and Silverton only had about a dozen or so families left.

"It seems to me," Marika said as she geared down, "that Gemma's gait looks a little worse. Did she have another stroke while you were gone?"

"I don't know. She hasn't said, and I haven't asked."

"C'mon, Alex. You guys talk about everything. What's going on?"

Alex shrugged noncommittally. He didn't want to talk about Gemma, not right now. He wasn't ready. But even as the excuse formed in his mind he knew he'd never be ready. Some things you can never prepare for, you simply deal with them, or you don't. Like some of the things you see on ambulance calls, spilled brains, dead children, burned carcasses that still breathed and talked, if only for a few minutes, families members stricken with grief as you work on their drowned toddler. It had always helped to talk about those things. So maybe he *should* confide in someone. Talk about Gemma, about her request and his promise. And why not Marika? They'd been friends since forever; he trusted her, and she had a good heart. He *needed* to tell someone. He needed to smooth some of the sharp edges off the stone sitting in his heart, and he knew the only way to do that was to talk about it. *She asked me to kill her.* He opened his mouth, but the words refused to be spoken.

"Uh-oh," Marika said.

"What?" He almost choked speaking that single word.

"That's not good, not good at all."

On the ridge high above them to the northeast, the ridge from which Silverton Creek spilled down into Silverton, it looked as if a monstrous festering wound had opened up, and flames, like an erupting infection, had thrust themselves up through the trees, driving clouds and clouds of bone-white smoke into the sky.

CHAPTER 5

Sage Van Peldt opened her eyes without moving. For a single nanosecond she believed she was waking up in her lovely form-molding bed in her lovely white stucco house on the outskirts of Seattle beside her husband, Quinn, with Maddie and Jovan snug in their little beds down the hall; then it flooded in, like the daily memory of cancer or Lupus or any other terminal disease, the ache and the chant of *Lucy, Lucy, Lucy* sawing through her brain. The disease, *devolution*—a frenetic retrovirus-induced backwards slide down the genetic hill into primordium—made your body a reverse timeline of the rise of *Homo sapiens sapiens*.

It was dark, though not dead-of-night dark, but the dim lightlessness of pre-twilight. The smell of dried leaves, dirt, pine needles, jammed her into the present: she was inside her sleeping bag a hundred and fifty meters up off the highway, scrunched in among broken bone-dry pine boughs and several sad-looking shrubs, having trusted that she was hidden well enough to risk sleep. So what had woken her? She strained to listen for footfalls, or the snuffling of wild dogs or a bear, or the distant crack and roar of a forest fire.

A week ago she'd blundered out of the burned apocalyptic forestscape almost without noticing. For some reason the fire had turned, fallen back on itself, headed more north than west, and Sage found herself, within a few strides, stomping on dried ponderosa pine needles, burrs grabbing at her pant legs, and the scent of green and tree and shrub wrestling with the thick stench of smoke and ash she'd become so accustomed to breathing.

She could hear nothing of consequence in the pre-dawn air, simply the chatter of early-rising birds she couldn't identify, the nylon-like rustle of dry pine needles in a breeze blowing fresh from the east, the nattering of a squirrel several trees over. Perhaps, because she'd slept in the graveyard silence of the burned-out forest the past three weeks, and inside a dead-empty house the last few nights, it was the heart-sounds of a living forest that had disturbed her.

Something rattled through the tree above her: *thwack, thwack*, then *thud* onto the ground half a meter in front of her, a fist-sized ponderosa pine cone, barely visible, bouncing and rolling to standstill amongst a shadowy team of other cones, none of which had been lying there when she'd made camp last evening.

Sage let out the breath she'd been holding. From her burrow under the trees she could see where the slope fell away, dropping to the dilapidated highway below, then rising to the far ridge, and above that the sky where, just above the tree-toothed horizon a meteor flashed and then was gone, leaving a scar of light on her mind's eye. Another flash, another short-lived descent, like a life, born in darkness, flourishing brightly, then returning to darkness, quick as that.

Sage steered her mind away from such thoughts. She needed to remain as frozen as the comet that birthed those meteors, a stone locked in ice, trying to return from whence it came before it lost too much of itself and died en route. She huffed at the metaphor, annoyed that she couldn't recall the name of the kind of orbit most comets enjoyed. What was it? *Elliptical?* Was that right? This loss of vocabulary irritated her. She'd have to look it up later. Monkey-mind seemed, slowly but irrevocably, to be winning territory in her brain, and she'd be damned if she'd give up without a fight, an epic fight if need be, battling with armies of definitions, chariots full of mathematics, sieges of scientific concepts, an immense cavalry of mounted historical facts! Pah!

She could feel the baby move inside her, jamming a foot or an elbow into her bladder, making her suddenly desperate to pee. She pushed back the boughs and rose fully clothed, boots and all, from her sleeping bag as if from a grave, shivering in the pre-dawn chill. She uncovered her bicycle and her panniers, dug out her pack, checked quickly to make sure all her worldly belongings were intact and safe. She knew from hiking experience that her food should have been strung between two trees to keep it safe from bears and dogs—squirrels were a whole other problem—but had decided, firstly, it would be like raising a flag to mark her position, and secondly, it would mean leaving everything behind if she needed to make an emergent retreat. Better to be forced to frighten off four-legged predators with hysterics and a brandished axe handle than risk leaving everything behind simply to escape potential predators of the two-legged kind.

As the baby moved again, she found a spot away from her gear, dropped her pants, and squatted as best she could with her bulging belly. Thirty-two weeks along—but still peculiarly small for eight months pregnant—her belly was a taut moon pushing out above the waistband of her pants, which made riding her newfound bicycle rather uncomfortable. It was far better than walking, however, despite the constant exposure and vulnerability of being perched on two wheels on a barren strip of pavement. But she didn't have that far to go: today she'd make the border; by tomorrow's dawn she'd be back in Canada for the first time since before the outbreak.

When Quinn decided to take the kids to Disneyland that infamous March week, she had considered popping home, just a short flight from Sea-Tac to Vancouver, then another into Castlegar, to spend the week with her mom and dad in New Denver, in British Columbia, Canada. Just to get away for a while, maybe visit the hot springs, do a little fishing with her dad on the lake, ride the ambulance with her mom if she got called out, or help out at the bookstore her folks owned. Sage had been sick for a couple of days, though, so she decided against making the trip, opting instead for the peace and quiet of an empty house. After a few days, however, she got called back to work—she worked as a librarian at the Tacoma Public Library—because one of her staff had a family emergency. As Sage dragged herself back to work, she quickly realized that her illness had been morning sickness, that ironic proclamation of pregnancy—unplanned, it was true, but certainly and wonderfully, welcome.

Sage pulled on her backpack, secured the straps on her panniers, then pushed her bike down the embankment to the road.

She had to give that baby up, though; they took him away from her, out there in the camp hospital just outside Spokane. She saw him once, a nurse whisking him to her bedside, sneaking her a peek, the tiny undersized boy that had slipped out of her so easily, heavy dark down all over his body, thick ridge above his closed eyes, flat nose, tiny, tiny head. A lucy baby. They didn't know what they were back then. Neither the nurse nor the baby boy ever came back to her. Sage had called him Linus, because of the way his hair stuck up, like that Peanuts character with the blanket. And, ironically, Lucy's brother, she realized much later.

Everything has been taken away from me. The words staggered through her mind. She scattered them with a grunt of impatience.

She checked the road for signs of life, listening carefully, sniffing at the air, her flattened nose keen as a dog's. She felt safer in the burned out areas; here where it was untouched by fire there might still be people, those two-legged predators pretending at friendliness or hospitality, or feigning injury or dire need. She petrified her heart with dark remembrances of night attacks at the camp, fists through the blanket that had been cinched down over her head and torso, pummeling her face for failed alliances or perceived offences, leaving her to mix blood and tears into unsightly stains on her cot mattress. What was supposed to have been an emergency isolation from the larger population, a haven of safety while authorities and officials figured out how to win against this viral giant, had transmogrified over time into a prison-slash-sanatorium-slash-death-camp by default.

After sipping some water from the bottle on her bike, she eased up onto the seat and began to pedal, the fat tires bouncing easily over the cracks and holes in the neglected pavement. The border town of Danville, Washington, didn't look very far away according to her map. She had originally picked the more westerly route because it had been scoured by fire, even though it meant that scavenging for food would be nigh impossible. She had a couple of days' worth of food in her pack, so she was more interested in safety-through-stealth than in scavenging opportunities. If Danville proved to be an intact and thriving town, she'd be faced with finding an alternate location to attempt her border crossing, or with swallowing her fear and seeking help across the border.

Within an hour of pedaling, and much to her relief, the highway re-entered the fire zone, with its blackened stick-figure trees, some standing like shell-shocked sentinels, others like fallen soldiers crisscrossing the charred duff. Despite not feeling hungry—she hadn't been hungry much in the last trimester of her previous pregnancies either—Sage ate two granola bars and a handful of raisins and washed it all down with water, ruefully aware that she should probably be eating more to help feed the infant she carried. She pedaled easily in the growing heat, trying to remain hyper-vigilant to avoid being surprised by anyone. She had no real weapons with which to defend herself, save a hunting knife on a belt hidden inside the waistband of her pants and a wooden axe handle secured to her pack, and so was relying on her ability to flee on bicycle.

The house where she'd found all the treasures she now owned, bicycle included, offered up no guns of any kind, despite her desperate search. A lone house, abandoned in a rush, and somehow left standing when the firestorm razed the town—she had no idea which one of the many towns marked on her map—had gifted her with food, clothing, utensils, a sleeping bag, a tent (which she hadn't yet used), almost a hundred dollars in cash hidden in a jar in the clothes closet in the master bedroom, matches, soap and shampoo, and best of all, books. She spent several days there, camping a short distance from the house in case the owners came back to reclaim their belongings, or other scavengers appeared, ones willing to fight or kill for the right to take what was there, while she meticulously searched, sorted, and decided what to steal and what to leave behind. She crept through the two-story house like a cat burglar, emptying closets, drawers, cupboards, making piles on the plush living room carpet while she ate cold canned refried beans or salmon or creamed corn from the pantry. She studied the family photographs that hung in the stairwell up to the bedrooms, the high-school graduation pictures of two black boys and a girl, an older family portrait against an ugly fake-sky background, the parents smiling, the three children so much younger. She pored through the basement, hunting for anything of extraordinary value, but found herself returning to the floor-to-ceiling bookshelves in the living room, crammed with such a variety of books that Sage had momentary fantasies of living in this house, like some kind of self-appointed housekeeper, until the family returned, or not, and she'd have her baby and live out her life here in comfort and delicious isolation, teaching her child from the library of books at her fingertips. And because it was a fantasy, her devolution had miraculously reversed itself, and her child was born healthy and genetically modern, still a true *Homo sapiens sapiens*, with delicate features, strong dexterous fingers, and a precocious mind. She enjoyed this fantasy. It felt safe, almost attainable, in that mouth-watering way of true fantasies.

The fantasy, though, that she refused to entertain, refused to let leak into her conscious mind, was the one where she woke up, startled and breathless, to find herself with Quinn's arm draped over her breasts, and the knowledge that she'd been asleep, suffering only a particularly nasty night terror, spreading relief through her body like crisp winter air, like—

Sage thudded through a pothole in the pavement, almost spilling her bike. *Dammit*, she'd been daydreaming again, pedaling slowly in a too-easy gear, instead being vigilant and trying to cover as much ground as possible. She barely got her bike under control when something bolted out of the decimated forest, beelining for her. She jammed power into the pedals and was almost past it when it launched itself at her, catching the pack on her back with one paw, or hand, pulling her off balance, the bike twisting underneath her, handlebars wrenching sideways, and she tumbled, trying to protect her belly, trying to keep her head from striking the pavement, trying to scrabble to get her feet underneath her before the thing was upon her.

CHAPTER 6

Sage cracked the side of her head on the pavement, slid a meter or two on her side, scrubbing skin off her left arm, the bike sliding with her. They swarmed her, pulling at her pack, her clothes, her bike panniers, the bike itself. She shoved one away, kicked at another with her free leg, the other leg still pinned under the bike, and then struggled and twisted under the grasping, pulling hands. Sage finally freed herself from the bike and lunged to her feet with a roar of commingled frustration and fear, reaching behind her shoulder, jerking the axe handle out of the straps on the side of her pack and brandishing it.

They backed away, then, forming a ring, four of them: children, all under the age of ten or twelve. The two youngest, who were maybe about four years old, were naked and dirty and looked as if they were completely devolved, while the two older children, a boy and a girl, wore dirty T-shirts and shorts. They stared at her, breathing hard, covered in soot and dirt, bright eyes wide, skinny hair-covered bodies poised to fight or flee.

Warily, Sage reached down for her bicycle, still holding the axe handle high. They rushed at her again. She staved them off by swinging the handle and yelling at them, hoping they were young enough to be easily frightened off with bravado and, if needed, some well-placed but non-lethal whacks with her trusty axe handle.

Sage jutted her jaw at the one who looked to be the oldest, a female with budding breasts under a filthy yellow T-shirt and a blonde, almost white, head of hair, with darker blonde hair covering the scrawny limbs that stuck out of sleeves and shorts. "You talk?" Sage asked, and signed her question with ASL.

The girl simply watched Sage, her lower lip loose.

"But you understand me."

She nodded two sharp nods, her lip quivering.

Sage surveyed the others. "Where are you from?" The girl waved behind her to somewhere in, or beyond, the burned forest to the east. "What do you want? Food? Clothes?"

The girl just nodded.

"My clothes won't fit you. I do have some food, though. I will give you food if you leave me alone."

The girl stared at her as if she no longer comprehended. The boy nearest her, another even skinnier white kid with dark matted hair, muttered something to the white-haired girl, but Sage didn't catch what he said. Maybe it had been simply a grunt, not a word or phrase that the boy had uttered to the girl. Either way, Sage decided it was time to take the upper hand.

"I don't want to hurt you"—she swung the wooden handle to emphasize her next point—"but I will if I have to." She swept a hand under her bike and pulled it upright. Not one of them moved, for which she was terribly thankful. Her heart still cracked and snapped with fear: she knew how easily they could injure or kill her, or her unborn child, even if they hadn't a clue, and she wasn't especially prepared to be as vicious as she'd need to be to properly defend herself if they decided to attack her. They were only children after all, children morphing into something closer to animal than human, behaving out of need like little trolls or yahoos, it was true, but children none-the-less. It wasn't fair, what was happening to them, what they had become, and she wasn't particularly interested in adding injury to their already burdened lives. A bad cut or a broken limb could easily lead to a nasty death.

She eased her pack off her back, rested it on the bike seat, carefully zipped open one of the side pockets, which contained, among other things, a bag of hard butterscotch candies wrapped in gold foil. She crooked a finger at the youngest child, a tiny white boy, who inched forward, glancing again and again at the older boy, an anxious grin splitting his face. The older boy, who had said something to the girl earlier, growled at the younger boy, who froze in his tracks. The older boy came forward, placing himself between Sage and the youngest one. He cocked his head, just a little, and spoke to her, his voice like tumbling gravel, "Give me the food. I'm the one in charge." He stuck out his hand.

Sage dropped a handful of candies in his open hand, making sure several spilled onto the pavement. The younger children leaned forward, barely able to keep themselves from darting in to retrieve the fallen candy.

"More."

She put another handful into his other hand then casually flung the remainder of the bag's contents over the pavement, gold candies bouncing like coins, twinkling in the smoke-muted sunlight. The youngest children couldn't help themselves. They rushed forward snatching up their treasures, grabbing as many as they could, shoving each other out of the way. The older ones abandoned their caution and leapt into the fray.

Sage jammed the handle behind the straps, flung her pack over her shoulders, jumped on her bike, and pedaled away as hard and as fast as she could, leaving the pack of kids scrambling over the broken pavement like puppies after spilt kibble. She couldn't think about what was going to happen to them, growing up wild like that. Short, terrible lives, that's what they'd live, dieing of malnutrition, injury and infection, abuse at the hands of adults or other older semi-devolved children, or simply from exposure to heat or cold. Most certainly not a one of them would survive the winter, if they lived even that long. It was a sadness that she couldn't afford to nurse. Her own children—

But she didn't want to think about that right now either.

Sage pedaled hard and long, trying to put as much road between her and the pack of children as she could. She scanned the ditches and banks, the decimated forest, and the way ahead, with greater diligence now, having needlessly fallen prey to a pack of mere children. She'd been lucky, very lucky. It could have been so much worse, has been so much worse before. But she didn't want to think about that either, about being chased and chased—it would distract her from what she needed to be doing. And right now she needed all her wits about her to get to the Wall and find a way across. She hadn't come this far, for this long, to get waylaid by a pack of anonymous devolved children, no different from the thousands that undoubtedly roamed the countryside, having fled the imploding cities and towns, or escaped the FEMA camps.

Just like her.

A week after Quinn and the kids had come home from Disneyland, Jovan came down with the flu, waking up in the night with a nasty fever, chills, and aches all over his eight-year-old body. When she couldn't break his fever with acetaminophen, she took him to the hospital, farming out six-year-old Maddie to friends. Quinn was on a United flight to Bangkok, co-piloting one of Boeing's rickety 7E7s. He never came home.

Jovan had been admitted, and she'd spent the first night with him up in Pediatrics, the night his fever broke. Two representatives from the airline—a man and a woman—found her the following morning drinking bad coffee in the cafeteria and staring at a half-eaten bagel on a plate. Jovan was sleeping finally.

They were sorry to hear her son had been hospitalized. They hoped he would be okay.

Probably just the flu, she'd said.

The woman looked at the man. Could they talk somewhere more private? she'd said.

Sage's heart stopped and her hands went to ice, trembling like the DTs. She knew what was coming: a bomb; a fire; a hijacking; a crash at sea; or all of the above. She'd lived this moment ten thousand times in the decade since they'd married, momentary starts of terror at an unexpected presentation at the front door, or heart thudding suddenly in the deep night, waking with Quinn gone, her head muzzy at first with sleep, thinking he should be home by now, shouldn't he . . .

Quinn had felt unwell during the flight to Bangkok, they said. His pilot found him dead in his hotel room when he didn't make an appearance at breakfast. We're terribly sorry. An investigation is underway in Bangkok, to determine the exact cause of death. Foul play is not suspected. The woman had been talking, and now she paused, pursed her lips. The World Health Organization is involved, seems he may have had some sort of new flu.

Sage sucked in air, as if were her last good breath before going under.

"You have food."

Sage spun hard, reaching for the knife on the belt hidden inside her waistband.

They stood there, all four of them, looking even hungrier and dirtier than they had yesterday, the two youngest hiding warily behind the others.

Sage had ridden almost an hour, finding Danville to be another fire casualty, but feared that it had not been wholly abandoned as she'd seen a group of homes that looked like they'd been overstepped by the firestorm. A dog had rushed out in her direction, then turned back suddenly. So she headed northeast, following Boundary Road until she found a place to camp for the night, not too far from the Wall, figuring she'd spend the next day or two searching for a breach before heading to the crossing to attempt the border gates there.

She scanned the burned forest behind the children, her eyes darting from charred tree to charred tree, then sweeping across the three burned-out homes near the road. She'd picked this place to camp because she was well hidden from the road behind the cement-block detritus of an old garage. It was just after five-thirty in the morning, the air still cold from the smoke-filled night, and here they were, dressed in the rags of clothing they'd been wearing yesterday, the two youngest still buck-naked.

"How'd you find me?" she asked the boy.

He pointed at the bike tire, and Sage grimaced.

"Are you alone?"

"No. We're four." He held up a hand to show her how many.

She wasn't sure if she should be reading sarcasm in his response or not. She slipped her knife back into its hiding place. "I meant: Is there anyone else besides you four? Adults? Other kids?"

He shrugged. "There's adults in Danville. They don't like us; we don't like them."

The blonde girl scratched at bug bites on her arm all the while staring at Sage.

"Sic dogs on us," the boy continued, "if we get close to their stupid houses."

"Why did you follow me?" Sage demanded again, reminding herself to be wary of these half-sized yahoos.

"You have food." He came into her camp, then, and the others followed.

Sage watched warily. "I thought you lived over there somewhere," she said, pointing vaguely in a southeasterly direction.

"Uh-huh, in Josie's house"—he nodded at the blonde girl—"the fire didn't get it. Can't go there any more. 'Sides, we ate up the food, now we go hunting."

"Hunting," Sage repeated, remembering how he'd bolted out of the forest and knocked her off her bike. She watched, still wary, as they wandered among her panniers and her bike, touched her sleeping bag, her pack.

"For food."

"I can give you some of my food."

"Okay," he said. "What's your name?"

"Sage. What's yours?"

"Carl. An' that's Josie—she doesn't talk much any more—and that's Ula and that's Isaac. They don't talk neither, never did. Total lucy from the get-go."

"Parents?"

Carl shook his head.

Sage took a deep breath. "Why don't you sit down and I'll get us some food and we can talk."

Carl dropped cross-legged on Sage's sleeping bag and thermarest and patted the sleeping bag with his hands until Ula and Isaac squatted on either side of him, still eyeing Sage with open suspicion. Carl touched each of them, just once, on the arm and they visibly relaxed, taking some kind of reassurance from his touch. Josie sat on the other end of the thermarest. Four children seated in a row in front of her, like an audience ready for story-time at the library.

Sage sighed. She retrieved her pack and handed out four apples—that left her only two more—and a granola bar each, plus one for herself, then settled cross-legged on the dirt with the pack beside her, her trusty axe handle within easy reach.

"So, why did you follow me? It must have taken you a long time to come this far."

Carl shrugged. "We're used to walking," he said, nonchalance emphasized with a wave of his hand. "You have food," he explained. "Maybe a house, too, with more food."

"I was in one of the camps," she said, shaking her head. "Do you know about those?"

Carl nodded. "Camps for lucies," he said without looking at her. Josie hung her head a little, picking at a sore on her knee while she ate her apple. Ula wandered over to a spot near Sage's bike and ate her apple alone, while Isaac simply rocked back and forth in a crouch ignoring his apple and waiting while Carl unwrapped the granola bar for him.

"Yeah, well," Sage said with a grunt, "sort of. The camp I was in was near Fairchild Air Force Base. Know where that is?" When Carl didn't say anything she simply continued. "Then the fires came and I snuck away."

"You got a house here?" Carl asked, his mouth full of bright apple flesh.

"I'm going home to Canada, to find my parents."

"Our parents, they're dead," Carl said. "We got no one left here."

"You're all from the same family?"

"Me and Isaac and Ula. Not Josie."

"Well, my parents might be dead, too, for all I know," Sage said, liquid fear suddenly spilling through her. "I hope they're not, but I won't know for sure until I get there."

"Is it far?" Carl asked.

"Yes."

"Is it burned up?"

"I don't know. I haven't been in touch with them for two years."

"Take us there," he said, and it was not a question or a request at all, but a simple, direct command.

CHAPTER 7

Sage let out a wry laugh. "Keep your shirt on there, mister," she said, and when he looked down at his dirty shirt and back up at her, she laughed again and shook her head.

"What?" He sounded angry.

She studied them: Carl's furrowed brow, arms crossed sulkily; Ula and Isaac, having gobbled up their apples and granola bars, chasing each other around a tree, looking alarmingly like a pair of scrawny straight-hipped chimps; and Josie still chewing methodically on her apple. "You mustn't live very far from here," Sage said. "You want to take me there?"

Carl tilted his head, squinted a "why" at her.

She moved into a kneeling position, to take some of the pressure off her lower back. The baby was moving again. "Look," she began, "I need to know where you come from, what happened to your people. I just can't take you somewhere."

"They're dead!" Carl said, his gravelly voice high with sudden frustration. "And I told you, we can't go back there."

"Because there's no food?" Sage prompted.

Carl stole a glance at Josie. "You don't trust us," he said to Sage.

Sage creaked to her feet, one hand on her round belly, the baby kicking under her palm. "I don't trust anybody anymore," she said and the thought saddened her. "Why are you trusting me? How do you know I won't try to hurt you?"

"We know," Carl said. Josie nodded.

"I could be crazy, you know."

"We seen crazy," Carl said. "And you're not it."

Sage laughed at that.

"Besides," he added, "you'll need help. With the baby."

"So why can't you stay at your house?" She needed to get to the bottom of this: in the eyes of their parents she'd be kidnapping these children if she took them home with her. A memory flashed, of her at seven years old, coaxing a puppy she'd seen loose in a front yard to follow her home, convincing herself it was a stray, then trying to convince her mother, who simply directed her attention to the collar and the tiny lump in the puppy's scruff where its owners' microchip had been inserted.

Carl looked at Josie again. Josie's head bobbed up and down in slow, deliberate affirmations. "We show you," Carl said to Sage, "then you take us."

"Your house?"

"No, no. The hole. In the Wall." He waved his hands in exasperation. "Canada." Isaac and Ula stopped their play and stared.

Sage's heart thumped. She climbed to her feet. "I can't make that kind of promise, Carl. Show me your house first." Four mouths to feed; four bodies to clothes; four minds to educate. Four hearts and souls to protect and hold. And a fifth to make its debut in four weeks or so. She wasn't sure she could handle that much responsibility, or the grief if things turned out badly. She'd tangled with enough grief over the past few years to last her several lifetimes. What if she couldn't get enough food to feed them all? What if there was no one left in New Denver, neither her mom nor her dad, nor anyone she'd grown up with, to help her with all these children?

Carl was swinging his head back and forth, slapping the thermarest with the palms of his hands. Isaac and Ula scampered behind a tree. "Not going back there. Not going back."

Sage crossed her arms over her breasts. "Well?" she asked Carl. "What's it going to be?"

He jumped up. Josie watched him, still gnawing on her apple. He scuffed the dirt with the heel of one foot.

Half-turning, Sage retrieved her pack. She'd traveled for four terrifying weeks just to get this far and she wasn't going to get stalled on the wrong side of the border arguing with a ten-year-old kid.

"Tell you what," she said finally, feeling a little deceitful—she couldn't take them with her, could she? Could she actually leave them behind, though, to continue to fend for themselves. That'd be as good as killing them. "You take me to the hole in the wall, and I'll let you try to convince me to take you into Canada."

"Convince? What's that?"

She sighed. "Persuade. Sway." Carl was still frowning. "Give me reasons why I should take you."

"What reasons?"

"That's up to you."

They took her directly to a gap in the Wall, about a three-kilometer walk from where she'd camped, and there it stood, the absence of Wall, like a chip out of a front tooth. The gap was almost two meters wide, and because the fire had been so fierce here—the forest heavily wooded, and this section of wall boasting a guarded outpost, which housed electronic detection and drone-activation equipment—the concrete had crumbled, every last molecule of moisture wicked away, into a brittle pile of rubble and powder.

"There," Carl said. "All burned."

"Hmm," Sage mused as she studied the gap and the melted chain link fence beyond. The Wall had served several purposes, firstly as part of the undaunted anti-terrorist campaign by Homeland Security, fueled by Canada's inability to track down and deport anti-American terrorists hiding behind strangely worded Canadian refugee and immigration laws, and secondly, by the astonishingly tenacious cross-border drug and tobacco trade, which had continued to figuratively and economically moon the USDA, and thirdly, as a politically-sequined boondoggle to boost the economies of border towns economically crushed under the giant absence of Canadian tourist and gambling dollars. The drones, which could be activated by sensing equipment anywhere along the meter-thick, seven-meter high wall, had been armed with lethal-force weapons of undisclosed power. Chronically, though, the failure rate of the detection equipment was staggering over the first couple of years due to software problems with viruses and worms, and so Wall breaches were almost a daily occurrence.

To these children, the Wall was just another ruin.

"How did you find it?" Sage asked.

"Hunting," was all Carl said.

Silence blew like smoke between them.

"Convince?" Carl said, looking up at her with his head tilted. His brow ridge hid his dark eyes.

She nodded.

He looked back at Josie who stood with the twins about two meters behind him.

"You need to go home," Sage said. "Where you belong."

"No!"

She pushed her bike through the breach, bouncing the tires over the mounds of crumbled concrete, down through the ditch on the other side, then up and across ten meters of no-man's land to the remnants of a half-melted chain-link fence five meters high, at one time decorated with curling strands of razor wire.

Finally, rather anticlimactically, Sage found herself in Canada.

"Stop!" Carl was running after her. "Stop!" He ran up, grabbed at her arm. She jerked away from his grip, her hearth thudding, the memory of his attack on her the day before flooding her with sudden chills. Isaac and Ula were screaming at being left behind, standing on the other side of the hole in the Wall, too afraid to come through. Josie followed Carl like an automaton, a wasted stray.

"I killed a man," Carl blurted out all in one breath, his eyes wide and scared. "I killed a man, in the house. He's there."

Sage watched his face, how suddenly vulnerable he looked. "Tell me what happened."

Carl talked to the ground. "He broke a window. Just us there. Living. A long time just us four. Days ago, maybe . . . hmm, five, this man broke a window and come in. It was night." Carl scuffed at the ground with his foot. "We hide. He grab Josie's leg—didn't see me and Ula and Isaac. She screamed a lot. She never screamed before. Or talked. He rip her clothes and hit her and yell at her. He lay on top of her. I got my knife, the big one from the kitchen, from under my pillow. I stabbed him right in the back with my knife." His face, anguished and afraid, immersed in the memory, looked far too haggard for a ten-year-old boy.

"I'm so sorry, Carl," Sage said.

"He kept getting up, crashing around, yelling. Then he just laid there. He got real quiet. In the morning he was dead." He looked up at her then, and said, his voice almost a whisper. "He's still there."

Sage wanted to pull him into her arms, to comfort him, tell him that it wasn't fair he had to go through that, tell him how brave he'd been, how strong. Instead, she waved toward his brother and sister. "Go get Isaac and Ula," she said, unsure if taking them with her was truly helping them or pointlessly postponing the inevitable. But she just couldn't leave them behind. *These children need a parent,* she thought, *and this parent needs children.* Sage turned and pushed her bike along the gravel service road that bordered the fence on the Canadian side.

She was half-way home.

Jovan was transferred to a special isolation wing of the hospital for contagious diseases. Five of the nurses from Peds ended up there as well. One died three days later. Three more children joined Jovan, all from his class at school.

Sage found herself a prisoner in her own home, quarantined with Maddie. The family Maddie had been staying with had been quarantined as well, as were the families of the other children, the ill nurses, and all those who had had contact with Jovan during his initial stay at the hospital: a dizzying domino effect of precaution and escalating paranoia.

She called Jovan constantly on her cell so that he wouldn't feel abandoned, emailing him his homework assignments, and streaming him DV of Maddie singing him different silly get-well songs she'd make up. It proved to be a Herculean chore keeping Maddie busy enough with school assignments and games and art projects when confined. And suddenly Sage could think of a million wonderful places to take Maddie, exciting activities to do *outside*; suddenly she felt a driving desire to take up vegetable gardening, to ride her road bike, long forgotten in the garage, to visit her mom in New Denver. She found herself missing her job at the library with biting regret. Mostly, though, she moved through her day in a haze of grief and distraction, finding herself staring out the window at the overgrown front lawn, realizing that Maddie had been speaking to her or that the telephone had been ringing.

She talked to her parents every day by phone, mopping up their support, keeping them apprised of what little she knew of Jovan's condition. The US-Canada border had closed like a vault door. The first documented cases of the new flu in North America had surfaced in Vancouver, and the US, taking no chances, locked the border up even tighter than it was already. Under the WHO's direction, all flights to and from Canadian destinations were cancelled, stranding thousands of US citizens; cross-border commerce ossified, with transport trucks queued up at either side of the Wall for a dozen or more kilometers. However, when reports of American flu cases such as Jovan's hit the press, diplomatic retaliation from the Canadians was loud and potty-mouthed, with inane threats of redirecting power away from the US grids and inciting rolling blackouts if the border wasn't reopened for trade PDQ.

The WHO caught up with the times, finally announcing that the crisis had reached *Preparedness Level 1, Initial Reports of a New Strain in Humans*.

Sage fielded calls from the media, which had found out about Quinn's death in Bangkok and Jovan's hospitalization, but she was unable to answer most of their questions because she knew so little. She hadn't heard back from the airline people, nor had Jovan's doctor been giving her any other information than what she already knew, that Jovan was fighting some kind of new flu. When she tried to get some specific answers via phone, all she found out was that Jovan's doctor was now ill as well, and a new doctor, a specialist who was arriving from LA tomorrow, would call her as soon as he knew something.

She kept CNN on all the time, partly for the company and partly because it was a Quinn thing to do, to have the TV unscrolled, filling a whole wall in the living room and playing constantly, the news jabbering away in the background like a verbal waterfall. It kept the aching grief at bay during the daylight hours; at night the grief overwhelmed her, wracking her body with such heartache that she thought she might not live to morning.

The mornings always came.

Six days after Quinn's death in Bangkok, the news broke like an amniotic membrane, flooding the world with a wash of doom and gloom prognoses. This flu was another avian influenza, like the H5N1 outbreak at the turn of the century. However, an antigenic drift had occurred somewhere, forming a highly contagious—between humans—H5N2 Type A influenza. The World Health Organization was investigating more than one hundred cases in several countries, trying to determine where the new flu virus had first sprung up in hopes of successfully containing it before it reached pandemic proportions.

A long labor of inciting and controlling hysteria battled on the news channels.

More and more families were being placed under quarantine. The names of the countries where new cases were popping up grew longer, almost all of them first-world nations. The WHO's investigation suggested that the epicenter of the pandemic had been Disneyland, in California, although they had no evidence yet for how or why the H5N2 flu had erupted there. The central issue that seemed to tie all the earliest reports together was that, over a period of a week in March, all thirty-three individuals who were denoted as the primary cases had been visiting Disneyland.

And then the monster began to be born.

A letter wormed through the Internet like an urban legend, surfacing on late-night TV talk shows, hosts clambering about in their business suits hooting like chimpanzees, and daytime talk radio, where mostly people were just blowing smoke, thinking they knew who the author had to be, and what the hell he, or she, was talking about.

"Dear Angry Apes,

It is the nature of extreme self-lovers, as they will set an house on fire, and it were but to roast their eggs.

Your house is on fire.

Sincerely,

The True Gorilla"

Copycat letters hit the Internet like a blizzard. Discussion roared, about the Francis Bacon quote, about whether or not "fire" was to be taken literally or metaphorically, or both. CNN then received, among several hundred other letters purporting to be from "The True Gorilla," a handwritten note that caught the attention of more than the mail clerks.

"Dear Angry Apes,

The desire of power in excess caused the angels to fall; the desire of knowledge in excess caused man to fall.

You are falling.

Sincerely,

The True Gorilla"

It was not so much the letter but rather the lengthy block-capital post-script underneath the sender's moniker that caught Homeland

Security's attention: a crisply written sequence for an avian H5N2 Influenza A virus. By then, the WHO had announced that the situation had progressed from a *Novel Virus Alert, Preparedness Level 2 (Human Infection Confirmed) to Preparedness Level 3 (Human Transmission Confirmed).*

Jovan died on April 12th of complications of the Disney flu. Without his mother at his side. Without any family at all. He died alone, in an isolation unit, with masked and bio-suited nurses wrestling with a terrified four-year-old in the bed next to him.

Jovan had ended up in such a weakened state that he developed a pneumonia in his lungs which the medical staff could not get under control. Sage simply couldn't fathom it: first Quinn, and now Jovan. And three days before Jovan's death, Maddie had come down with the avian flu symptoms.

Still stunned by the news from the hospital, Sage pumped up the volume on the scroll TV and sat on the coffee table. Maddie lay on the couch, wrapped in a sleeping bag, with her pillow and her stuffed giraffe. Sage hadn't yet told her about Jovan. CNN was broadcasting the press conference being held by the Director of Homeland Security, a fierce-looking black woman. Sage had trouble paying attention, even though she knew she needed to hear what the woman had to say. She could barely make herself care, though. Twenty-eight days had passed since the kids and Quinn had returned from Disneyland. Less than a month, and half her family had been taken from her.

The Director reported the WHO estimated that almost a quarter of the population in the continental US had been infected with the Disney flu—almost one hundred thousand people—and upwards of two to five million worldwide. The death toll in the US alone was staggering with one thousand and seven confirmed cases, and four thousand probable cases. The real problem, she said, was that, with so many people ill and unable to report to work to do their jobs, simply keeping the country running and safe and secure was becoming extremely difficult.

And then the director took a deep breath. Sage realized she had been holding hers; she realized that everything the Director had said up to this point had been mere preamble. The Director looked into the camera and, under orders from the President, declared martial law.

CHAPTER 8

Ronnie Sapriken tried to shake the fatigue and tension from her muscles. She thumped her thighs and her hips with the heels of her hands, shook out her feet, which were cinched tight in her least-shabby pair of runners, and rolled her head around on her neck. It didn't help. The tension in her neck and shoulders radiated down between her shoulder blades. Her headache now fully encircled her skull. She windmilled her arms in the early morning chill—it was just getting light and the August mornings now had the bite of Fall to them—but the tension wouldn't let go. She gave up on her pre-run stretch, too impatient to simply get moving.

She tapped the center of her chest, starting up the heart monitor in her running bra. The familiar tone tip-tip-tipped through the receiver behind her ear. She cracked her neck first one way, then the other. Her joints ached, not from the training schedule she has maintained these past few months but from the devolution. Swollen knees and elbows, puffy, achy hands and feet. She cracked her neck again, and began to run.

Last November she'd had a bout of the flu which never really went away. By the spring she knew that it hadn't been the flu but rather the signs and symptoms of the beginning of mid-stage, and that realization threw her into a funk, which seemed to piss Matt off, her moping around the house when she wasn't working. The only thing that punched holes through her dark cloud was running, so even though the forest-fire smoke rubbed her throat and sinuses raw, she'd be damned if she'd let it keep her from pounding the pavement.

As such, as far as she was concerned, mornings belonged to her and her alone. They were the only time she seemed to have to herself. She set the alarm for 0430 and was usually running by 0445, sleep or no sleep, light or no light. These days she didn't need to be on shift until 0700, and Matt would never in a million years get up before she was long-gone to work if he didn't have to, and anyone she came across on her run, out tending their gardens or their animals, had learned to just nod or wave and let her be, undoubtedly thinking her loopy for maintaining a training schedule when the world was going to hell in a hand basket.

She was the only RCMP officer left in New Denver, the other two vanishing last summer—one of them taking the only ham radio around—with the big exodus from the valley, not wanting to be stuck out in the boonies when things got worse. And they certainly had. But Ronnie didn't want to leave. She felt an obligation to the community, to the people she'd come to know over the decade since she was posted here, and besides, Matt liked living in New Denver, liked the laid-back lifestyle, so that made it easy to stay. And she hadn't ever wanted to do the big city thing anyway: live in the suburbs, white-picket-fence and all, commute to work, deal with gangs and shootings and skid row bullshit, and all the freakin' politics that came with being a big-city cop. Besides, the RCMP were a cut above city cops, hands down. Two cuts above, as far as Ronnie was concerned.

The tension slowly leeched from her muscles and her stride became full, fluid, and easy. The beep of her monitor relaxed her and the ache between her shoulder blades melted. Her caffeine-addict's headache vanished as if she'd bathed her brain in coffee.

The sky should have been bright and blue but the smoke from the fires had dulled the morning to a peculiar tone of rust. She ran away from the house toward the lake, with it's surface quiet and steel-gray, the Valhalla Mountains stolidly rising from the far shore with its trees air-brushed to the color of iron by the forest fire smoke. She turned along the lake, ran past the Nikkei Internment Centre, which memorialized the internment of Japanese immigrants and Canadian citizens in New Denver and elsewhere during World War II, then cut over a block, and ran up the next street all the way to the highway. New Denver also had the ignominy of being the town where government officials institutionalized Doukhobour children during the 1950s after forcibly separating them from their parents in a series of nighttime raids, raids led by the RCMP.

Ronnie liked using the street grid of this part of town to pile up the kilometers. Today was her long-run day, twelve kilometers. She wiped her face with the back of her arm as she took the road that led to the old hospital, long since boarded up and abandoned after government cutbacks. She had started training a number of years ago with the goal of competing in a local triathlon. Then the Lucy virus gouged a huge hole in the population. Triathlete-type races fell away as issues of basic day-to-day survival took precedence in everyone's lives. Now Ronnie trained because she couldn't *not* train. It satisfied her in ways she was unable to express, a daily release of the pressure that roiled inside her, an addict's fix. And as her body began its four-wheel skid into mid-stage, she knew that, despite all the anger and darkness she'd been pummeled by, she had to fight to control those changes with everything she had. She'd begun to loose mass, but her strength was improving and her stamina was light-years beyond were it used to be. Cardio-wise, she'd never been fitter, with a resting pulse of 40. And besides, training helped her focus her attention on something other than the job. Or on Matt, and all his bullshit.

With the flash of Matt's face in her mind's eye, anger spit white-hot into her psychological atmosphere, tightening her neck and resurrecting the ache between her shoulder blades. Ronnie fought resolutely to relax her shoulders: she adjusted the swing of her arms, gave her neck a quick crack, lengthened her spine.

"I don't know why you're still going to work, Veronica," Matt said to her last night when she told him she was heading to bed. He'd called her Veronica since forever—at first she'd thought it sweet that he used her full name, but now it just annoyed her, like lots of other things about him she used to find alluring. "You're not getting paid anymore," he continued, "far as anyone can tell. So why do you put yourself through all that crap, dealing with all those low-life pukes, like that Walter guy, and those Gargoyle kids."

Gardener, she corrected mentally, but said nothing, because she knew he was trying to be funny, or at least amusing, and he didn't like it if she corrected him. He'd complain she had no sense of humor. And these days she was afraid he might be right. The Gardeners, all three of them boys—young men, really—in their mid-twenties had shown up in the late afternoon behaving like outlaws from a bad western flick, shooting off a hunting rifle, pissed to the gills as they pounded on the door at the bar, which had closed down back in May when their supplies ran out. She threatened them with a night in jail and for some reason they decided to leave, to go back up to wherever they were squatting up on Red Mountain Road, mouthing off only a little.

"Well?" Matt had said, startling her—this was how things had been for some time now, these layers of thoughts, feelings, even daydreams, all distracting her from what was going on at the moment, in the present. In the now. As if some sort of attention deficit disorder had invaded her brain, its lurking announced by that interminable low-grade headache that she tried to convince herself was from lack of coffee. When honesty got the best of her, she knew that being easily distracted was probably just the devolving. Monkey-mind setting in.

Matt had been sitting on the floor in the living room sorting through his fishing gear, a good-sized joint burning in an ashtray beside him—pot from the mayor who grew a rather sizeable plantation in her backyard these lax days and was quite generous with her produce, trading it for vegetables, or meat, or in Matt's case, fish . . . and maybe even sex, so the rumor mill had hinted. All Matt seemed to want to do these days was challenge Ronnie, digging at her insecurities, like using a barbed fishhook to worry out a sliver, telling her things she already knew, demanding to know what she was going to do about it: "So you arrest those bastards 'cause they beat up Walter, then what? Lock 'em up for a couple of months?

Who's gonna feed them? Us? You've got no courtroom, no judge, nothing, just you. And, frankly, you're going to end up just getting yourself killed. You know that? People don't give a damn about the law anymore. And there's nothing you can do about it. You're only one person, Veronica. No matter how many *deputies* you sign up, you're fighting a losing battle against human nature."

Auxiliaries, she had corrected mentally but hadn't said anything. She just watched him as he talked, his attention darting from object to object, like a kid circled by toys. The headache pounded with every word he said and her inner critic took up his cause, echoing his words like gunshots.

She tried to shake away these dark thoughts as she looped back and took the path through the campground where a number of evacuees from Nakusp had taken up residence, setting up tents, doing nothing, sitting about looking shell-shocked, having lost loved ones to the Lucy Syndrome, or homes to the fires, or jobs to the fallout from both.

She upped her speed as she pounded the path above the beach, her breath coming hard now, dry and coarse with the smoke. Sweat ran down her temples. She loved this part of the run, pushing herself, all other thoughts fleeing as she concentrated on breath, form, stride, the fluid movement of muscle and sinew.

She ran like an animal.

Easing back, Ronnie relaxed her pace, slowing her stride to an easy eighty-to-the-minute. She headed up to the highway to run the three kilometers over to Silverton, and then back again, and settled into her distance pace. Her breathing slowed, and with the aftermath of endorphins from the sprint came her fantasy-lust, thick as blood. She had a whole series of these fantasies—afterMatts, she called them, fantasies about her life after Matt. They'd started out innocently enough, evenings when she was alone because he'd gone off hunting for a week with his friends. They'd started showing up during her run when she'd dropped her m-scroll on the pavement last year and no longer had music to keep her company.

AfterMatts. She'd hated the thought of fantasizing about someone else, even someone imaginary, with Matt still in her life—a smoky guilt always invaded her, laced with a ridiculous paranoia that somehow such fantasizing would poison their marriage and make her uncharacteristically vulnerable to a stranger's advances—so she set up a back story in which Matt had been killed in a hunting accident, dead for a couple of years, and she'd grieved and grieved (oh, how she had grieved) but was slowly healing . . .

She flicked through the opening scenes of several afterMatts as she leaned into the climb up out of New Denver.

She parks the RCMP SUV behind the aqua-blue Chevy pickup she'd been following and gets out. She climbs the trail through hemlock and cedar. It's winter, the new knee-deep snow betraying his crisp boot prints—he'd come this way barely an hour before her. The trail empties into a clearing with a small log cabin, smoke rising from the metal chimney, yellow candlelight glowing behind white-curtained windows. She steps up onto the porch, her winter boots clumping loudly, and raps on the door, which swings open with the simple force of her knock. Inside the cabin the air is thick with steam. She pulls off her hat, closes the door behind her. A clawfoot tub, brimming with steaming water, fills a corner of the one-room cabin, a bed fills the other, and between them, a woodstove chugs out heat like a Roman bloomery. To her right, a wooden table with pinewood ladderback chairs, and a note on the table, addressed to her, is held down by a bottle of blush wine and two glasses—

An unbidden memory from their first anniversary pushed into her mind: wine and two glasses on a table: for their first anniversary Matt had surprised her with wine and candles and dinner—corny and deliciously romantic—with sex and crème caramel (drizzled with dark chocolate) for dessert. She and Matt had been married barely a year before she'd been posted to New Denver. And he'd loved the idea, moving to a small town smack dab in the middle of great fishing and hunting and hiking, but he hadn't been able to find work in his field, no surprise to either of them, New Denver—back then—being a town of only 350 residents and Matt being trained as an urban geographer. Not exactly a glove-like fit. Finally, he'd landed a job with an eco-tourism company and that seemed to keep him satisfied for a number of years. They tried to have kids. After the third miscarriage, though, they both gave up without even having to talk about it. They should have talked about it, but they didn't. Their not-talking seemed iconic of the devolution of their marriage. And now Ronnie couldn't seem to stop not-talking.

You see, she should have said to him, at least as a police officer I still have something to do, I still have a purpose in life. Sure, she wasn't getting paid, but that didn't matter to her. She had a reason to get out of bed every day, and she was the only one left to do her job, even if that meant she had to deal with more than her fair share of low-life pukes. A town needed law enforcement, even if the absence of a judicial system made the whole process rather fuzzy. Matt was right, of course, both deterrence and punishment-by-incarceration were out of the question. People had to do what was right because it was good for the community as well as for themselves—that's what Ronnie believed, that's what she had always believed—otherwise they were all screwed, with everyone devolving to the lowest common denominator, the proverbial every-man-for-himself, full-speed-ahead-damn-the-torpedoes. And Ronnie just couldn't abide that. And these days she could no longer abide Matt believing that.

She shoved thoughts of Matt to the back of her mind.

Walking to the table, she sheds her parka, drapes it on the back of one of the chairs. She's sweating, just a little, under her vest. The note is folded, a simple cream paper with her name scrawled across it. She opens it. 'Take a bath' is all it says in his large crisp script. There is no sign of him in the single room cabin. She locks the door behind her, pours herself some wine, and unbuttons her uniform shirt—

Lust arced through her—not the thin arousal of the afterMatt but something stronger, fuller—and in that moment, a vision arced like a meteor across her mind's eye, of the Gardener boys, their insolence more vituperative than usual, mouthing off at her when she told them to go home, the two youngest finally turning away, while the oldest boy, Roy, his lucyized face making him look even stupider than he was, held his ground, his big chin jutting. Lust roared through her like an old Saturn V rocket—not for him, but for his blood—and *as he jerks the rifle up and toward her in sudden crazed defiance, the scenario keys into slow motion. She slides her 10 mm out of its holster, easy as undressing, slips off the safety and puts the first round oh-so-beautifully into his right shoulder, throwing him backwards, and sends the second slug into his chest just above the fourth rib. He falls like an action hero, all slow motion and drama, red flowers blooming on his chest, rifle sliding impotently across the pavement.*

The endorphin rush howled through her. Ronnie staggered mid-stride, legs suddenly weak, heart jack-hammering, disturbed by how deliciously aroused she was by those two shots thunking into Roy's flesh, terminating a tediously everlasting problem in one simple, perfunctory moment. It was as good as licking ice cream, better than an afterMatt. *Hell, much better.*

She crested the summit between the two towns on a wave of rising bloodlust that left her confused, dizzy. The smoke at the summit seemed unbearably thick. She wiped her face as echoes of the vision flashed across her mind's eye, then staggered to a standstill: below her parts of Silverton burned, flames puking smoke high into the morning sky. She stood, momentarily stunned. Her monitor beeped frantically. She cursed herself for not carrying her portable radio—which she never carried on her run anyway—then spun and ran, as hard and as fast as she could, to sound the alarm before the fire spread, before it consumed all of Silverton and swarmed up and over the bluff to consume New Denver, her home, her life.

CHAPTER 9

Ronnie wrestled into her uniform in the RCMP station, her skin still drenched with sweat from the mad run back into New Denver to the church to ring the bell and sound the alarm. The Emergency Team Leaders had responded quickly, mustering at the church for a briefing. She didn't have much to go on but told them to prepare for a big firefight, potentially with casualties in Silverton.

Sweat soaked right through her uniform shirt and into her vest as she jumped down the station steps, unplugged the RCMP SUV from the solar feed before leaping inside. She threw it into reverse and squealed out of the driveway onto the street, where she stopped, took a couple of breaths to calm herself even though the church bells were still sounding the alarm, calling for the whole community to respond, and the fire trucks, with Matt on board, had already rolled, but she knew in the pit of her gut that unless they somehow got a handle on the house fires in Silverton the whole mountainside would go up in flames.

Irene and some new guy whose name Ronnie couldn't recall flew by her in the ambulance, using their siren to add to the call-to-alarm. What Ronnie dreaded most were the possible burn victims—house fires before full daybreak could easily be fatal, homes filled with sleeping residents—especially given that what they called their makeshift hospital was really nothing more than a glorified first aid room set up at the school. Only a dozen or so families still lived in Silverton, though, so most of the houses were boarded up or just sitting empty, abandoned. Word from the evacuees coming down the valley was that the hospital in Nakusp had been gutted when their town was overrun by fire in mid-July. Nothing had been saved. Thirty people died—that they knew about—and most people lost their homes, although miraculously a few were spared here and there, given the strange wiles of the fire. Ronnie still hadn't finished interviewing them all.

She followed in the wake of the ambulance, up over the crest where she had aborted her run and down through the outskirts of Silverton, crossing the bridge over Silverton Creek. She parked at the Museum a car length behind the ambulance. The Silverton Inn, at the south end of town, was completely engaged, spitting snotballs of fire up into the treed hillside. The fire hall, situated behind the Museum, was in flames. One of the fire trucks had been pulled out into the street, but was already lost. People were scurrying around like panicked rats. Several houses a block up from the Inn were also engaged. The New Denver firefighters threw in with those from Silverton to save the fire hall, or at the least the other truck, the turnout gear, the SCBA equipment—all irreplaceable.

A crowd of people milled about the dead lawn in front of the Museum, where rusting mining equipment from the region's mining heydays lined the sidewalks. Several people were weeping, holding onto each other. A woman wearing only an ankle-length nightgown ran toward the SUV, hollering something at Ronnie, arms reaching, her tear-streaked face twisted with anguish. The woman was Deloris Kessler, the Museum's caretaker.

Ronnie climbed out of her vehicle, slipped her shock-baton in her belt. The paramedics were heading toward the crowd.

Deloris came around the vehicle, grabbed at Ronnie's arm. "They took my Thea!" she cried out through the tears. "They *took* her! And they killed my Peter when he tried to stop them!"

Molten steel swirled through Ronnie's gut. She held Deloris at arms' length. "What happened?" she said.

Deloris, one hand going to her mouth, simply pointed at the crowd on the lawn with her other hand. The crowd had opened up like a wound for the paramedics. Ronnie let go of Delores and stepped over the concrete parking barrier. Six bodies lay on the brown lawn. There was a lot of blood. Irene moved from body to body, assessing, while her partner, the young man whose name Ronnie still couldn't recall, slowly backed away, the red jump bag clutched to his chest.

Suddenly other people noticed Ronnie and rushed at her, all of them talking at once. She held her hands in front of her. "I'm going to want to hear from everybody, but right now I just want one or two people's stories. The rest of you—I know this is hard—need to go do what you can to help fight the fires. We *have to* get those fires under control. Understood?"

There were nods and grunts of assent, then they talked among themselves, deciding who would stay. Ronnie delivered Deloris into their midst and went over to Irene.

"What have we got?" she said, but didn't need the words to tell her what her eyes already saw: six dead from gunshot wounds—rifle and a small shotgun, probably a 4-10, from close range—two shot point-blank in the face, the rest with various GSWs to the chest and abdomen.

"I've never seen anything like this before," said Irene, who was the same age—fifty-six—as Ronnie's mother would have been if she were still alive. Ronnie and Irene had never been close, but they shared an easy camaraderie that came with doing calls together in the middle of the night, and Irene seemed to have a bit of a soft spot for Ronnie, if only because she was the same age as Irene's daughter.

Irene straightened up. "One of them said it was the Gardener boys. They came into town about two a.m. all pissed up and raring for a fight. Somebody else said there were a couple of other neanderthals with them. That *they* took Deloris's girl."

"Yeah, I'm going to talk to her." The salacious chunk-chunk of fantasy bullets hitting Roy Gardener's body echoed inside Ronnie's head and she couldn't help but think if she'd killed him yesterday afternoon none of this would have happened. She slapped the thought away. (*Killed him for what?* her inner critic demanded, *Just for being an asshole?*) "Are they sure it was the Gardener boys?"

"That's what I heard."

"I'll get the story."

"Nothing we can do here," Irene said. "We're going to head over to the fires, see if everyone got out okay."

"All right." Ronnie's head throbbed. An explosion further down the street made her duck automatically, the morning sky brightening as flames shot upward. One of the houses must have had some propane left in a tank for a BBQ. A tree behind the fire hall erupted in flames.

Ronnie motioned to Deloris and to the man standing with her, one arm around her shoulders, and led them to the other side of the SUV where she convinced Deloris to climb inside. The man introduced himself as Josh Pierce and Ronnie recalled that he'd lost three or four kids over the past couple of years to complications from the Lucy Syndrome. He drove snowplow in the winter.

"They showed up about two, two-thirty," Josh began, worrying strands of beard between a finger and thumb. He was fully mid-stage, a small scrawny man with a narrow chest, jutting jaw and protruding orbits, which interfered with how his glasses sat on his nose.

"Who showed up?" Ronnie asked.

"Those Gardener boys—Roy, Willis, and Levi—and two others. Didn't recognize them, though, but someone said they knew who they were."

Ronnie simply nodded to keep him going as she glanced over his shoulder at the scramble to get the trees on the hillside behind the Inn knocked down before the fire jumped further up the mountain.

"They broke into the Inn, looking for booze or cigarettes, whatever. Lots of yelling. I could hear them from inside my house over there"—he pointed across the street—"so I came out and there was already a bunch of people out there in front of the Museum arguing with them and yelling at them, including Peter Hlookoff." He nodded at Deloris, then, who was crying into her hands with such ferocity that Ronnie felt tears welling up in response. "They'd grabbed Peter and Deloris's girl, Thea, who had come out of the house—she's a pretty little thing, about sixteen, most of the way through end-stage, but smart as a whip. They meant no good, saying they'd trade her back for beer and cigarettes and pot, and they were laughing and holding a gun to her head like it was some sort of game. Peter tried to grab her back and they just shot him point-blank." Josh swallowed.

"Who shot him?"

"One of the others, I don't know his name. The older one, guy in his late twenties, heavy-set, lots of muscle." He toed the pavement for a moment. "Then it all went to hell after that. People screaming and running and all kinds of shots being fired. I ducked back into the house, figured I needed to get some protection, so I grabbed my 12-gauge and some shells, but by the time I got back outside those houses over there were on fire, and they had set the fire hall on fire.

"I ran down the sidewalk figuring I could get to their trucks, maybe blow out their tires, anything, 'cause of them taking Thea, but they shot at me. Anyway, I couldn't get close enough. They set the lawn in front of the Inn on fire then burned out of here in their trucks, heading south. Folks figure they're squatting someplace up on Red Mountain Road, there's a bunch of big fancy houses up there that have been abandoned. A bunch of us talked about going up there after them, but they're pretty heavily armed."

Ronnie took a breath. She knew what they'd be doing to Thea right now. "Nobody's going after them without me," she said. "Thanks, Josh. I'll find you, okay? Right now, I'd like you to take Deloris and help her get me a picture of Thea, okay?"

He nodded, looking relieved that she'd given him something to do.

Deloris slid out of the SUV. Josh took her arm, led her up the street away from the fires and the bodies on the Museum lawn.

It was hard to tell that it was fully daylight now, the smoke was so thick and ash was falling like snow.

Ronnie tucked the pre-lucyized photo of Thea into the breast pocket of her vest: an attractive girl, but not pretty, just ordinary brown hair with typical hazel-green eyes and a largish nose. Ronnie tracked down Josh Pierce for a more recent and realistic description.

"She had on a jacket, orange, I think, over top of some pajamas, flannel ones, the kind little kids wear. She pretty much looks like the picture, except her nose is flatter and the openings bigger, you know, and she's got a pretty prominent ridge, more than most. She doesn't talk much anymore either—don't know if she can't, or if she just doesn't want to." He shrugged, ducked his head.

"What?"

"Poor kid. Just can't help thinking what those bastards are doing to her."

Ronnie simply nodded. She wished she could call in the regional Emergency Response Team, but she couldn't: the RCMP infrastructure (bureaucratic and electronic) had disintegrated along with the rest of the government. She wished this responsibility wasn't hers, but it was, she'd chosen it and she had maintained it, despite Matt's recent protestations. She wanted to put a rescue team together immediately, something small because she wasn't sure how many bodies the community could afford to free up before the fires were under control.

She found Darcy Khaira, the fire chief. "Can you spare a couple of my auxiliaries?"

Darcy just held up his hands: "Do what you gotta do, Ronnie, but frankly I was just coming to find you to send you back into New Denver to get us warm bodies—anybody, even those shell-shocked Nakusp folks—we're in some pretty deep shit here, and I'm not sure we're going to get out of it."

Ronnie rubbed her forehead, trying to settle her headache. "I want to set up a roadblock on the highway. You know, to keep the riffraff out, or at least trap them if they decide to come back into town. And I want to go after the Gardener boys. They took a sixteen-year-old girl."

"Yeah, I heard." He shook his head. "Nothing three bullets wouldn't solve."

Ronnie's heart danced up into her throat.

"I'm kidding," Darcy said. "Well, sort of kidding, if you know what I mean." He wiped his face on the sleeve of his turnout coat. "We're gonna be here all day, for sure, and all night. Could you let Polly Sherstibitoff and the rest of the Dragon Ladies know before you bugger off, maybe get some food coming down the pipe?"

"I'll take care of it," she said, then headed over to the Museum to photograph the slain bodies before returning to New Denver. She had to have a visual record of this crime. In all her years in New Denver, she had never had a homicide: she'd had lots of suicides, two attempted murders—both perpetrators had been too drunk to do the deed properly—and various and sundry traumatic fatalities, but never a homicide. Now she had six. And a *bona fide* kidnapping—not the usual kind, the estranged dad running off with a kid he doesn't really like just to piss off his ex-wife, nor the ones where rumors of an absentee parent kidnapping a child turn out to be tall tales surrounding the countless devolved kids who simply go missing, wandering off to join the packs when they hit puberty, or succumbing to the elements or injuries before someone in the community realizes they've become orphans.

Someone had covered the bodies with taupe fake-suede curtains taken from one of the abandoned houses. She took her pictures, then covered the bodies back up.

After a bit of searching she found three of her auxiliaries, piled them into her SUV, and headed back to New Denver. She sent two of them to ferry anybody who could walk and follow instructions over to Silverton, and delegated the third auxiliary to come up with some sort of security perimeter they could easily set up around the twin towns.

Priorities, she grunted to herself, knowing full well what the continued delay in rescue would be costing Thea. *Goddamn priorities.*She'd kill the bastards when she found them; no, she wouldn't, she'd do her job and arrest them and stuff them in a cell at the station. *And then what*? Matt had said. *And who's going to feed them? Us?*

Like hell, she thought in response, bitterness fomenting her base-line anger into a simmering rage.

CHAPTER 10

"Turn up here," Alex said to Marika, who cranked the wheel to the right and bounced the truck up a gravel road. Smoke billowed into the sky; towers of flame shot high above the ridgeline as tree after tree candled.

Yuri pounded on the roof of the cab. "Hey, take it easy! You just about bounced me—! Holy Christ, have you see the fire? Jesus Mary Mother of God."

"There are a couple of places," Alex said to Marika, "before the road starts to hook back down to the highway where we can probably get a good look at the ridge and maybe see how big this fire is. The folks in Silverton and New Denver might want to know what they're up against."

"The smoke's so thick I can almost chew it," Marika said.

Yuri was pounding on the roof again. "Hey, stop the truck. Stop the truck!"

The truck crunched to a halt then was enveloped in a cloud of dust from the gravel road. Yuri clambered off the load, hopping on one foot, and climbed in the back seat.

"Back this thing up," he said. "Back up to that driveway there on the right."

"Did you see another fire?" Alex asked.

"No. Not sure what I saw. Just want to check it out. Here, here: stop." He had the door half-open before Marika had halted the truck.

Alex looked at Marika. She shrugged as she kicked on the parking brake and turned off the motor. Yuri was already out and hobbling up the gravel driveway. Alex jumped out of the truck.

"Let me know if it's worth a look-see," Marika called after him.

A sun-faded yellow vinyl-sided garage was perched at the top of the driveway in a grove of trees. Through more trees but further back on the left Alex could see a two-story house the same ugly color as the garage, with a monstrous overgrown lawn and several weedy-looking perennial beds, and an older Honda SUV parked half on the lawn. Straight ahead beyond the end of the driveway stood a small barn with run-in sheds for horses, long empty, and a dried out paddock. In the paddock, slumped on the ground, her hands tied above her to a hitching post, was a young devolved woman, an adolescent really, maybe fifteen or sixteen years old. Alex couldn't see her face as her head hung forward. She was naked except for a torn baby-pink pajama top, which hung open at the front.

Alex skidded to a halt, suddenly afraid. *She sure as hell hadn't tied herself to that post.* Before he could call out to Yuri to be careful, she had lunged to her feet, and even from where Alex stood by the garage he could see her eyes widen with immediate terror. She started to pull at her bindings, twisting and writhing, then began to screech and scream.

Curses erupted from inside the house. A head pushed out an open window on the second floor. "Shut up, bitch!" the man yelled, then stared. He pulled inside.

"Yuri! Get the hell out of there!" Alex called out.

The front door of the house slammed open. The man who had stuck his head out the window—an unshaven man in his mid-twenties looking rather hung over, with longish dark hair and wearing only a t-shirt and underwear—shook an arm at them. "Get the fuck out of here!"

Yuri froze at the edge of the paddock while the young woman continued to screech and pull at the rope binding her wrists.

Another man appeared on the steps, then, older than the first, built like a steroid-assisted weightlifter. He swung a rifle up to his hip and gunshots cracked through the air. Alex bolted back toward the truck, waving an arm at Marika, who had been standing on the road, leaning against the truck waiting for them. "Start it up!" he hollered.

"Were those gunshots?" she said, eyes wide.

Alex could hear his name being called. He stopped.

"Alex! I've been hit!"

Marika jumped in the driver's seat and fired up the engine. Alex's stomach clenched. He could still hear the screeching of the young woman over the growl of the motor. He turned, glanced at the porch in time to see the man with the gun descend the steps to the lawn. Alex bolted back up the driveway.

There, behind an overturned picnic table, Yuri lay on the ground, trying to get up, a bloody hand against his belly.

The two men were making their way across the lawn, moving carefully. Two more shots barked, hitting a tree just behind Alex as he slid in beside Yuri.

"Shit, Alex," Yuri said, "this really hurts."

"Just hang on, okay. We gotta go, and I mean right now."

"I can walk," Yuri said with a grunt.

Alex hooked an arm under Yuri's armpit. He poked his head up over the edge of the picnic table. The two men had angled closer to the paddock, in order to come between them and the woman. Several trees offered some protection.

"Let's go," Alex whispered. He pulled Yuri to his feet, jammed his shoulder up into Yuri's armpit to support him, then ran in a crouch, half-dragging Yuri. More shots. Alex grunted with the exertion, but fear drove him, his legs pumping hard. Yuri simple hung his head and endured, running as best he could.

Marika had the doors open, and the jumpkit sat on the floor in the back seat. Alex levered Yuri into the back seat ahead of him. Yuri grunted in pain. Marika floored the accelerator, slamming Alex's door shut and shooting the truck ahead in a spray of gravel and dust. Bullets thwacked into the side of the truck bed.

Alex squished onto the floor of the back seat and pulled on a pair of chloroprene gloves. Yuri was still laying mostly face down, groaning. There was a bloody hole in the back of his T-shirt. Alex cut the shirt open. The exit wound was a hand span below the ribcage, twoonie-sized and ragged, which meant the bullet had passed right through and had taken most of its kinetic energy with it. The exit wound was bleeding, but not heavily, and there were no air bubbles. Alex taped a trauma dressing over it, then helped Yuri roll over onto his back and inspected the entrance wound, which was dime-sized and leaking quite a bit of blood.

"You didn't get hit anywhere else?" Alex asked as he taped a dressing over the entrance wound. Yuri shook his head, but Alex checked him over anyway as the truck bounced and fishtailed over the gravel road.

"Can you ease up a bit, Marika? I want to start an IV."

"They're coming, Alex," Marika said. "I can see that SUV behind us every once in a while through the dust."

"Great," Yuri muttered. "Just fucking great."

Alex prepped a line, braced his body between the seats, and tried the antecubital fossa anyway. "Got it," he said as he taped the catheter in place.

"What are we going to do?" Yuri said. "Drive 'til we run out of gas?"

"I'm going to drive right up the front steps of the New Denver cop shop, thank you very much."

"What if there's no one there? What if they've all left already? Can't you go any faster?"

The truck slid sideways around a corner.

"How about you just shut up and let me drive, okay?"

Suddenly the truck bounced hard and settled smoothly onto pavement.

"Thank Christ," Yuri muttered.

"I'm going to give you some morphine for that pain," Alex told him.

Yuri wrapped bloody fingers around Alex's arm. "No. It's not that bad. Save it for someone else."

"You're kidding me, right?"

Yuri shook his head. Alex shoved the vial back into the drug kit.

The engine roared as Marika floored the accelerator on a straight stretch, then she banked hard through several curves.

"They're still there," she said, watching the reflection in the side mirror. "I can see them clear as anything now."

Yuri moaned. Alex started a second IV.

Marika slammed the tires over several small trees lying on the pavement. Near the top of a rise, a section of the road had sloughed away, so she drove hard against the ditch, alder and conifer branches scraping paint off the side of Mickey's truck.

"I knew we should have brought a gun," Yuri said as he tried to sit up a little.

Alex held his hand on Yuri's chest to keep him still.

"Yeah, right," Alex said, "you said for protection against bears, not people."

"One of you would have just ended up blowing a foot off or something," Marika said through gritted teeth as the back end of the truck skidded to the right.

Gemma's voice invaded Alex's brain: *It'd be quick, right? They say your body's so shocked you don't feel anything really, right?*

"I don't like guns," Marika said. "Never even shot the one we have."

Grampa's old gun is still in the basement, and there are bullets. I checked.

"You don't have to like them, you just have to respect them," Yuri said, grunting with the pain. "Everybody should know how to use a gun, anyway, especially now that we have to be our own police."

"Our own police," Alex echoed.

"There's still one cop left in New Denver, last I heard," Marika said, then, "Jesus, they're gaining on us."

What if there are complications and I'm in so much pain, but I can't tell you, or we don't have medicine anymore?

"Shit!" Marika braked hard, the truck skidded, tires squealing on the hot pavement. Alex strained around to look out the windshield. Marika fought to control the pickup.

A massive conifer blocked the highway, lying crosswise like a dead giant.

The truck lurched to a halt several meters from the tree.

"Hey . . . " Marika said. "I can see people moving through the bush over here. Oh Christ, they've got guns, too."

She rammed the transmission into reverse, floored the accelerator. The truck didn't seem to move at first, then suddenly it was flying backwards, the motor screaming. But then she braked hard, tires screeching, jerking the truck to a standstill.

Alex stuck his head out the window. Behind them the SUV that had given chase was nowhere in sight, but a tree, a cedar, even larger than the one they'd just about hit, crashed onto the pavement twenty meters behind them.

Then there was a shotgun jammed against Alex's ear and someone he couldn't quite see was yelling at him, at them, ordering them to get out of the vehicle right fucking now or his brains would be all over the side of the goddamn truck.

CHAPTER 11

They camped south of the town of Grand Forks in a log barn that had withstood the fire. To Sage, it seemed much safer to go to the trouble of hauling her bike and panniers up into the loft, with the swallow shit and bat shit and mouse shit on boards rubbed smooth by years of moving hay bales, than it was to camp out in the open. At least up here they could fend off attackers. Sage had brought up a pitchfork she'd found—it was as good a weapon as any. She doubted there would be any attackers, though; in fact she wasn't sure there was anybody left in the whole town. She'd heard no untoward sounds—no motors, bells, shouts—just this weird quiet, punctuated by crow calls and a barking dog somewhere in the distance, which seemed to fill a world that, too, felt mostly empty.

With a flat-nosed shovel she'd found in the barn next to the pitch fork, Sage scraped away the guano while Carl dragged over a couple of old, forlorn bales. Josie helped him spread out the straw to use as a mattress.

An eastern breeze wandered through the loft, cooling it, picking up the dust they'd made and pushing it out the opening at the west end. The sun, a coppery smudge in the smoky sky, threw warm light across the loft floor. Sage set up her hiking stove—the stove she'd taken from the house along with her bike and all the other camping gear—and filled a pot with water to boil. She had several packets of hot chocolate left, and now was as good a time as any to make some of it up and drink it. Then she'd cook up two packets of Japanese noodle soup. That would probably hold everybody until morning. After dinner, they'd string up her panniers to protect them from the mice, climb down and have one last pee, then she'd make up a little nest in the straw for the kids with the musty horse-blankets she'd found in the tack room. And as the sun fell away into night, she'd tell them a story, as she'd promised, and they'd all go to sleep. Librarian or not, she simply had no idea what story to tell them. Nothing twigged her imagination; no story hopped forward making her heart flutter, as it usually would. When the time came, she decided simply to ask them.

"What kind of story do you want to hear?" she asked.

Carl took a sip of hot chocolate, then handed Sage's lidded coffee mug to Isaac, who took it eagerly in both his hands. Ula crouched beside him, barely able to contain her impatience. "Hot," Carl said. Isaac frowned at him, not a confused look, but rather one that clearly said, I know, I'm not a baby—how many times had Sage seen that look on Maddie's face when Jovan was being bossy.

"A story about a princess? Or a wizard? Or about a great warrior who is trying to get home to his—"

"Tell us a story about you," he said. "And it can't be sad."

Ula tried to grab the mug from Isaac, who screeched at her, jerking the mug away. "Hey, hey," Carl said. "You gotta share, Isaac." He held out his hand until Isaac, ruefully, finally gave up the mug.

And it can't be sad. For a moment, Sage thought she might cry. Agreed, there was already too much sadness in the world.

Ula grinned at Carl when he handed her the hot chocolate.

She settled herself onto her sleeping bag, then told them about the time when she was fourteen years old and on a camping holiday in Canada with her parents. She told them about her best friend, a Shepherd-Rottweiler cross she named Crease because when he was a puppy he had this crease across his nose, and how Crease saved her life by keeping her warm when she got lost in the woods one night after following a trail from her family's campsite high up into the mountains.

"I had a dog," Carl said. "Her name was Ripper. I had to leave her. Dad said he was going to get Ripper, and come back. To the cabin. But he didn't come back."

"I'm so sorry, Carl."

Ula had clambered behind him in order to hand the mug of hot chocolate to Josie. "That's right, Ula," he said to her. "Good sharing." Ula flopped onto her behind between Carl and Josie.

"I like dogs," he said to Sage. "Nice ones. Not the bad ones."

"I like dogs, too," Sage said, her voice choking at the thought of all the loss Carl had already endured in his short life.

"When I'm grown up, maybe twelve, or even eleven, I'm going to have another dog."

Sage nodded, words of reply trapped and burning hot in her throat.

After tucking in the children, she sat in the dark with her sleeping bag wrapped around her against the August night, tears streaming down her face. The sentimentality of her life's version of a girl-and-her-dog story coupled with the naked loss on Carl's face as he talked about Ripper had melted away some of the ice she'd layered over the nucleus of her pain, as though the nearer she got to her destination the less able she was to protect herself, from either the present or the past.

With hundreds of others, Sage and Maddie were transported in a special bus by soldiers in bioprotective gear to a FEMA mobile isolation hospital near Fairchild Air Force Base just west of Spokane, Washington. Rows and rows of barracks had been assembled in a hayfield near the base to house the quarantined families, while sealed hospital tents became home to the ill and the dying. A nasty-looking perimeter fence had been erected to keep intruders out and infected persons in.

There had been no funeral for Jovan, nor for Quinn. The whole country seemed to be drowning in a stupor of disbelief as the death toll from the Disney flu clambered upward. In turn, cascading disasters wracked the country: rolling blackouts, factory shutdowns, inner city fires. The freeways were clogged with dead vehicles, making it difficult for the National

Guard to patrol. The infrastructure of the American economy was girded by people, by millions of individuals who went to work and who consumed, and with over a quarter of the population ill, the infrastructure, like a massive bridge on rusted supports, began to creak and crack and sag, which in turn led to more deaths than the influenza had already claimed. Hospitals turned away patients; FEMA camps proliferated; soldiers shot on sight looters who broke curfew.

Maddie didn't die from complications of the flu, as had Jovan and Quinn. She'd been feverish for five days while they had been quarantined at home and she had become quite weak; however, by the time they were evacuated to the camp, she'd bounced back to her normal animated self. Sage didn't come down with any untoward symptoms at all.

They took only one suitcase of belongings each, it was all they were allowed, which they packed while armed soldiers stood in their house, their bug-faced biosuits frightening. There had been no warning. A pounding on the door. Shouted instructions. Sage tried to call her mom, but the circuits were all busy, and she couldn't get a signal with her cell. She sent a quick email, dictating it to the house computer as she helped Maddie pack.

Sudden anger scoured away the torpidity of the past weeks. Why hadn't they tried to make a run for it like so many others she'd seen on the News? She was angry at herself for sitting open-mouthed in front of the TV, stunned by the disintegration of her family, of the country, when she had Maddie's welfare and safety—and the baby's welfare and safety—to consider. *What kind of a mother was she*? Briefly, she considered making a run for it right then and there while the soldiers waited in the living room, sneaking out the back door into the wet April night. But where would they go? They'd never make it past the first military checkpoint. And if you got caught out after curfew, or if you ran into one of those gangs out there the News reported on . . .

Simply going with the soldiers seemed the most reasonable option, and so they did, ushered out the door of their house, their home, setting the biometric lock, the soldiers unable to tell Maddie when they'd be allowed back, and Sage, the answer burning in the pit of her stomach like dry ice, fed Maddie patriotic platitudes. She knew the answer, and it was this: *never.*

The camp did *not* at all make her think of the summer camp on Kootenay Lake she got sent to when she was eleven. It made her think, instead, of the Japanese Internment Camp in New Denver, where the Canadian government forcibly removed Japanese Canadians during World War II; it made her think of photos she'd seen in Montreal's Holocaust Memorial Museum when she was sixteen, photos of *those* camps; it made her think of the documentary she'd watched, interviews with Doukhobour men and women living in the Slocan Valley, quite elderly at the time of filming, who as children were stolen from their parents on midnight raids by the RCMP during the 1950s and imprisoned in New Denver in a boarding school surrounded by a tall chain link fence.

Even though the Director of Homeland Security had said this was the only way to get the virus under control, Sage felt a terror that turned her muscles to slush as she climbed down the metal steps of the bus, gripping Maddie's hand, and stepped into the mud that was the parking area in front of rows and rows of prefab metal-walled barracks, and beyond the barracks stood a five-meter chain-link fence topped with a curl of wire that glinted scalpel-sharp in the wan early morning light.

Maddie changed before Sage's very eyes. The cheer drained from her cheeks. She stopped running everywhere, complained that she hurt all over, her knees, her elbows, her shoulders. Even her teeth ached. She missed home. *When are we going back home, Mommy?* She missed Daddy and Jovan. *Are we going to die, too?* As they slept together in Sage's cot, Maddie refusing to sleep in her own, even with the two cots pushed together, she'd ask Sage to sing to her, and Sage would sing quiet, happy songs until Maddie finally slept or one of the other families complained. And then Sage would lie there, in the never-dark of the crowded, stuffy barrack, listening to snores and farts and tears and sudden night-terror shouts amidst the pounding of the May rain on the metal roof, all-the-while fighting her own despair. She wondered if Maddie would be able to continue to cope if this incarceration lasted too long; she wondered if *she* would be able to cope. She wondered if her mother got the email message she'd dictated to the house computer. She wondered, once it was all over—hopefully by September, if not sooner, the Director had promised—what kind of world she would be bringing her new baby into. Her and Quinn's baby. Loss lanced her like hot shrapnel.

The "campers," as they called themselves, were put to work, depending on their backgrounds and skills, cooking in the main kitchen, cleaning, assisting in the tent hospitals to care for the sick and the dying, supervising and teaching the children. The non-infected workers, the outsiders, bug-eyed in their biosuits, dwindled in numbers as the summer wore on, replaced by already-infected newcomers with the same skills or expertise, but without suits. Most of them were not happy to be posted (read quarantined-slash-incarcerated) at the camp.

Sage volunteered to help administer the elementary school program so that she could be with Maddie most of the time. It was clear to her that the promised September deadline for finding a treatment for the Disney flu and returning the campers to their homes was going to fly by without apology from Homeland Security. Supposedly the influenza virus didn't normally survive well in warmer weather, but this strain seemed to do just fine. Something about it having been bio-engineered to be more heat-tolerant, CNN said, the TV in the camp dining room scrolled down and on all the time.

The camp filled to overflowing by mid-August. Additional barracks were brought in. Sage helped assemble them.

Sage brushed Maddie's hair, working out the tangles that seemed to create themselves over the course of a day. It was early evening toward the end of August, and the air felt cool despite the day's heat still radiating off the barrack wall. Several kids and adults played soccer on the hard-packed parking area. Maddie sat silently between Sage's legs on the wooden stoop at the front of their barrack as Sage worked the brush through her hair. Other adults sat near them, absently watching the game or staring off beyond the fence at the Air Force base.

Maddie wore shorts and a T-shirt that needed laundering, and bare feet, dusty brown from playing all day out on the dirt parking area. Maybe it was the angle of the light, yet it seemed to Sage that Maddie's arms and legs were covered in long sun-bleached hairs that she hadn't noticed before, thicker and heavier than her normal little-girl down. She glanced around her to see if other adults were noticing. She looked at Maddie's neck, pulled the back of her T-shirt away and looked inside.

"What?" Maddie asked, turning.

"Nothing, love."

"Did a bug fall down there?"

"No, no. Just tucking in the tag," Sage lied.

Maddie frowned at her as she turned back to watch the kids playing soccer, reaching behind her, trying to scratch the imaginary bug away. Sage scratched for her. Maddie rounded her shoulders with a groan of pleasure so that Sage would scratch her whole back. Sage set the brush down and scratched.

Maddie shook herself like a dog when Sage finished.

"I'll brush *your* hair now," she said, so Sage handed her the brush and Maddie stood behind her, judiciously moving her hands over Sage's hair, deciding where she was going to begin. "Do you want me to make braids, Mommy?"

"Sure, honey. Braids would be nice."

Linus was born on the third of November, 2016. Sage was told that he hadn't survived, that they'd taken him away for specialized care because his lungs were underdeveloped and he hadn't, however, responded to the treatment. She saw him briefly, though, a nurse rushing him behind the curtain for Maddie to hold, just for a moment. *You're not supposed to see him*, she said to Sage. *He's the third child in the camp born this way. I thought you should know.* Sage stroked his hair-covered arms, his flat-nosed face, smelled his baby smell. And then the nurse was gone. And Linus with her.

When she told Maddie that her baby brother had died, she felt traitorous in her lie. Maddie said little, sitting primly on the edge of the hospital bed, a nurse busying himself within earshot. Several children Maddie had come to know in the camp had died over the past months, mostly from strange pulmonary and cardiac conditions, so perhaps, Sage thought, Maddie was simply—sadly—becoming accustomed to the fact of death.

Sage had felt numb since Linus' birth, overwhelmed with loss and confusion. She saw his strange little face in her dreams, sometimes he spoke to her, but she could never recall what he said. She laid on her bed most of the day, feeling frozen outside time. At night she stared into the semi-darkness, sleepless.

What had happened to him? What disease did he have? How could there have been three born just like him? Questions arced through her mind's atmosphere, one after the other, lighting up her mental sky then vanishing without resolve.

"What did he look like?" Maddie asked one evening as they snuggled in Sage's cot in the barracks a week after her release from the hospital. Sage's heart thudded.

"Well—"

"Was he a monkey baby?"

"What are you talking about?"

"Rachel's mother, she got out of the hospital two weeks ago, Rachel says she had a monkey baby, but no one's supposed to know."

"Yes," Sage said in a sudden whisper, unsure as to why she was giving Maddie this knowledge.

"He was? I thought . . . "

"You can't tell anyone," Sage whispered. "Not yet. I wasn't even supposed to know. They told me he died, but I saw him. You can't tell anyone. Promise me you won't tell?"

"I promise," Maddie said.

The announcement came from the Director of the World Health Organization, carried on most news channels. The camp dining room overflowed.

We have determined, he said, *that the so-called Disney flu, the bioengineered H5N2 avian influenza virus, was used as a Trojan horse. Hidden inside the flu virus was a retrovirus of an undetermined nature. As far as researchers can tell*, he continued, *this retrovirus, which is able to cross the placental barrier, can invade a human fetus in vitro, the result being significant reconstruction of the fetus' DNA while the fetus continues to develop. Genetically speaking, the fetus devolves into a more primitive version of a human being during gestation. The survival rate of these infants is currently less than one percent. In addition, studies are now being conducted to determine the effect this retrovirus may have on children and adults who have already contracted the Disney flu.*

Sage couldn't help but touch Maddie's arm, fingering the long soft hair she felt there.

A reporter nicknamed it the *Lucy virus*, after the 3.5-million-year-old female skeleton found in Hadar, Ethiopia, in the 1970s. *Australopithecus Afarensis*. The mother of modern humankind.

CHAPTER 12

Carson Road paralleled the border, its pavement pocked and rumpled. The fields on each side were scorched, with jungle-green spikes punching up through the blackened hay. Crows circled above the fields while Sage pushed her bike, and Carl and Josie piggybacked the younger children. They'd set off without breakfast, Sage hoping to get a couple of kilometers covered during the cool of the early morning before stopping to eat. At this pace, however, even if they walked all day, they wouldn't get a tenth of the distance Sage could cover alone on her bicycle. As such, they would need a lot more food to make the journey to New Denver. *A lot more*. Children didn't eat that much, compared to the average adult, but the walk might take ten days, longer if they ran into trouble, or if they had to carry Isaac and Ula most of the way. What she needed was a wagon, or a couple of strollers, something with wheels they could push or pull so they wouldn't have to carry the twins, and so that they could bring along extra food—if they could find it—without having to carry it.

Sage took a long deep breath. It was clear they were going to have to detour north into Grand Forks proper, see if they could scavenge what they needed, or, if the town was still populated, maybe buy or trade.

The fire that had whipped through here had done its peculiar hopping and skipping, leaving the odd house or pickup or tree untouched. They stopped and stared at a white farmhouse, an overgrown shade garden with hostas and ferns on one side, a willow looming over the roof on the other side. The willow's tendrils moved in the breeze that came off the Kettle River just to the north, otherwise there was a stillness about the place that raised the hairs on the back of Sage's neck. *It's too quiet here*, she thought. *The whole world is too quiet.* But the possibility of what they might be able to salvage from the unscathed property drew her up the gravel driveway.

None of the kids followed her. She turned back, shielding her eyes with a hand from the glare of the morning light. "Are you coming?"

Carl shook his head.

"I want to see if there's food. And maybe a wagon, so you wouldn't have to carry Ula and Isaac."

That convinced him.

"It feels bad," Josie said, the words falling out of her mouth like jagged stones. She backed up until she stood on the far side of Carson Road.

Carl stared at Josie. Chills whispered down Sage's back. Those were the first words Sage had heard come out of Josie's mouth and her fear was infectious.

Cut it out, Sage told herself as she laid her bike on the gravel and shed her backpack. "Wait here," she told them as she pulled the axe handle from her pack and headed toward the house, trying to appear casual and unconcerned to the children, the axe handle swinging easily at her side.

"Don't go!" Josie shouted, and Carl started yelling for her to come back, Josie's panic infecting him, his voice loud and high. Ula and Isaac started to whimper and scamper about waving their hands.

Sage stopped, her heart hammering like a hailstorm in her chest, and she felt the fear of being a child all over again, going down the basement to get some potatoes or onions and bolting back up the dingy stairs as if a devil were on her heels. She pulled in a lungful of dry summer air, thick with smoke. "What are you so afraid of?" she asked Josie.

"Let's just go!" Carl demanded, motioning for Isaac to climb up onto his back, which he did in a mad scramble, almost knocking Carl to the pavement.

Josie stared at the house, as if stuck, frozen.

Sage saw them, then, in the bottom corner of the front room window, faces like Ula's and Isaac's, fully devolved but older, larger, with wide grins of fear, pressed against the glass, then turning, bolting into the darkness of the house and appearing just as suddenly in the opposite bottom corner of the window.

"They're just kids," Sage said, trying to believe it herself, yet her heart still hammered wildly. She continued up the gravel driveway. Cold sweat dampened her armpits. There was nobody in the front room window now, just a reflection of the burned out ridge south of town and the gray sky above it.

Sage knocked on the front door. Hoots and screeches erupted inside the house, and crashing sounds as if furniture were being overturned, or pots thrown. When no once came to open the door, she felt only relief. Determined, though, she headed around the side of the house, ducking under the sweeping branches of the willow tree. She could hear Josie crying loudly out on the road. The sudden cool of the shade under the tree rippled shivers up and down her back.

Flies buzzed over three partially devoured humanish carcasses on the weedy lawn in the back yard. The stench hit Sage like a fist. She detoured, not looking very carefully, to the back door where she rapped on it with her axe handle. More hoots and screeching inside. She called out and banged on the door again. After a moment, she gave up and began to search the yard, moving carefully between the outbuildings, axe handle held high at ready. She found a green plastic gardening cart on its side near an empty chicken coop and pulled it upright. It would do. She rummaged through the buildings without finding much of value—they looked like they had already been ransacked. She took some nylon rope she found, and something that looked like a dog harness or seatbelt, just in case she could rig up a way to pull the garden cart. Back outside she threw her findings into the cart and headed toward the road, moving away from the half-consumed, decaying bodies on the back lawn. No sense in trying to get into the house to look for food—she didn't really want to see what the inside of the house looked like, didn't really want to know what had happened there. Nor did she want to think about the kind of existence those two devolved kids were living. The dead on the back lawn had been graphic enough. And the cloying sense of fear she felt drove her back around the side of the house to the driveway.

She wheeled the cart out to the road, shedding her fear and feeling almost triumphant as the distance between her back and the house increased.

Josie ran up to Sage, threw her arms around her bulging waist. "I could smell them," she said. "They smelled dead. I don't like dead."

Sage stroked her hair, her back. "They weren't dead, honey. They looked very much alive to me; however, there were dead people in the back yard, it's true. That's probably what you smelled. You don't need to be afraid of dead people. They can't hurt you. And you don't need to be afraid of *them*, either, Josie," she added pointing back at the kids in the window. "They're only children, just like you. Nothing to be afraid of."

Her blonde head swung side to side against Sage's T-shirt, smearing tears and snot. "I'm *not* like them. I'm not!" She squeezed Sage even harder.

Unwrapping Josie's arms from around her waist, Sage crouched down to look her in eyes. "Why do you say you're not like them?" she asked.

Josie rubbed her nose with the back of her hand. "They're lucies; I'm a people."

"Aren't Ula and Isaac people, too?"

Turning, Josie looked back at the two youngsters, Isaac up on Carl's back, Ula hiding in the ditch on the far side of the road, only her head visible above the rim of the pavement. "No. Lucies."

Sage pushed to her feet, knees cracking. She didn't say anything—there wasn't any point. What was going to happen would happen, whether Josie liked it or not. As far as Sage knew, pretty much everybody, at least in North America, had probably been exposed to the Lucy virus. Some devolved more slowly than others, particularly adults, but sooner or later everybody would devolve. Or die devolving.

Sage felt pleased, though, that Josie was talking, that she could in fact talk. She took the handles of the cart and pushed it out to where the others waited. Behind her she could feel the eyes of the two housebound children staring through the living room window, watching her steal what belonged to them. A shiver ran up Sage's spine, but she refused to turn around. In some ways Josie was right: they *were* dead.

It bothered Sage to leave them behind even though she knew there was no saving them. Their fear had become impenetrable, insurmountable. It would take a long time to win their trust, time she could ill afford with her baby due in barely four weeks. Josie, Carl, Isaac, and Ula would at least have half-a-chance at surviving with an adult looking out for them. And, really, only because they could ask for help, only because they were still—the older ones, anyway—capable, functioning *human* children, only because the violative Lucy virus hadn't yet had its complete and pernicious way with them.

Maddie, like many of the other children at the camp, the younger ones in particular, devolved rapidly during that first winter, the pain from the physiological transmogrification at times unbearable—aching joints, sore muscles, stabbing headaches. Some nights Maddie would cry until she fell asleep, Sage's touch providing little comfort, especially during those times when her skin became hypersensitive. Anti-inflammatories were prescribed by the nurses but to little effect; mild analgesics and anti-migraine medications were brought in. When stronger synthetic opioids, more effective for pain, were introduced, a whole other set of problems evolved—addiction, theft, extortion. A black market had already sprung up, and within a few weeks after Christmas, a camper could purchase just about anything they might want from the outside—food, toiletries, toys, books, sexual aids, clothing—if you had cash or other valuables, or if you were willing to perform sexual favors or bully others.

Sage fought—sometimes with her fists—to keep intimidators at bay and to protect herself and Maddie and what few possessions they owned.

She could no longer delude herself: the FEMA camp had devolved into a prison, whose inmates' only crime had been illness, or exposure to illness. Perhaps, she mused, the camp had always been a prison, had always been *categorized* a prison, filled to capacity with lifers of various ages, and now the inmate population was simply playing cultural catch-up. Of one thing she was certain, though, prison was no place to raise a child.

During the long nights of January and February, sleep continuing to elude her, Sage began to fantasize about escape, not plotting it, *per se*, merely daydreaming about it, wishing for it, all the while automatically grouping that fantasized outside-life into categories and subcategories of simple, desired, nostalgia-laden living: 600s Technology (Applied Sciences); 640s Home Economics & Family Living; 641s Food & Drink; 649s Child Rearing & Home Care of the Sick; for cool mornings, 635s Garden Crops (Horticulture); and for lazy, summer afternoons or dark winter evenings, Fic for fiction.

As the camp's school year progressed, it became evident that most children were suffering emotionally and cognitively: inability to concentrate, outbursts of frustration-induced anger and violence, withdrawal and depression. Sage received shoulder shrugs and empty-handed gestures from camp officials whenever she shoved her way into their on-site offices. *Resources "out there"*—a nod beyond the fence—*are as scarce as hen's teeth, so why would you think you'd get any special treatment in here? In fact, you should consider yourself goddamn lucky to be in here, the bad shit that's going on out there now. Jesus God, makes me want to fuckin' cry some days. Now get the hell out of my office before I ask the guards to throw you out.*

Maddie seemed to shrink as she lay beside Sage night after night. The body hair grew thicker, her head literally changed shape—nose flattening, brow ridge protruding, jaw becoming wider and squarer. The mental lapses and peculiarities bothered Sage the most, in particular the way Maddie would stall right in the middle of doing something and simply stare, or the times when she believed with utter disregard of their current surroundings that they were living in Cleveland, in Quinn's parents' house, and, more eerily, the plummeting decline in her vocabulary, reading comprehension and problem-solving skills. By her seventh birthday on March 20th, Maddie tested out as a pre-schooler, no longer the bright, sunny child soon to go boldly into second grade. By the official end of the school year in June, Maddie could no longer read.

By then, the FEMA camp had been Sage and Maddie's home for fourteen months, and Quinn and Jovan had been dead even longer. Sage had born a child, an undersized devolved baby boy, whom they had taken from her.

Now, Sage's wintertime fantasy of escape seemed cartoonish, juvenile, and no longer provided her with even threadbare comfort. Summer came hard and hot. In the soul-numbing July heat, anger erupted and spread like fire through the FEMA camp. On July 24th, the campers rioted, surprising and overwhelming the diminished force of National Guard, breaching the front gate with a hotwired truck. Tear gas, stun rifles, and shock batons were used initially to combat the rioters, but when it became evident to the guards that an unconfirmed number of rioters were armed with guns, they exchanged riot-control weapons for the real thing. Sixty-seven FEMA camp residents were killed, including nine children, five of whom had been hidden away in the school portable when stray automatic gunfire penetrated the pre-fab metal walls.

One of those children was Maddie, a bullet punching through Sage's hamstring, her body wrapped tightly around her daughter, hidden away in the storage room in the school portable with several other camper parents and their children. The bullet shattered Maddie's sternum, tunneled through her heart and lodged against her spinal column. She was dead before Sage took her next breath.

CHAPTER 13

Alex was frozen in place, staring back at the cedar tree lying across the highway, blocking their retreat, while crisp circles of metal bruised his ear, his skull, and he knew that those circles were a side-by-side shotgun, *and* he knew far too intimately the kind of supreme damage a shotgun could do to a human head. In that skidding moment, he understood with a clarity as startling as ice water that he could *not* die right now because he could not leave Gemma to die alone.

Yuri groaned, tried to sit up.

Marika eased open her door, climbed out onto the pavement—Alex felt her movement more than saw it.

"Slowly," someone said, voice serrated with warning.

"Now you." The shotgun jabbed harder against his ear, as if tagging him, then moved away.

Alex, his eyes still fixed ahead of him, groped for the door handle. He turned as he climbed down onto the highway, blood-stained gloved hands in the air, to look at his assailant and assess the scene. Alex felt relief blow through him like a cold wind. Ronnie Sapriken, New Denver's only RCMP officer, held the shotgun. He sagged a little.

"For the love of God, Ronnie, put the gun down. I'm Alex Gauthier, with the ambulance in Winlaw."

She hesitated, then her face visibly paled. "Jesus fucking Christ," she muttered as she lowered her shotgun. She looked for a second like she might be sick. "Didn't recognize you," she said, "out of uniform, and such. And besides, I remember you as being a bit, well, bigger, last time I say you."

"Yeah, that's what a whole winter without burgers and fries will do to a guy."

"It was at Tom Rilkoff's funeral last year, when I saw you last, wasn't it?"

Alex recalled that Tom had been friends with Ronnie's husband, Matt, that they sometimes went hunting together. Alex jerked a thumb at the truck. "I've got a guy in here with a gunshot wound to the abdomen. You still have that doctor—what's her name?—the one with the South African accent?"

Ronnie shook her head. "No doc. Just head up to the elementary school in New Denver. We've set up a kind of field hospital; got a handful of nurses. And just so you know, the hospital in Nakusp got burned out along with the rest of the town, so don't get your hopes up." She motioned a man over who was dressed in a uniform with a rifle crooked in his arm. "Get the barricade moved, and get these people through. Warn Darcy so that they don't get held up in Silverton."

Alex climbed back into the truck. Slammed the door shut.

"Sorry about the ERT-style welcome," Ronnie said, leaning on the door. "Gunshot wound, Jesus. What the hell happened?"

"One of your locals had a devolved girl tied up in a horse paddock. Yuri went to check her out, and some lunatic comes out of the house, shooting."

"What did this girl look like? Teenager, end-stage?"

"We can go now," Marika said over her shoulder. "There's enough room to get around the barricade."

"Fifteen, sixteen years old, wearing a pink pajama top," Alex said. "You need to get her out of there."

Ronnie shoved a photo in front of him. "Is this the girl you saw?"

"Could be. I didn't get very close."

Yuri was diaphoretic now, and starting to look pale. Alex checked his radial pulse. It was there, but barely, so his pressure was dropping. "We need to go," he said to Ronnie.

Marika eased the truck around the barricade.

Alex propped Yuri's feet up on the door, his dusty boots sticking out the open window, using gravity to keep as much blood around the vital organs as possible. Alex checked the dressings. Yuri had bled through the dressing over the exit wound.

"It's not good, is it?" Yuri said as Alex stuffed another dressing under Yuri's back.

"No," Alex said. "It's not good." He'd never been one to lie to his patients, and he wasn't going to start now. Especially not with Yuri.

"I wish Mickey was here."

"Yeah, I bet you do." Alex pumped up the manual BP cuff. He wished he had the monitor, but it was back in Winlaw in the main ambulance. All he'd taken were the basics. BP was 85/50. Not good at all.

Despite the absence of any respect for Yuri Evdikimoff, Alex felt sorry for him, his life bleeding away like this, without his brother to talk to and to comfort him. *Mickey's heart is going to break in two*, Alex thought.

Out the window he could see fire raging over the hillside behind what was left of the Silverton Inn, smoke roaring into the sky. Wind whipped through the truck from the west, from the lake, the fire greedily pulling in fresh oxygen. Two mid-sized cats were blading a wide break up the side of Silverton Creek in the hopes of containing the northern flank of the fire to prevent it from reaching New Denver. But the southern flank was wide open and the fire could easily begin to trek south down the valley, chewing up hectares and hectares of forest, roaring and spitting all the way to Winlaw.

Marika braked suddenly, slowed to a crawl. "Oh my God," she said.

Alex craned his neck in the opposite direction to see what she was looking at. On the Museum's overgrown lawn, now all trampled, and contained inside a barrier of old police tape, were six bloodied bodies, barely covered by wind-blown blankets, scattered through the grass. Several crows picked at the carcasses.

"I wish I'd stayed home," Marika said, and let out a long sigh.

"You sure as hell aren't the only one," Alex said.

Yuri's eyes were closed. Alex rubbed his knuckles on Yuri's sternum. "Yuri! Hey! Wake up!" Yuri's eyelids fluttered, then remained open.

"What?" he muttered.

"Just making sure you're still with me."

"Where's Mickey? I gotta talk to Mickey."

"Mickey's down at the fire. Remember?"

"Oh, yeah. When's he coming back?" Yuri was slurring his words now.

"Marika, you'd better pick up the pace."

Marika ran inside the school to get help. Alex opened the back of the ambulance parked at the front entrance to get the stretcher, but it wasn't there. Neither was their monitor. Must be inside the school with a patient.

The front door flew open, Marika ran back to the truck. "They're on their way," she said.

Irene Rilkoff, dressed in her uniform, white shirt crumpled and dirty, drove the motorized stretcher out the open doors and down the sidewalk to the truck. She'd grown her hair out since Alex had seen her last. It was now shoulder length and mostly gray. Her face hadn't changed much, a few more wrinkles, the smudges under her eyes a little darker. She grinned at him. "Damn nice to see you, Alex," she said.

Alex grinned back. He'd met Irene not long after he'd moved to the Slocan Valley. He'd dragged eight-year-old Gemma into Irene and Tom's bookstore—they'd been to the Nakusp Hot Springs and had stopped in New Denver for ice cream—just to poke around. He and Irene fell into conversation; he found out she'd recently become a member of the ambulance crew in New Denver, just as he had in Winlaw; they both had a daughter, Sage sixteen years old to Gemma's eight; she talked him into buying a book of poems—though he had never much liked poetry—by a local poet, now dead, who had lived not far from the house Alex had just bought on a bluff on Perry Ridge overlooking the Slocan River.

"What have we got?" Irene said.

"This is Yuri. Forty-year old male, GSW to upper right quadrant of the abdomen, with an exit wound. BP's under 90 systolic."

"So what the hell else is going to happen today?" she said with a shake of her head.

They slid Yuri out onto the stretcher and Irene drove it back into the school.

The hospital was a series of classrooms down one hall. Irene picked the first one.

"What's the story?" said a woman in her thirties with muddy brown hair, a strong brow ridge protrusion and the squarest, thickest jaw Alex had ever seen.

"Lindsey," Irene said, "this is Alex; Alex, Lindsey."

Alex nodded and gave a report as they slid Yuri over onto what looked to be a padded massage table. A nurse, introduced as Terry, entered the room, and suddenly Alex needed to get out, to breathe some fresh air.

"You're looking a bit pale, Alex," Irene said and took him by the arm. "We'll be outside if you need us," she told Lindsey.

Alex let himself be led, feeling the comfortable warmth of Irene's hand on his arm. Nausea blew through him in icy waves. He just needed to sit down, relax for a few moments, regain his psychological balance.

Irene sat him on the back bumper of the ambulance, handed him a plastic bottle of water. Ash whirled about on conflicted breezes. He took a few sips, handed the bottle back. Wiped his face with the back of his arm, then rested his elbows on his knees and let his head hang. Cold sweat chilled his back. He knew this was simply the aftermath of all that adrenaline shot into his system.

Marika popped her head out the school door. "Lindsey needs you guys," she called out.

"You ready?" Irene asked.

Alex stood, feeling his hip crack. "I'm too old for this shit," he said to her, making a face.

Irene headed up the sidewalk to the school. "Marika's a physiotherapist, right? Does she still live in the same place, just north of you?"

"Yeah, her and Bill have lived there for as long as I've known them. By the way, their son, Colin, died last year, some sort of pneumonia, and Darlene, their ten-year-old is end-stage and running full tilt into puberty."

"Thanks for the heads-up. And, dare I ask, how's Gemma?"

Alex pulled the door open. "She's okay. Late mid-stage now. She's had a couple of strokes, though. Marika's been treating her. She walks with a cane, but can still ride her bike, is as opinionated as ever, and regularly hikes the ridge with Coyote. Well, not so much this summer, with the fires."

"That's good news," she said, relief relaxing her face. "That's really good news."

Alex grinned at her. "Damn, it's good to see you, too," he said.

She laughed.

He hugged her, then, almost fiercely. Last time he'd hugged Irene had been at Tom's funeral, and then she'd felt limp, small, crushed. She felt strong and solid this time, and as she pressed her head against his shoulder, he could smell her sweat, the musk of her skin, the wildfire smoke in her hair. She hugged him back so hard he almost couldn't catch his breath.

"I've gotten so that I hate to ask anyone anything these days," she said as she let go of him. "Let's go check on your friend."

"He's not my friend," Alex said. "He's Mickey Evdikimoff's pain-in-the-ass brother, and word has it he's started drinking again."

"Evdikimoff? The drunk driver who killed that kid?"

"One and the same."

Lindsey met them in the hallway. "I need you to help hold him down. I've already stitched up the exit wound so that he won't bleed out while I work on him. I can't tube him 'cause I don't have any paralytics and or sedatives. I've loaded him up with analgesics, but that's the best I can do. Looks to me like the bullet went through his liver—which is big enough for a frickin' elephant, by the way; he's a drinker, right? Doesn't seem to have hit any bowel, from the smell of things, but I have to take a look to be sure. Don't want him getting any more septic than he's going to get as it is." Then she shrugged. "He's probably not going to make it anyway, so maybe you"—she pinned Alex with her eyes—"should give him the choice. I don't mind practicing, but he's the one being cut open."

Alex pulled in a deep breath. "Yeah, I'll talk to him."

Marika was standing beside the table, holding Yuri's hand, and not appearing particularly happy about it. She took one look at Alex's face and said to Yuri, "I gotta go." Yuri didn't want to let go, but she pried his fingers out of her hand. "*I'm not his goddamn confessor*," she muttered to Alex as she passed him. She stopped. "I'll be in Silverton at the fire if you need me. I'm sure they can use an extra set of hands."

Alex leaned his hip against the table. Yuri had that gray look to his skin—pallor gone to shit. His eyelids drooped. Alex rested his hand on Yuri's arm to get his attention.

"Al? Mickey here yet?"

"Mickey's not coming, Yuri, he's at the fire. Listen to me. Lindsey says it doesn't look good. The bullet went through your liver. She's going to go in and fix it, but she doesn't have the right drugs to put you under. Do you understand? You'll be awake through the operation." Yuri nodded, but a drugged nod. "And there's a good chance you won't survive. She can't seem to keep your blood pressure up enough. Do you understand what I'm saying?"

"You're saying I'm probably going to die."

"That's right, Yuri."

"Whether she does anything or not." Yuri looked away. His hand found Alex's and squeezed, cracking knuckles. "If I die, tell Mickey I forgive him. Okay? You tell him that."

Frowning, Alex nodded. *What could Mickey have done that the likes of you would be offering forgiveness*? "I'll tell him," he promised.

"All right, then. Let's just get this fucking thing over with," Yuri said.

CHAPTER 14

Ronnie trembled from the fall-out of adrenaline, from the bloodlust that had roared through her, lascivious and obscene. It had taken every single molecule of Ronnie's self-control to *not* squeeze that trigger and blow Alex Gauthier's brains all over the side of the truck.

She needed to go after Thea, or if that wasn't her tied up in the paddock, to at least rescue *that* poor girl, but her internal white noise distracted her. Where had all her training and discipline gone? She hadn't felt any fear at all; it seemed that what she'd felt could only be described as an endorphin-fed predatory drive—like a cougar chasing down a rabbit and nailing it. She'd wanted the kill. *Really* wanted it.

"If we don't go now, those bastards'll just vanish to who knows where with that girl—" It was Kevin Bryant, one of her auxiliaries, talking to her.

She held up a trembling hand. He clamped his mouth shut. It took tremendous effort to focus on his face. "You're right," she said. "We can't wait any longer." She called Janice Goffin on her radio, told her what she wanted. Janice was ex-military; Kevin was a hunter friend of Matt's.

Ronnie walked past the barricade to her SUV, clamped the shotgun into its mount. *Get control, girl,* she told herself. She climbed in and fired up the SUV, checked her ammunition supplies, grabbed her binoculars.

Kevin opened the door behind her.

"Sit up front," she told him.

Janice pulled up beside her in a sedan, threw a bag of gear in the back, then climbed in behind Kevin.

Ronnie gunned the SUV, heading south down the highway to the far entrance of the Red Mountain Road loop. Kevin, a relative newcomer to New Denver, was early mid-stage, and could have some changes happening, or he could have always looked that way—a kind of heavy-browed, strong-jawed masculine look—and so ironically would be the only guy the Lucy virus actually made better looking. He looked paler than usual—no surprise given the rush on the vehicle from Winlaw—but Ronnie knew she could count on him because he still had all his smarts. Janice looked the same whether she was on a call with Ronnie or over for a barbeque. And she looked pretty much untouched by the virus.

She hid the SUV in an empty carport at a house half a kilometer down road from the address Marika had given Kevin. She pulled her shotgun from its mount, automatically checked it, shoved extra ammunition in her pockets. They all bailed out of the SUV.

"Okay, kiddos," Ronnie said, as Janice and Kevin geared up, "I want the girl, and I just want to talk to the guys in the house. But don't be afraid to defend yourselves if you have to. And remember: check your targets. No friendly fire, okay?"

Janice grunted.

"Kevin?"

"Ten-four, Ronnie. No friendly fire." He was sweating pretty badly.

They hiked up the gravel road. There was an SUV parked through the trees. It wasn't the red Ford pick-up the Gardener boys usually drove. Ronnie pumped the 12-guage in anticipation.

She waved them to the side of the road and pulled out her binoculars, but couldn't see much from such a low vantage point. "We'll circle around through the bush," she said. "I'd like to get a little above the place to get a better look."

They hiked to a wide bench high up behind the paddock, which was now empty, with a good view of the house and grounds.

"Place looks abandoned," Kevin whispered, still breathing hard from the uphill hike.

"Could be," Ronnie said as she pulled out her binoculars. "Or they could be sitting in one of those upstairs rooms with a hunting scope just waiting for us."

Kevin didn't say anything.

"Here's what I want to do. Janice—"

Janice tugged on Ronnie's vest. "The front door!"

Ronnie looked. The front door had opened. "Get back," she whispered as she scrambled over dry conifer needles into deeper cover, getting most of her body hidden behind the trunk of a thick Douglas fir tree.

A man in his twenties stuck his head out the door, took a quick look around the yard, then shoved a devolved child—a ten-year-old boy—out ahead of him. A girl in her mid-teens came out next. Ronnie heard the man growl something that sounded like "Don't move!" before disappearing back into the house.

"Let's just see what they're up to," Ronnie said. Five years ago, she'd have simply called in the regional Emergency Response Team and they would have handled the whole damn thing. Mind you, five years ago nobody would have kidnapped a teenager and shot six people so publicly, then camped just outside of town because they were pretty sure no one they couldn't handle would come looking.

"That's the girl in the picture," Kevin whispered, watching through his scope.

Sure enough, Thea Hlookoff, hands bound and still wearing nothing but a pajama top, was shoved out the door ahead of a heavy-set man with an older M4-style assault rifle.

"And that looks like the muscle guy Josh Pierce described," Janice said.

They pushed the devolved children into the back seat of the SUV. The younger man got into the driver's seat, started the motor.

"Kevin, take out the front tire. Janice: if it looks like the guy with the gun is going to hurt those kids, take him. Wound him if you can; kill the bastard if you have to."

Ronnie covered her ears, but still the crack of Kevin's Weatherby almost deafened her.

The front end of the SUV sagged. Through the binos Ronnie could see the man with the gun waving at the driver and yelling as he wrenched his neck around looking for the source of the shot. The engine roared and the SUV bolted backwards.

"Hit as many tires as you can," Ronnie told Kevin as he worked the bolt.

Crack. Crack. Crack.

The closest back tire flattened. The SUV braked, turned and charged down the gravel driveway to the road.

Kevin took three more shots before the SUV bounced onto the gravel road, swinging left to the highway.

"Shit!" Janice said.

"Let's go!" Ronnie pounded downhill at a dead run. She needed to get to her vehicle before those assholes got too far ahead: there were way too many perfectly good places to nip off the road and set up an ambush.

Ronnie raced across the overgrown lawn, past the faded yellow garage and down the driveway, her breath coming hard, legs pushing, pumping. She was running like an animal. A predator.

She skidded to a sudden halt at the end of the driveway, almost falling. The SUV had rolled on the turn, the two flats on the outside throwing it off balance. It was upside down in the shallow ditch, the driver's side jammed hard against the bank. She could hear the kids screaming and one of the men yelling at them to shut the fuck up. The passenger door creaked open and the muscle man spilled out onto the ground, assault rifle clenched his right hand.

Ronnie jerked her shotgun to her shoulder as she ran. "Drop your weapon! Drop your fucking weapon! *Right now*!" She was thirty meters away—hard to be very accurate at a dead run, and he was right beside the vehicle with those kids inside. She ran straight at him. He was on his knees now, swinging the gun up. Twenty-five meters.

She squeezed the trigger. The blast knocked him backwards, but not down. He fired as he swung the gun up at her, as he made it to his feet on the gravel. She shot him again, wide spread across chest. He went down this time, his rifle clattering beside him on the stones.

She slid in the gravel, on her knees, knocking the gun away. Quick look: wide hole across his chest filled with ripped cloth and hamburger and bone splinters. Second look: inside the SUV at the driver. He was suspended upside down and still trying to untangle himself from his four-point. "Get out of the car!" she yelled at him. His eyes were wide with fear. He stopped struggling with the buckle and just hung there upside down, showing her his hands. "No gun," he said. "Got no gun."

Janice ran up behind Ronnie, panting hard. "Holy shit," she said. "You get hit?"

Ronnie shook her head. "Check on the kids," she said, keeping her gun leveled at the driver. "Tell me if we need the ambulance."

Kevin looked like he was about to have a coronary as he rested, bending over with his Weatherby braced across his knees, his chest heaving. "Man, if we're gonna do this kind of shit, I gotta start working out again," he muttered. "Shouldn't we maybe cover up this guy?" he added. "You know, the kids . . . "

"Why don't you get outta here, Ronnie?" It was Lindsey. She was stitching the cut on Thea's face. Thea lay as if dead, heavily drugged. "Go home, get cleaned up, take five. And get some food into that bone rack of yours. Polly came by and said The Dragon Ladies have a meal going on over at the church. Bunch of the firefighters are there, chowing down. Including Matt."

Ronnie didn't want to be around people. She wanted nothing more than to go home and crawl into a hole and hide for a while. But she needed to track down the Gardener boys. The dead guy's partner, Chris Plenta, sitting in one of the cells at the RCMP station, had told her where to find them, and she didn't even have to hit him.

"It's been a helluva day," Lindsey added.

Ronnie took a deep breath, but didn't say anything. Her brain seemed to crackle with white noise and her headache pounded right at the base of her skull. She stared past Lindsey out the schoolroom window at the mountainside. The fire spit and swirled, coughing smoke into the air, but so far it hadn't jumped the new firebreak Darcy's crews had been cutting.

Ronnie skipped the meal at the church and headed home. She plugged the SUV into the solar recharger, then let herself in the basement entrance off the carport. She started up the stairs, en route to the master bedroom to see if she had a clean uniform left, but found herself in the guest room in the basement. She was suddenly tired and her uniform stank of sweat and smoke and blood. She peeled it off, left it heaped on the carpet, and crawled under the duvet on the guest bed in her underwear and bra. Her sticky skin rubbed against the clean sheets like Velcro. The headache crashed, an oversized engine roaring inside her cranium. She wriggled out of her underclothes and threw them on the floor.

She had killed a man today. And even though she had prepared herself for this possibility—or so she had thought—from the very moment she decided to go to the RCMP Depot in Regina for her basic training—the reality of the shooting jangled her brain. What troubled her most, though, was how easy it had been. Anger roiling volcanic at what they'd done to Thea Hlookoff, at what they had probably done to the other kids; anger at herself for not getting the search underway faster, and for not knowing about the other two children; plus, combat-style fear pumping out the adrenalin, endorphins popping, as she ran right at him. He was the rabbit; she was the cougar. And, with a simple, gentle squeeze of her index finger he was rocked backwards. Then another squeeze, the second blast tearing a hole in his chest the size of a watermelon. *Cougar kills rabbit.*

No one yelled at her, no one pointed fingers; there was no media to come after her, no supervisors to challenge her choices. In fact, she was a hero according to most. Some, like Darcy Khaira, also felt sorry for her. "I'm not sorry you did it," he'd said to her, then added, as if she were a vet who'd had to put down a dangerous animal, "I'm just sorry you had to be the one."

But *she* wasn't sorry. And that was what bothered her. She was *supposed* to be sorry, to feel remorse, or regret, or sick to her stomach. Instead she felt nothing, a vast and wide absence: no anger, no guilt, no fear. However, some other feeling, crouching deep inside her, was coming out of hiding, out of the tiny shielded pocket where it lived: a kind of exhilaration gleaming down inside that pocket, the kind that made you want to kick your feet and grin like an idiot to yourself, the kind of painful delight that you had as a kid as you crawled into bed Christmas Eve, the kind of tortured pleasure you want to prolong just microseconds before you come, your hips turning to stone in anticipation of the wild, fluid bucking just beyond that precipice.

Ronnie shook her head at the thought. *She shouldn't think that; she shouldn't feel that.* Is this what devolving was doing to her, turning her into some sort of amoral animal, clapping her bloody hands in sadistic delight? Or is this who she was, who she had always been?

She *killed* a man today. No matter that it was justified, no matter that it may have been the right thing to do, no matter that he may even have deserved it. Or that it was in self-defense.

No, the problem was—

Her hand reached between her legs and she touched herself. A gasp leaped from her throat. She jerked her hand away from her skin, laid it carefully on top of the duvet, and ground her eyes shut against the throbbing headache. The hand trembled.

No, the problem was this: she *liked* it—no, too weak a word—she *enjoyed* it. She felt excited by it, exhilarated, all her senses stuck open on alert, on high-speed. This is probably what coke is like, she thought.

This is wrong, she told herself. *Think about something else. Do something else. Get up, get dressed, go split firewood, or go for a run, or . . .*

Matt. Think about Matt: he was at the church, loading up on food so that he could get back out there to fight the fire, back to humping gear and hoses up to the pump they set up a little higher on Silverton Creek where they started the new firebreak.

The fire.

She couldn't hide like this. She had work to do. She had those Gardener yahoos to hunt down. And besides—

The basement door crashed open. Ronnie's heart raced.

"Veronica?" It was Matt. He thumped to the bottom of the basement stairs in his heavy boots. "Veronica!" he called up the stairs.

She could see his shoulder, the dirty yellow of his turnout coat, through the doorway. She flung back the duvet and rose from the bed to stand naked in the doorway to the guest room barely an arm's length away from him, breathing in the reek of smoke and sweat that swirled about him.

He turned toward her, seemingly having felt more than heard her appear beside him. His eyes widened. She reached for him, pulling his face to hers, wrenching the thick coat off his shoulders, drawing him toward the bed, biting his lip, his neck, the sweat-smoke smell of him almost overwhelming her.

He said something, but she was pulling down the suspenders of his fire pants. She peeled his damp t-shirt off over his head. He was grabbing at her breasts now, kissing her face, her shoulders. She jerked his pants and boxers down all in one motion, and hauled him down onto the bed on top of her.

The sex was rushed, almost violent, leaving Ronnie panting and unsatisfied, wanting more of him. She took his head in her hands and pushed his face down between her breasts, over her stomach, between her legs, and held him, held him there until he finished her, and then he was almost hard again and she took him inside her and wouldn't let him go.

For a long while she lay under him, feeling drowsy, enjoying the weight of him on her, her mind's eye watching as he raised his head, began to work again on her breasts. He licked her belly, then leaned up and kissed her on the mouth, his unshaven face rough against hers, while his hand played up and down her labia.

Ronnie moaned, just a little.

Blood spewed from his chest, then, splattering hot all over her skin. He pushed up and away from her, fingers embracing the red cavern just center of his left nipple and he looked down at her, his blue eyes surprised, accusing her, while his mouth opened and closed in silence.

Ronnie jolted awake, her breath coming in hard gulps.

"Hey," Matt said, from beside her. "You dozed off for a bit there."

Ronnie hurled the lingering remnants of the dream away, sudden anger displacing the dark river of loss that had flooded her, and flung the sheet and comforter back to sit on the edge of the bed. She could smell herself. And him.

"Darcy was trying to get you on the radio," Matt said. "So he sent me home to see if you were here. Glad I came." He laughed at his own joke.

Ignoring him, he gathered up her uniform, then went upstairs to wash herself at the kitchen sink, scrubbing dried blood and sweat and dirt from her skin. After getting dressed, he followed her up the stairs, and watched as she washed.

"I heard you killed a man today," he said, then: "Are you all right?"

She could tell by the set of his mouth, the openness it belied, that he really wanted to know. His vulnerability sanded some of the roughness off her anger.

"No," she said, then, "Yes, I'm all right." She dressed in her last fresh uniform, hauled on her vest, which stank of smoke and sweat and had flecks of blood splashed up the front.

"I know this is something you'd hoped you'd never have to—"

"What did Darcy want? You said he was trying to get a hold of me." Ronnie keyed her radio. Nothing. "It's dead again. Goddamn batteries won't hold their charge anymore."She dropped into a kitchen chair to pull on her boots, the toes scuffed raw.

Matt sighed. "He's talking about evacuating."

CHAPTER 15

Alex folded himself onto a child's chair in the school library and sipped water from a glass. Alex couldn't believe Yuri was still alive. He'd endured the surgery with his usual acrimony, Lindsey periodically threatening him with sundry evils if he didn't shut up and let her work, but all in all she looked pleased with the job she'd done. She certainly looked like she'd had a lot of practice cutting and sewing people up. Whether Yuri made it through the next few days and the inevitable infection that would follow was a whole different matter. Thankfully no emergent cases came in from the Silverton fire that needed Lindsey's attention, just those poor kids Ronnie Sapriken brought in from the house where Yuri got shot. When it was over, Alex had gone outside, but the air was so thick with smoke and flying ash he couldn't stand it. Although the air inside was more breathable, the child-sized furniture in the library reminded him of the tiny wooden table and chairs he'd bought Gemma when she was five, after the divorce. Little hearts carved into the chair backs and painted red. On the weekends he had her, Gemma would orchestrate tea parties with him and her various stuffies that she carried in her backpack—"bagpag"—to his apartment, and they'd sip iced tea out of plastic teacups, their pinkies raised and all conversation delivered with British accents.

Gemma gave the table and chairs to Darlene when Darlene turned five. They were a big hit; the gesture made Marika cry. All along Gemma had wanted to save them for her own children, but she came to Alex asking him if it would be okay—she was sixteen, then—that she wasn't sure she wanted children of her own and leaving them in the basement collecting dust was wasteful. "They were a gift, missy, and so they're yours to do with as you please," he'd said to her, although secretly he coveted them for his own nostalgic reasons.

A head popped through the library doorway: Irene. "Hey," she said, sounding a little winded. "You want to do a call? We could probably use an extra pair of hands."

"What's up?" He downed his water, using the moment to wash away the memory, and left the empty glass on a table.

"Somebody rolled a truck. Might be nothing, but I doubt it. The call came in on the fire channel—caller was pretty panicked."

Outside, ash fell like bone-colored snow. He swung up into the jump seat in the patient compartment, closed the side door. Nathan pulled out of the parking lot onto the road.

Alex sighed. It used to be that emergency calls would jack up his heart rate, get his adrenaline pumping. Now his heart rate didn't even change. Maybe it was experience, just doing lots of calls over the years, or maybe it was because most *real* emergencies nowadays were simply tragedies that hadn't yet finished unfolding, and that there was little he could do to affect the outcome. And he'd had his fill of tragedy. He'd rather be sipping iced tea out of a tiny plastic teacup with his pinky pointed at the ceiling making up regal gossip with five-year-old Gemma. He'd rather be cooking up mac and cheese while she chatted to him about what had happened at school that day, how she liked it when Mr. Kelly read to them on Friday afternoons. He'd rather be—

Loss ran through him like a dark river.

"How's your guy?" Irene asked over her shoulder.

"Yuri? He's still alive. Lindsey figures if he survives the night, he might actually have a chance." He pulled gloves from a box on the wall.

"Well, she *is* the best veterinary surgeon in these parts," she said, her voice sly.

"Lindsey's a vet? You're kidding me!"

Nathan turned on the siren to shoo a couple of loose dogs off the highway. "Have you heard how those kids Ronnie Sapriken brought in are doing?" he asked Alex.

"All I heard was they beat up the girl—Thea?—pretty badly, and Lindsey said she's been raped, probably a couple of times already. Same with the other girl. Doesn't seem like they molested the boy, but he's pretty traumatized, all the same. They're trying to figure out whose kids the boy and girl are, in case the parents are still around."

"Jesus."

"Yeah."

The ambulance crested the summit between the two towns. The fire was a monster, filling the whole side of the mountain, hurling lumps and wads of flame down on the town and the humans below and titanic columns of smoke into the sky. They dropped down into Silverton, and before they got to the bridge, waving arms directed them up this street, over here, further up the hill, across the fresh firebreak, over there. They parked.

They had to hike a hundred meters through smoldering duff and burning deadfall, carrying their gear, to get to the vehicle. The scene had that panicked look to it that bad scenes tend to have: people's movements are jerky, rushed; there's shouting and anguished faces; the shell-shocked get in the way or wander aimlessly.

A truck had been ferrying people down from the fire line along a makeshift road cut into the hillside by a cat. A piece of the road sloughed under the weight of the midsize pickup, sending the truck and its six occupants pinballing downhill through burning trees to stop finally, miraculously, on its wheels with its nose crushed against a boulder.

Alex was sweating hard, the heat from the fire pummeling him from all directions. The smoke was thick, and harsh, like breathing fiberglass, making him cough. Irene had ash smeared across her forehead as if she'd been consecrated. Nathan hugged the red jumpkit to his chest like a kid squeezing a stuffie for comfort.

Darcy Khaira was there, giving report to Irene: three serious, still trapped inside the truck, three with minor injuries out of the vehicle, walking and talking (they'd been riding in the back and had time to jump). Then he was showing her the direction of the vehicle's descent.

Alex touched Nathan on the arm. "Find the three walking wounded and assess them," he said, taking the jumpkit from him. The hillside was steep, and the burned duff puffed ash into the air with every step. Frantic hands waved at him from the other side of the vehicle. He circled around until he was among the bystanders there talking to the patients inside the truck. The roof was crushed in, but not flattened, and the whole truck was arched in the middle, looking like a dog throwing up its breakfast. There were three people in the cab of the small pickup, the driver not moving much, the woman in the middle thrashing about, trying to free herself, and the passenger was just making moaning sounds.

It seemed as though every single person fighting the fire had come to the accident scene to help. These were their neighbors, friends, trapped in this vehicle. They had the driver's door open and bent forward, but the driver's legs were crushed between the seat and the dash, which had been rammed down on top of his legs. "He's not talking anymore," somebody said to Alex. "It's Josh, Josh Pierce."

Alex pushed his way through until he was beside the driver. He couldn't rouse him. The woman in the middle—Pamela—yelled at him to help her, blood seeping from a gash above her left eye. He told her they'd get to her in a minute. The driver's face was a mess, teeth missing from hitting the steering wheel, blood matting his beard, and his respirations were noisy. Alex did a quick listen to the chest: nasty slurping sounds. The driver hadn't been wearing his four-point, so his chest hit the steering wheel sometime after the airbags all fired and deflated. Pulse was pitiful, weak and fast. Where his legs were crushed between the dash and the seat, they formed ugly little right angles. Not good at all.

Irene appeared on the passenger side of the truck. "I've got a decreased level of consciousness here, with head trauma, and a dislocated shoulder. Legs are trapped, but not pinned."

"Get me the fuck out of here!" the woman in the middle yelled at Irene.

"Just take it easy, Pam," Irene said. "We need you to stay calm."

There was a flurry of activity behind Alex. He ignored it as he told Irene about the driver's condition. Somebody tapped his shoulder. It was Darcy Khaira. "You need to get them out," he said. "Wind has changed direction."

Alex looked at him, frowning.Darcy jerked his head. Alex could see it then, flames coming at them through the trees, maybe a hundred meters away. He scrambled around to the other side of the truck. Nathan was there, handing Irene equipment.

"Can we get your guy out?" he asked her.

"Yeah, they're just getting a jack to push the dash up a bit, then I think we can pull him out."

"Fire's coming this way again."

"How much time?"

"I didn't ask."

"Well, I'm sure I know the answer."

Alex leaned in close to her, then. "We'll have to leave the driver," he said. "He's trapped. He's not going to make it anyway."

She wrapped a collar around her patient's neck. "We can't leave Josh behind," she said. "He'll be burned alive."

"Unless they can get the dash off him by the time we're done here—"

She turned then, hands still working the hard collar into place, and pinned him with her eyes. "I won't leave him."

Alex pressed up against her, his mouth against her ear. "Irene, his legs are crushed, pinned. We'd need to amputate to get him out. I know he's your friend, but he's got massive chest trauma . . . "

"I know, I know." She turned away.

Alex scrambled to the back of the truck. Nathan grabbed his arm. "We can't—"

"It's called triage," Alex said, his voice raw with sudden anger. He jerked his arm away. But then he stopped, turned back to Nathan, whose mouth open and closed and opened again, and added, more gently, "We have to make choices, and sometimes none of the options are any good." He climbed up into the box of the pickup to help lever the passenger out by reaching through the back window.

Darcy organized stretcher-bearers, the rest of the bystanders he sent back to the fireline.

The passenger became more alert when they pried his broken legs out from under the dash. They slid him onto the spine board and handed him off to Nathan and the stretcher-bearers.

Pam was still combative, but was becoming drowsy. She screamed when Irene tried to move her legs.

"How much morphine do you have?" Alex asked Irene as he scrambled out of the back of the truck.

"Enough, but it's gotta go in intravenously. Intramuscularly won't work fast enough."

"Let's get a line in, then."

Darcy called down from the road: "How much longer?"

"Ten minutes," Irene called back.

"You might not have ten minutes!"

Irene wiped her mouth with the back of her arm. "Shit," she said. "She'll fight us if we try to pull on those legs."

"Okay, I'll hold her down, you get the line in."

Alex clambered up onto the seat, broken glass stabbing through his jeans. Heat from the fire pounded the truck. On the other side of the woman, Josh Pierce, still unconscious, was gulping huge wet breaths. The woman moaned and struggled but didn't open her eyes anymore. Alex pinned her arm while Irene poked her.

"Got it," Irene said. She taped the line down and let it run wide open. Then she drew up the morphine and injected it into the port. Within half-a-minute, Alex could feel the patient relax under his grip.

Irene called out for extra hands and the stretcher-bearers who had been hiking back from the ambulance, ran to help. They pulled Pam out of the truck, straightening her broken legs as they laid her on a spine board.

Alex could feel the furnace heat of the fire at his back, threatening, as they carried the patient away from the truck. He wondered if Josh Pierce, trapped in the driver's seat, knew they'd left him behind, that they weren't coming back for him. Maybe it was simply his reptilian brain keeping his heart pumping and his lungs gasping, and all Josh's awareness had fled, or had drowned in the static of dying. That's what Alex hoped, but in his heart of hearts he knew that Josh knew, and understood, that he was going to die alone. Before they drove Pam and the first patient away, Alex ran back into the truck. He clambered up into the cab, drew up the last of morphine and plunged it into Josh's deltoid muscle. It wouldn't be enough, but he hoped it would help some. Then he leaned over, his mouth close to Josh's ear, and told him. Alex never lied to his patients. Not even by omission.

The metallic stink of Josh's blood, and his deep gurgling gasping breaths, followed Alex back to the ambulance.

He'd heard a story once, a call that another paramedic had done up north somewhere twenty years before, of a truck driver pinned against a wall by his fuel truck, crushing his pelvis and upper thighs. The rear tires had caught on fire—hot brakes, or something, Alex couldn't recall—and they couldn't free him, or pull the rig off him and he screamed at the paramedics and the firefighters to kill him, kill him now, because he didn't want to burn to death.

At least Josh Pierce wasn't able to ask Alex to kill him.

Word spread that they'd left Josh behind. That the fire had been too close to allow them to bring out his body. Alex realized that people presumed Josh had died at the scene, that he wasn't still alive when the ambulance left with its two patients, that Alex and Irene would not have left him unless he were already dead.

Alex slipped outside, found a secluded spot at the back of the school, sat on the concrete with his back against the wall, coughing and choking on the smoke and ash. He felt angry, bitter, frustrated. He wanted to go home, wrap Gemma in his arms. But he wanted the Gemma who hadn't yet started to devolve, who hadn't yet had three strokes, who hadn't yet asked him to promise to kill her. He shouldn't have come. He should have stayed home, with Gemma, with devolving, beautiful, darling Gemma. With his missy.

He pushed his sore body to his feet.

He'd left a man to die alone. The stink of his blood overran the stench of the smoke. He imagined himself sitting there, trapped, trying to breath, the fire coming on, its heat monstrous, demonic—

"Stop it!" he shouted, at himself, at everything.

This is a normal response, he reminded himself. *These feelings, they're normal. What you have just experienced is abnormal, but the response to it is normal.* He'd been through the aftermath of difficult calls before and knew the ugliness of the fallout, knew that it would take time to process what had happened, to come to some sort of terms with it.

He knew the rhetoric.

CHAPTER 16

After bouncing along Red Mountain Road for far too long, Kevin tapped Ronnie on the shoulder. "Isn't that the Gardeners' pickup over by that woodshed up on the left?"

Ronnie squinted. Sure enough, it was the red Ford half-ton they'd been barreling around in, parked most of the way up the gravel driveway of a ritzy log house with panoramic windows. She parked the SUV. "If those little shits haven't heard us already, I'd just as soon surprise the piss out of them."

Kevin laughed. He looked pale again, and was sweating already.

Ronnie sent Janice and Kevin around the back while she eased open the unlocked front door. The stench of food gone bad and stale marijuana smoke assaulted her. A mouse scurried across the floor.

She heard shouts out back, then, and the clatter of metal patio furniture on concrete. A gunshot cracked the air. She crept into the kitchen at the back of the house. Garbage was strewn all over the counters and floors. Through a set of wooden French doors she could see all three Gardener boys face down on the aggregate concrete patio, Janice pinning them there with her revolver. Overturned patio furniture littered the yard. Kevin was cuffing each of them with disposable restraints.

Ronnie pushed through the French doors. "Nice work, kids. Anybody else in the house?" she asked Roy, the eldest Gardener boy.

Roy shook his shaggy head as he lay facedown on the concrete. He was the least devolved of the three. "This place is ours. We found it. Nobody else is here."

"You mean, Chris and Don aren't holed up upstairs somewhere, waiting to blow my head off?"

"Who?" Roy said.

Kevin and Janice hauled the brothers to their feet.

Ronnie flipped the patio chairs back onto their legs, nodded for the boys to take a seat, while Janice and Kevin headed back inside to search the upstairs.

"Cut the crap, Roy," she said. "I'm talking about the two neanderthals who were with you when you took that girl last night."

"We didn't take the girl!" Levi blurted, eyes bulging under the thickest brow ridge Ronnie had seen on an adult.

"Shut up, Levi," Roy said, giving him a long, acidic look.

Ronnie pressed on. "They said you took the girl and were doing really nasty things to her up here. So, where is she?"

Willis spat on the concrete. "That's a fucking lie." He wiped his mouth on his shoulder. "I told you they'd screw us, Roy."

"Shut up."

Ronnie turned another chair right side up, sat on it backwards so she could rest her elbows on the chair back. The shotgun lay across her arms. "Well, it doesn't really matter, does it? They said you took her, and the whole town thinks you took her, and, well, folks are talking about just, you know, hanging you . . . " She let the lie drop, like a burning ember on tender skin.

Levi squirmed in his chair. "*They* wanted her. They were going to trade her—"

"Shut the fuck up, Levi, or god-so-help-me I'll beat the living shit outta you."

"Well," Ronnie said, "it's your word against theirs."

Levi squirmed some more in his chair. Willis stared at the big wad of spit he'd hawked onto the patio. Roy shook his head, just a little.

"We don't have the girl," Roy said finally. "And that's all we're gonna say."

"That's all right. They're going to hang you anyway for killing all those six people in Silverton. And for starting the fire."

"We didn't start the fucking fire," Roy said. "And we didn't kill anybody. Besides, they won't hang us 'cause we don't have the death penalty in Canada. It wouldn't be right."

"Nobody seems to give a flying fig about what's right anymore." Ronnie offered a one-shoulder shrug for effect. "Hell, I've got orders just to shoot you down like dogs if you give me any trouble."

"That's bullshit."

Ronnie jerked her shotgun to her shoulder, squeezed the trigger, and blew apart the patio table lying on its side next to Roy. The blast deafened her.

"Jesus fucking Christ!" Roy yelled, ducking, pinpoint spots of blood rising on his face and arm from the exploded glass tabletop. Levi screamed and screamed. Kevin's head popped out of a second floor window. He looked around for a moment, the ducked back inside.

"Who were they going to trade her with?" she asked Roy.

Levi kept screaming. Willis simply hung his head. He looked suddenly very pale.

She pumped the shotgun. The roar of the blast, the power of the recoil, the primal terror on Roy's face: she was grinning inside, now, her muscles like oiled metal, while the quiet hiss of exhilaration in her brain muffled Levi's screaming. She wondered suddenly if she were actually going to kill Roy, and realized she didn't know. It all depended. And besides, what difference would it make if she killed him? If she killed them all? *The three-bullet solution*, Darcy had said.

Nobody seems to give a flying fig about what's right anymore . . .

Ronnie aimed the shotgun at Roy's chest.

"No!" Levi yelled. "Don't hurt him! Don't!"

"She's not going to shoot me, Levi," Roy said, although he didn't sound all that certain.

Janice and Kevin came through the French doors. "All clear," Janice said.

Ronnie ignored her. "Roy, seems to me you're trying to escape."

"No! No, he's not!" Levi was almost in a complete panic now, on his feet, yelling.

"Ronnie, what the hell are you doing?" Janice demanded.

Ronnie kept her eyes locked on Roy. She sighed for effect. Roy cringed.

"The Sun people!" Levi yelled out. "They were going to trade her to the Sun people!"

"Shit," Roy said, mostly to himself.

"Where are the Sun people?"

"Up the top of Stellars Jay Road." Levi jerked his head back, indicating up the mountain, in the direction of the fire.

Ronnie looked at Roy down the barrel of her gun.

"Look, they'll kill us if we say anything."

"Hell, everybody this side of the goddamn highway is going die anyway, unless they evacuate. That fire you set in Silverton, it's completely out of control. All this"—she swept an arm wide—"will be in flames by morning. Sooner, if the wind picks up."

Roy stomped his right foot on the cement. "Goddammit," he muttered as he let out a long, slow breath. "Don and Chris, they were going to trade the girl to the Sun people for, you know, booze, meth, food. *Stuff.* The Sun people, they keep lucies."

"What do you mean, 'they keep lucies'?"

"They keep them, you know, like slaves. They make them work the gardens, the pot plantation, mill wood for construction, cook for them. They fuck them whenever they feel like it. Got a whole pack of them up on their farm and they'll trade all kinds of shit for them if you can get your hands on one."

"You mean that old commune on the bench way at the end of the road?" Ronnie asked. She used to get called up there regularly by Social Services.

"Yeah," Roy said. "Used to belong to a bunch of hippies who wanted a place where they could worship the moon, be one with nature, that sort of bullshit. Used to run around naked all day long. We'd hike up there as kids just to see the naked girls. We called them the Moon people, 'cause they did this kind of orgy, free-love thing, on nights with a full moon.

"But these aren't the same people," he explained. "Don't know where these people came from. Two years ago they chased off what was left of the hippies and moved in. Then we saw that they started to have a lot of lucies around, working out in the fields. They wear these collars—like shock collars for dogs, eh—and they use them to keep the lucies from running away. Don and Chris were in pretty good with them."

"We called them that," Levi piped up, "because they're the complete opposite of the Moon people." Roy scowled him into silence.

"Don and Chris traded kids for things?" Ronnie felt sick. Not just at what they'd done, but that they'd done it on her watch. Clearly, she hadn't been paying attention; clearly, she hadn't had a very high level of suspicion about all the kids who had 'run away' or 'gone missing' when they were well into end-stage. It's true, if they hit sexual maturity during late end-stage many would abandon their families and homes for life with the packs who roamed the bush, squatting in empty houses, searching for food. But clearly some of them at least had been kidnapped instead. Sold into slavery.

Jesus God.

Anger and frustration roiled like magma. Her whole body was in flames. She lunged at Roy, jammed the muzzle of the shotgun hard up under his chin. "You piece of shit," she growled at him. "Didn't you even think you should do something about this? That it was your fucking responsibility to protect those children? That you should have come to me and told me so that *I* could stop them?"

Janice grabbed Ronnie's arm, jerked her backwards, twisted the barrel of the shotgun up and away. "Cut it out!" she said to her.

Ronnie let Janice drive her backwards. She was drowning in anger. Her heart was molten steel in her chest.

Levi cried and howled, tears and snot running down his chin. Willis threw up, then, spewing alcoholic vomit all over the concrete patio.

Kevin pulled the shotgun out of Ronnie's hands. Roy sagged in his chair, as if already dead. Kevin was shaking. "Didn't you think," he said to Roy, "that when you or your brothers were devolved enough, they'd make you slaves, too?"

Roy shrugged. "Who'll care by then? Once you're a total lucy, you're nothing. You're an animal. Like a dog or a pig." He shrugged again. "So, what does it matter?"

Ronnie jutted her chin toward the brothers. "Let's go find the Sun people."

Roy swung his head from side to side, grunted. "They'll kill us. All of us."

"So, *what does it matter*?" Ronnie mimicked.

It took them half an hour after parking the vehicles to hike up through the bush to the bluff where the Gardener boys had come to ogle the naked moon worshippers. On her belly at the cliff edge, Ronnie studied the farm through her binoculars. It was early evening and there wasn't much movement, save for some livestock—a couple of hogs, some goats, a dozen cows, and lots of chickens. The farm, sitting on a long, wide bench two-thirds of the way up the mountainside, included half-a-dozen sheds, a Quonset hut, a barn and two separate houses, as well as a huge vegetable garden, an even bigger pot plantation, pastures and paddocks, and a high perimeter fence that made the place look like one of the American FEMA camps Ronnie had seen on TV a few years ago. The forest had been clearcut thirty meters back from the perimeter fence. Fire break, Ronnie presumed.

What was missing from the scene, though, were all those kidnapped children Roy talked about.

She handed the binoculars to Janice and scrambled back from the cliff to where Kevin had the brothers sitting on the ground. "So, where are they, asshole?" she asked Roy. "I didn't see any slaves wearing dog collars."

Roy squinted at her. "It's supper time, right? They'll be in the Quonset hut. At least the girls will. It's like an army barracks. That's where they sleep and get fed. The guys are in one of the other sheds."

"You've seen this with your own eyes, or is this just some crap Don and Chris have been feeding you?"

"My own eyes."

She crouched in front of him, her face close to his. "Bullshit," she said.

He rubbed his cheek on a shoulder, wriggled his arms, still cuffed behind his back. "Don and Chris took us up there once, all three of us." Willis and Levi nodded in agreement. "To show us the kinds of lucies they wanted. You know, how old, how big. Showed us what they'd trade." He spat on the ground. "It was pretty fucking creepy, really. We were in the Quonset hut, talking. Then, one of them farm guys went in to where the lucies were eating, grabbed one of the girls, brought her back to where we were. Then he fucked her from behind, right then and there. Right in front of us. Asked us if we wanted to have a go." His eyes were on the ground. "We didn't, though."

"Those two guys did," Levi said, as if trying to be helpful. "Big grins on their faces."

"Makes you wonder who the goddamn animals are," Kevin said.

For a second, Ronnie thought she might throw up.

On the hike back down to the vehicles, Ronnie tried to make up her mind. The farm needed to be evacuated because of the fire. If it came over the ridge, those measly thirty-meter firebreaks wouldn't slow it down at all. She doubted, though, that the Sun people would be particularly happy seeing her show up to ask them to evacuate. But she didn't want to risk sending civilians up to the front gates either. She had no idea how paranoid these people would be—given that they had every reason to *be* paranoid.

"So, how many lucies did you trade in, Roy?" Kevin asked, breaking the silence.

"Fuck you," Roy said.

"No, I mean it. Was it worth it? What'd you get? A six-pack, a couple of kilos of BC bud, all-you-can-eat pussy?"

Roy stopped dead in his tracks and spun to face Kevin, looking ugly and mean despite having his hands still cuffed behind him.

"Whoa there, mister," Kevin said, "I was just asking. You know, making conversation."

"Watch yourself, fag-boy."

"Ouch. Name-calling. I'm really hurt, now."

Janice gave Roy a shove to keep him moving. "Knock it off," she said to Kevin. "Move your ass, Roy, we're almost there."

Ronnie could see the RCMP SUV through the trees ahead.

"*Yeah, Roy, move your ass.*" A voice to Ronnie's left, and slightly behind. Ronnie spun, pumping her shotgun.

Half-a-dozen men swarmed out of the bush, dressed in fatigues and armed with assault rifles.

Something slammed into the side of Ronnie's face, knocking her backwards over a stump at the edge of the trail. Her brain roared as she fell.

She scrambled to her knees, her vision still muzzy from the blow, and jerked her shotgun to her shoulder.

Then her vision cleared.

One of the men had the muzzle of his weapon jammed up under Kevin's jaw. The Gardener brothers were all on their knees. Janice was standing with her hands on her head.

"Don't even fucking think about it." The muzzle of a handgun butted up behind her ear. A hand reached out for her shotgun. She placed it in the open hand. "Get up," he said as he moved in front of her. She'd seen him once or twice in the hardware store in Silverton, a tall man in his mid-to-late fifties, thick and muscular, perhaps with some lucy changes, perhaps not, it was hard to tell with those gray caterpillar eyebrows and that brick-shaped jaw. He looked like a weightlifter.

"Now the service revolver," he said to her. "And the radio."

No point telling him the batteries were dead, she thought.

"Nice to see you again, Corporal Sapriken," he said after she'd handed over her revolver and radio.

"*Freakin' Sapriken*," chimed the man with the gun shoved up under Kevin's chin. He had the same thick build and heavy eyebrows as the man in front of her, but wore his shit-brown hair long and looked half the older man's age.

Ronnie's cheekbone throbbed. Blood ran down her jaw and dripped onto her vest. She mustered as much cop persona as she could, straightened her shoulders. "You need to evacuate. There's a firestorm on the other side of that ridge, and the fire chief estimates that it'll take this whole valley by the end of tomorrow."

"Yes, I'm sure that Mr. Khaira is concerned for our safety. Is that why you're here, Corporal, to warn us about the fire? Or have the boys—whom I can't help but notice have been restrained—been telling you tall tales?"

"We didn't tell her anything, Mr. Kratky," Roy said.

"Shut up, Roy," Mr. Kratky said, "or I'll put you out of my misery right here and now."

Roy shut up.

Ronnie's head pounded. She tried to think.

"Let's move along, Corporal," Mr. Kratky said. "Don't want to waste the evening, do we?" One of the other men laughed and Mr. Kratky smiled.

CHAPTER 17

Alex followed Irene up the concrete walk to her older two-story house. She'd offered to put him up in her guest room until first light when he and Marika were to head back to Winlaw to apprise folks there of the fire situation in Silverton. Marika had found a bed at the Khaira's—Darcy's wife, Amanda, had been a patient of Marika's off and on over the years.

The evening was cool and the light was beginning to bleed away. The blue paint had faded and the wooden steps to the front door sagged. But the border gardens thrived despite the summer's relentless heat, and up against the house white climbing roses spread across the wood siding like a lush skirt. Irene pulled open the metal screen door, led him inside.

He pulled off his boots and socks then followed Irene through the house to the screened-in deck off the kitchen, the wood floors cool on his bare feet.

"You want a beer?" she said.

"Yeah. A beer would be great." Alex dropped into a chair on the deck.

She disappeared back into the kitchen, and he heard her stomp down the basement stairs.

He ran his fingers through his dirty hair, rubbed his gritty eyes. His sinuses were raw from the smoke, and his back and legs were sore and stiff. From half-dragging Yuri down the driveway, from helping to carry Pam through a hundred meters of smoldering forest to the ambulance, from running back to the crashed truck to pump some morphine into Joshua Pierce and to tell him that there was nothing they could do, the fire was too close, they had to leave him—

News about the fire wasn't very good. According to Marika, Darcy Khaira had cut the crews back to a minimum for the night, sending everybody he could home to rest them up and get some food into them, advising them all to be back before sun-up, though. Plus he had put the town on a one-hour evacuation notice.

Floorboards creaked and Irene came out onto the deck with two brown bottles in hand. She handed him one.

"Hey, it's cold," he said.

"I have an electric cooler in the basement. Works just fine on the solar feed. Not as cold as a real fridge, but good enough. I keep a few things in it. Sometimes run some lights with the feed. Mostly I've just gotten used to not having electricity."

Alex took a pull on his beer. "Damn, that tastes good."

A tired laugh was all Irene seemed able to manage.

He didn't want to think about Josh Pierce. "So how are you doing these days?" he asked her.

She looked over at him, took a swallow of beer. "Better," she said, "much better."

They sat in silence for a while. Josh Pierce hung between them. Cool air blew the scent of roses and fuchsias across the deck as the night deepened. Irene set her bottle on the table between them and stretched her legs out in front of her.

"It hasn't been the best year, though," she said. "And it's days like this that make it extra hard." He could barely see her now: a silhouette, the lines of her hair, her shoulders, her legs, etched like charcoal on dark paper. "I've never left someone at the scene like that before, left them to die all alone."

"Me neither," was all he could get out.

"Tom's dying took a lot out of me. The house was so empty all the time. It was like I didn't know who I was anymore, or what I was supposed to do. Everything had been about us, together." The line of her shoulders moved up and down: a shrug. "I've seen so many people die these last few years, so many families grieve, and live their lives, and grieve some more, and go on living. I knew that's what would happen to me, that I'd grieve but go on living."

Alex took another pull on his beer.

Irene sighed. "Of course, I closed up the bookstore when Tom died—there hadn't been any point in keeping it open anyway (we just did it out of habit, familiarity), it's not like we'd been able to order any books for quite some time. Without the store, there was only the ambulance. But at least it got me out of bed every morning."

She sipped at her beer. "I hated the idea of Tom dying alone, laying on the kitchen floor like that. That's what bugs me about Josh, leaving him there like that."

"Nobody could stay with him. The fire." It sounded so lame, stating the obvious.

"I know. It's just not right, though."

The August night's dark should have been absolute under such a thick seam of smoke, however the southern sky over Silverton loomed bloody and virulent. Irene asked him about Gemma again, and about folks she knew in Winlaw, how they were. She asked him how *he* was. Alex didn't want to tell her, although it had always been an easy thing to do with her. But he couldn't make himself open that door. If he told her of the promise he'd made to Gemma, if he let *those* feelings out, that jagged stone in his heart would turn to magma and burn him hollow. So he deflected, talking about Yuri getting shot, about how he felt leaving Josh behind; he asked about the bodies on the lawn in Silverton, about the girl tied up in the paddock. And Irene let him.

Finally, when he'd finished the last of his beer, his heart heavy with death, he said, "I think I need to call it a night. It's been a long day, and tomorrow's probably not going to be much of a picnic, either."

She nodded slowly.

He stood, and she stood with him. "Will you come to bed with me?" she said. She came around the table, touched her hand to his chest, to the place where his heart lay leaden. She kissed him tentatively on the mouth. "You can say no."

Loneliness flashed through him, smudged dark by sadness. He stroked a finger along her cheek, kissed her, then followed her through the dark kitchen into the living room, where he picked up his pack, and climbed the stairs behind her.

Sleep evaded Alex. He checked his watch, shifted the comforter. Dim bloody light invaded in the open window.

"What time is it?" Irene said, voice muffled, her head half-buried under her pillow.

"Just after two."

She rolled up against him. Her face was creased from sleep and her hair stuck up on one side. He smiled at her, reached over and pushed her hair down. She kissed his arm. He propped himself onto an elbow and pulled the comforter down far enough to expose her breast. He ran his finger around the nipple, then kissed it. He pulled the comforter down on the other side, ran his hand across the flat sheet of rib where her right breast used to be, traced the scar. "When did this happen?" he said.

"A dozen years ago."

He kissed her shoulder. "Tell me."

She rolled onto her back, shrugged a little. "It was a long time ago. Seems almost inconsequential now." She picked up Alex's hand, rubbed it against her lips. "Tom's gone; so are my grandchildren; I haven't heard anything from Sage for two years; most of the friends I had here in town have died or left the valley. The cancer is nothing."

He leaned over her and kissed her on the mouth. She wrapped her arms around him, pulled him down against her. Alex could feel her heartbeat against his chest and the smooth waves of her breathing. He wanted to stay like this forever, skin to skin.

Alex eased out from under the comforter, trying not to wake Irene, who quietly snored, her head once again half-buried under her pillow. He still hadn't slept. As tired as he was, his mind was spastic with flashing images: of Yuri bleeding in the back seat; of the girl in the paddock screeching with fear; of Josh Pierce gulping thick wet breaths; of Pam screaming at him to help her; of Gemma, her face turned toward his, pale as death in the starlight, weeping. He stood in front of the window, the night's cool air raising goose bumps on his skin. He hugged his arms across his chest.

He knew that the stress of the last couple of months was eating him up. And he knew that Yuri's shooting and Josh's abandonment would haunt him for a while to come. He expected that. It was Gemma who weighed on him most of all, and how all the avoiding, all the time spent busying himself with work, all the hopefulness he'd laboriously engaged in over the past year had simply gone up in smoke the other night as they lay out under the stars watching for meteors.

"Dad, I don't want to end up like Darlene. Or like Colin. If I get so that I can't talk anymore, or think anymore—so that I'm not me anymore—I want you to kill me. Okay? Grampa's old gun is still in the basement, and there are bullets for it. I checked . . . I'd rather be dead than live like that. Promise me you'll do it."

Alex hugged himself in front of Irene's dark window. *He had promised to kill his own daughter.* He could no longer lie to himself: Gemma wasn't going to get better. Just because he wanted her to be whole again so badly it made him ache didn't mean it would happen. He imagined himself as Josh, the fire approaching, trying to wish himself out of that truck.

The universe doesn't work that way, Dad.

How does the universe work, then, missy? he should have said. And what if she asked him the same question? What would he say to her? In this moment, his mind flickering and snapping with grief, it seemed to him that the universe's *modus operandi* was nothing short of perverse cruelty. Otherwise there wouldn't be cancer, or the Lucy virus, or wars or starvation or earthquakes. Or trucks trapping good people that had to be left to die alone. In fact, some days it seemed as if the universe were intent on torturing, and eventually exterminating, *Homo sapiens sapiens.* Is that what he'd tell her? That the universe was vindictive and malevolent?

On the other hand, Yuri Evdikimoff was still alive. And there was no goddamn reason for that at all. "Too pickled to die," Marika had suggested.

And Ronnie Sapriken had saved that girl, Thea.

It was as if the universe had wanted Yuri to live, had wanted Ronnie to rescue those kids.

Is that what he'd tell her, that the universe, despite appearances, can indeed line up small miracles, tiny salvations?

The universe doesn't work like that, Dad.

But what if it does? Isn't that something to hope for? That the universe could save her?

The bed creaked behind him. "Can't sleep?"

Alex turned. Irene was sitting, her single breast splashed with rusty light, her face open and soft. He sat on the edge of the bed. She wrapped her arms around him, pulled his face into her neck.

"How can you stand it?" he asked her softly.

"Stand what?"

"Not knowing about Sage. Tom's dying. The cancer."

"You either stand it or you die." She rubbed her cheek against his shoulder, her skin cool and soft. "Things were bad after Tom died. Suddenly it seemed like all I'd done was grieve, first the cancer, then my breast; the list goes on, all the friends who died because of the Disney flu and the Lucy virus; Quinn, Jordan, Maddie; maybe even Sage; then, last year, Tom. Working for the ambulance helped, you know, by giving back. But it also made it worse. I ended up knee-deep in everything ugly and sad and hard." Tears dropped onto his shoulder burning his skin. "But somehow I got out of bed everyday. There was always somebody who needed something. And there was always the thought that maybe today would be the day I'd hear word from Sage." She slipped out of Alex's arms, wiped her eyes with the back of her hand. "Eventually I realized I still had the rest of my life to live, and that I had choices I could make about that. Not the same choices I had before—because Tom is gone—but choices none-the-less, and they were mine to make. They're all I have, really, my choices." She rummaged in her nightstand until she found a handkerchief and blew her nose. "I'm not sure why, but knowing that, that I still have choices, good or bad, makes me think that somehow it's all going to be okay."

Alex swallowed. "That's what I want. That's *all* I want. To know it's going to be okay." *That Gemma will be okay.*

"I can't give you that."

"I know."

"If I could, I would."

He laughed a little, but sadness swept through him like scorched wind.

Irene touched his face. "I can't save you," she said. "All I can do is hold you when I can, on the days I feel strong enough. I can listen if you need me to. But in the end, you have to make your own choices. Every single day, you have to choose. You have to save yourself."

"I just don't know how." *Gemma asked me to kill her, and I said yes.*

"You'll find your way. You're a kind man; trust what your heart tells you."

Tears fell, burning long streaks down his chest.

CHAPTER 18

Sage pushed Isaac and Ula in the garden cart while Carl rode ahead then circled back on the bicycle. Josie walked beside Sage, once again an automaton of a girl.

Sage directed them along a road heading north toward the center of town. They still needed food supplies and fresh water, and some place safe to stop for breakfast. A chain link fence appeared on their right, enclosing a long, straight street, with several large metal buildings in the distance, all untouched by fire. She stopped, cupped her hand over her eyes and studied the buildings for several moments. "It's an airport," she whispered, and then with a whoop started to push the garden cart at a jog.

"An airport?" Carl echoed. "Can you fly an airplane?"

"Actually, yes, I can. Quinn took me flying quite a bit. That was a long time ago, but, hell—" Tears spilled from her eyes.

Josie tugged on her shirt, forcing Sage to settle back into a walk. "Who's Quinn?" she asked.

Sage wiped her face with the back of a hand. "He was my husband."

"He's dead, right?" Carl said.

She nodded, wincing a little even after these long four years. "He was a commercial pilot, but he loved small planes."

"I'm not getting in no airplane," Carl said.

"Why not?"

"It might crash." He swung past her pedaling the bike.

"We're not even going to worry about crashing until we know for sure if there is even a plane to fly."

Carl wasn't about to let it go. "Why would we use an airplane that could crash? We got a bike and a cart and we can walk wherever we want?"

"Technology, kiddo. If you've got it, use it. You see, way back when, in the days of early humans—"

"Like back when Lucy was alive? The real Lucy?" Carl said.

"Not that far back. Maybe as far back as 750,000 years ago, though, someone figured out that rolling things around was much, much easier than dragging or pulling them. There are pictures from Sumeria—"

"Where's that?" Carl asked.

"Iraq."

Carl just shrugged.

"Anyway, there are these drawings showing a cart with wheels from about 5500 years ago." Sage turned right on the road leading to the airport entrance. "Once the wheel was invented, people found lots of uses for it."

Carl frowned as he pedaled toward her. "Like for bicycles," he said, then he scrunched up his face and added, "and cars, and airplanes, 'cause they need wheels to land with. And skateboards."

Sage laughed.

The chain link gate that led out to the tarmac had been crushed, as though rammed by a vehicle. The first building looked heartily ransacked, with broken windows and smashed office furniture.

"How come you know stuff, like Sumeria and the wheel?" Carl hopped off the bike and leaned it against the fence.

"I read a lot. And I was a librarian. It was my job to help people find the information they wanted."The frown on his face suggested to Sage that Carl thought she might be lying to him. "Didn't you ever go to a library?"

"Yeah. We had a library. I went."

"Can you read, Carl?"

"'Course I can read," he said and stalked off through a gap between the crushed gate and the fence. Sage pushed the cart after him. She let him be. There would be plenty of time later to talk about reading, and books, and history, and learning, and all those things she so loved that no one could take from her. They had taken everything else she loved, but they could not take—

Monkey-mind can take it, a voice taunted her. *Monkey-mind will scratch away all at those precious facts, all that knowledge, until it is shredded and scattered. And all those fond, loving memories? Pah! Monkey-mind will howl and screech them all away into senseless static, leaving your mind hissing in the dark like a dead radio channel.*

Sage shook the voice out of her head.

The side door on the first hanger had been jimmied open. Two helicopters, looking a little worse for wear, crouched in the dim interior like giant insects.

Carl was already over at the second hanger, swinging an arm for them to hurry up. "There's three planes!" he shouted. "Three!"

Sage leapt into a pregnant-woman's run. Ula shrieked at the speed of the cart, slapping her hands on the plastic sides in excitement. Isaac, on the other hand, crouched low, ducking his head and holding on, white-knuckled. Sage's pack bounced on her back, slowing her down, but she ran anyway, elation flying her feet over the pavement.

Maybe it was because planes evoked such fond memories of Quinn, maybe it was because the end of her journey seemed so much closer with the possibility of flight, maybe it was because, for Sage, the airplane symbolized the ability, and concurrently, the willingness, to think beyond self, to see beyond borders, to move between worlds.

And to drop bombs on unsuspecting civilians.

She told her inner critic to shut up. Now was not the time. Sage was well aware that technology carried with it the usual baggage of human decision-making, good and evil, just and unjust. Living with that dichotomy is the human condition, she reminded her critic. Wheel: bicycle; chariot. Gene therapy: the demise of Alzheimer's disease; the invention of the Lucy virus. It is always about choice. Sometimes the lines of choice you draw in the sand have to be moved. *ETHICS, you'll find that in the 170s, ma'am, if you simply want to browse the shelves. Did you have a specific field in mind? You just want to know what's right and what's wrong? Stealing airplanes? Hmmm. Let me see . . .*

The door was locked. Carl peered through the window into the dark interior. The glass had been broken from the outside and someone had tried, half-heartedly it seemed, to pry the security bars apart. Sage stuck her forehead against the bars. Inside there were two Cessnas, one a tired looking Skyhawk, the other a snazzier Skylane, and a basic Piper Arrow, the newest of the three, maybe only a decade old.

Sage tried the bay doors on the front of the hanger. They were all locked. No one had done much tampering. She found the back door locked as well, the security glass still intact in front of the bars. Well, she'd be damned if she'd let a couple of locked doors keep her from the possibility of flying to New Denver rather than walking there pushing a garden cart full of kids.

When she came back round to the side of the building with the broken window, she found Ula crouched behind the cart, pulling the contents of her backpack out onto the ground.

"Hey!" Sage hollered. Ula screeched, grabbed an apple and a bag of dried fruit, and bolted towards Carl who was rounding the corner from the front side of the hanger with Isaac riding piggy-back. Ula scampered behind Carl, whimpering, all the while cramming her mouth with dried fruit. Carl glowered at Sage.

"C'mon, Ula, you got to share," he said to her as he pushed her out from behind him. He shrugged Isaac off his back and onto the ground. Isaac raced after Ula, grabbing at the bag of fruit dangling from her hand. She screeched and tore off behind the hanger. Carl threw up his hands, the exaggerated gesture of a child imitating adults.

Sage gathered the scattered contents of her pack. "Obviously," she said, "I've asked everyone to wait far too long for breakfast." She looked at Carl. "If Ula eats that bag of dried fruit all by herself, she'll have diarrhea like you've never seen before."

Carl made a face, then went after Ula and Isaac, yelling and commanding, the irritation in is ten-year-old voice escalating. Josie, who had simply stood by while Ula emptied Sage's pack, stooped to help Sage gather her belongings.

Sage laid out the last of the granola bars, an apple that Ula had left behind, and a plastic jar barely a third-full of honey-roasted peanuts. The meager buffet would have to do. She didn't want to use up any more stove fuel until dinner, and they'd certainly have to head into Grand Forks proper—or what was left of it—to hunt for food.

A screech erupted from the other side of the hanger, and a cacophony of barking and snarling followed it. Sage's blood turned to ice. Carl was shouting. Sage wrenched the axe handle from her pack. "Josie! Get in the hanger with the helicopters! *NOW!*" Josie turned and ran.

The barking and screeching echoed off the metal walls. Sage raced around the hanger, almost knocking Isaac to the ground. Up ahead in a copse of scorched trees just outside the airport fence a knot of dogs and children writhed.

Sage found a hole in the fence, threw herself onto her hands and knees and scrambled through, points of torn chain link ripping through her T-shirt. She ran at the melee with a roar. The knot unfolded, two big black and tan dogs turned to run, while a third, a Border Collie cross, skulked away; Carl was pulling at a large shaggy-looking terrier cross of some kind which had its jaws clamped on Ula's upper arm. There were patches of blood on her arms and legs, and a nasty gash in her right cheek, just below her eye.

"Leave it!" Sage bellowed at the dog, rage erupting. She wielded the axe handle. Carl backed away, as if Sage had yelled at him. The dog spun, swinging Ula wildly, to make a run for it, its prey clamped securely in its teeth. Sage brought the axe handle down on the dog's back, two-handed, with as much power as she could muster. The dog staggered under the blow. The big head dropped Ula and swung around at Sage, jaws air-snapping, as it stumbled sideways. Ula tried to scrabble away, screeching and whimpering, her left arm useless. The dog snapped in her direction. Out of the corner of her eye Sage saw one of the other dogs dart in toward Ula, but Carl was there first, scooping her up in his arms and backing away. The big terrier scrambled sideways, out of the reach of Sage's axe handle. Sage turned her attention on the other dogs, putting her body between them and the children, and swinging the axe handle over her head to make herself look larger than she was.

After eyeing her for a moment, the terrier turned and loped away, followed by the rest of the dogs. They stopped at the edge of the next road to look back and watch as Sage orchestrated a retreat. She swept Ula up out of Carl's arms as they hurried back between the two hangers.

Josie stood looking through the barred window into the airplane hanger. "Isaac," she said.

"Goddammit!" Sage threw the axe handle on the pavement, shifted Ula's weight onto her other arm. "Carl, see if you can get Isaac to open the door. Josie, go to the edge of the hanger and tell me if you can still see those dogs." Ula whimpered and cried against Sage's neck, her breath hot and damp. Sage laid her face-up on the pavement. At a glance none of the bites looked life threatening. It seemed though, that her left arm might be broken above the elbow—which would also mean a lot of tissue and vessel damage.

"No dogs," Josie said, panic tightening her rusty voice.

"Carl?"

"Isaac's climbed up onto one of the planes and is just sitting here."

Sage glanced back at Josie. "Do you think you can fit through those bars?"

Josie gave a single nod.

"Carl, go watch for those dogs. Okay, Josie, I'm going to lift you up, and we'll see if we can squeeze you between those bars." Sage creaked to her feet. "Okay, make yourself stiff as a board." Josie complied. Sage lifted her—she turned out to be much lighter than she had expected—and eased her between the bars. "Turn you head; look at the ground. Good." Josie's scrawny upper body slipped between the bars. "Okay, honey, I'm going to ease you the rest of the way through, then lower you to the ground. Use your hands so you don't hit your head. Tell me when you can feel the ground."

"Ground," Josie said.

"I'm going to let you go."

Carl squeaked. "They're there, by the fence! They saw me!"

The door handle rattled.

"Josie?"

"It won't open."

Sage rushed to the door. "Honey, there's a deadbolt above the handle."

The deadbolt clanked back and forth.

Sage studied the door. "Look down at the bottom of the door. Is there a pin, or a latch, that you can lift?"

Click.

"Now look up at the top of the door. There's probably exactly the same thing there."

"Sa-age," Carl sang, warning in her voice. "I can't see those dogs anymore."

Click.

The door swung inward.

"Nice work, Josie!" Sage said. "Everybody inside. Now!" She lifted Ula with one arm, stuffed the innards back into her pack with the other. Carl followed her inside.

Josie slammed the door and locked it.

Maddie's death hit Sage's world like an asteroid, vaporizing a huge section of her soul on impact.

From everything else—Quinn's and Jovan's deaths, the loss of her devolved baby boy, Linus, the loss of her home and work, their disintegrating life in camp, even Maddie's own devolving—from all this, Sage seemed able somehow to protect herself, to burn up or at least grind down enough of the incoming pain with her psychological atmosphere to keep going, to continue to have hope. But not with Maddie's death. And not her dying that way, with Sage holding her still, breathless body against her chest and rocking her, Maddie's blood leaking through Sage's clothes and staining her skin, while Sage's own blood dripped on the linoleum floor, and the campers around her wept and screamed and rocked their own dead as gunfire outside continued to crack the day into white-hot fragments.

The dead were taken away and cremated without ceremony.

Sage was treated for the gunshot wound in her leg and released back to her barrack, which had been ransacked by the National Guard after the suppression of the riot. She had nothing left of Maddie's, save for a few clothes in the hamper bag under her cot. Everything else had been stolen or destroyed in the mayhem: all the photographs of Quinn, Jovan and Maddie, and of her parents, were gone. Everything had been taken from her but her pain, and now that nucleus of loss leaked up from her heart and pushed hot and molten out through the massive cracks in her frozen, protective exterior.

She curled up on her cot, pressing one of Maddie's T-shirts to her face, trying to breath her daughter's life out of the unwashed fabric. Sage could smell her child's sweat from playing on the hard-baked soccer field just days before.

Sage overflowed with a reckless bitterness, shunning all attempts by people to comfort her, keeping her eyes steadfastly averted, avoiding the mess hall, the games room, the playing field. She blamed her co-inmates—they were the ones who had rioted, who hadn't had the fortitude or the faith to wait this thing out—and she blamed the Guard, who had quelled the riot with injudicious and overwhelming firepower. She blamed the government, who let the virus get out of control; she blamed the True Gorilla, for having so little faith in humans to right the wrongs they had wrought. And she blamed God, who, given that He was supposed to be so goddamn omnipotent, had just stood by and let her family die. She hadn't realized how much she had believed in Him until the moment she denounced Him, running the perimeter fence like a caged animal under the stark September sky. And yet, despite her incarceration, in the moment of her denouncement she experienced a heady, peculiar flush of freedom. She stopped running suddenly, her breath biting back lumps of hot September air as she rested her hands on her hips, arms akimbo. Sweat rivered down her back and face.

God had been foundational to her understanding of life. She realized that the existence and attributes of God had given shape to how she viewed events in the world, the existence of good and evil, and humankind's role and responsibility in this world, *her* role and responsibility. She had taught her children that God loved them and would care for them. That God held the whole world in His hands.

She wound her fingers through the chain-link of the fence and tipped back her head to stare at the September sky, achingly blue, the glare of the mid-afternoon sun hurting her eyes.If there was no God, then there was no order. No externally imposed order, that is. If God didn't exist, theodicy didn't exist—all those 214s written for naught. If God didn't exist, then what were good and evil? So much for the elaborate discussions penned in the 216s. For that matter, the whole of the 200s was simply a waste of space, both mental and architectural.

She resumed running, her sweat suddenly cold against her skin.

There needed to be a new category. Sometimes a number home had no occupants, technically established as "Not assigned or no longer used." The occupants of the 200s needed to be recatalogued, repurposed even, into a new category, the 1000s perhaps, a home for those tomes whose *subjects* were "no longer used." That is where God belonged. He had outlived his usefulness. He was no longer needed.

CHAPTER 19

"Is Ula going to die?" Carl asked, his eyes frank and afraid.

"I don't know," Sage said. "Listen. I want you to make sure nothing can get in here," she told him, "while I look after Ula. Take Josie with you. Look for holes, gaps, anything that those dogs could get through."

Carl turned away, shoulders pulled forward.

Ula moaned, but lay still where Sage had placed her on the tool bench at the back of the hanger while Sage began at the top of Ula's head, looking for injuries she hadn't yet seen. A laceration on top of a growing lump behind Ula's left ear explained her lack of responsiveness. She probably had a concussion, getting her head whacked on a rock or a tree root when the dog had tried to run away with her. The cut seeped very little blood. Her left arm felt broken, though, halfway between the elbow and the shoulder, and the punctures there were deep, right to the bone. Ula moaned and tried to pull away when Sage palpated her broken arm. There was a tear in Ula's right cheek that needed a good cleaning, and, ideally, stitches to keep it closed. No bites to her back or chest, or her belly, just some scratches and bruises. Her legs had several punctures and tears, but the bones felt intact. The real problem was going to be infection. What Ula needed was antibiotics. And even though Ula was not going to appreciate having her wounds tended, Sage was going to have to clean them with soapy water, and simply hope for the best. Plus, Ula needed to wear a splint on that broken arm.

Sage wondered if the Grand Forks hospital still stood, or if it, too, had become a victim of the fire. If memory served, it was on the west side of town half-a-dozen kilometers or so from the little airport—a quick dash on the bike, she noted. She cringed, though, at the thought of leaving the kids alone in the hanger.

Sage spent an hour carefully cleaning Ula's wounds, using up almost all their drinking water to do so. Then she bandaged them, gutting the contents of her tiny first aid kit.

Meanwhile, after the kids had reported that the hanger was secure, she had them search the cupboards, the airplanes—if they were unlocked—for another first aid kit or other items they might be able to use, like flashlights or batteries or canned food.

Ula, who had slowly returned to full alertness, whimpered under Sage's ministrations, even cried once or twice, but never pulled away. Carl stayed close by, reassuring her, while Isaac, warily watching out of the corners of his eyes, kept his distance, seeming to think that somehow he might be next. Finally, Sage splinted Ula's upper arm, adjusting the size and the Velcro straps with care, then undoing the valve and letting in enough air to make the splint rigid.

When it was all over, Ula appeared quite drowsy, the trauma and the treatment having taken a lot out of her. Sage convinced her to swallow an acetaminophen caplet with some water and to curl up in Sage's sleeping bag on the workbench. She gave Carl instructions to wake Ula in an hour, and every hour until she came back, and gave him her watch. Carl nodded dumbly. Neither he nor Josie put up any fuss when she told them she needed to find antibiotics for Ula.

Sage retrieved her bike, pedaled it back to the hanger where she dumped the contents of her panniers and backpack out onto the floor, and then piled in all their empty water bottles. She left the children her axe handle for protection and kept only the knife hidden inside her pants. Then she wheeled the bike back outside where she waited until she heard the locks fasten before heading out through the broken gate to the airport road.

She pedaled hard, sticking to the middle of the streets and avoiding blind corners. It became clear when she crossed the small bridge over the Kettle River that the fire had taken the whole town proper, coming down from the north and the west. People seemed to have had warning enough to flee, though, for vehicles were few. The Kettle River had shriveled into a ghost of a river, its bed looking like an oversized Japanese dry stream. She'd stop on the way back to get water: she wanted to get to the hospital as fast as she could. Since leaving the FEMA camp, she'd felt exposed and vulnerable outside, and the attack by the dogs had only amplified her sense of exigency. She concentrated on the environment around her, scanning for predators and for debris on the road that might blow a tire or cause her to take a spill.

Grand Forks had been a pretty town, with sweeping deciduous trees lining the main street that doubled as a highway, and lovely, tall heritage homes. All of it had been razed. Concrete basements, like open maws, were filled with the ashes and detritus of their burned houses. Sage pedaled and sweated while the thick stench of the burn clotted her lungs. The fire must have been driven by its own ferocious winds, hurling a storm of burning branches and embers ahead of it, because even the stores and restaurants with wide paved parking lots as firebreaks had succumbed. The hospital had fared no better, the roof caving, pulling the concrete block walls in with it.

Sage leaned her bike against one of the scorched pillars at the Emergency entrance. The burned-out subdivision to the north of the hospital blew ash and dust at her. She felt a terrible need to rummage through the debris, to at least make a search for the medication she needed for Ula, but there was no point. Better off seeing if the pharmacy in the downtown core had perhaps suffered only partial damage. She felt little hope, though. Seeing the destruction here only made her feel more afraid that she would find New Denver, too, had been consumed by fire, and that her mother and father had been relocated to some other town, maybe even to another province. Maybe they weren't even alive anymore, her mother's cancer coming back, chewing her life out of her, perhaps leaving her already long dead, like Jovan and Maddie and Quinn.

She mounted her bike and pedaled back through town, which was a wasteland. Her fear and grief spread, feverish and virulent, threatening to lay her to waste like the town around her. Yet, she knew that if she let despair win—if she did not get to New Denver, if she did not find her parents, the only people to whom she could truly and fully tell the stories of Quinn's and Jovan's and Maddie's lives and deaths—she will have let the ones she loved slip into oblivion unremembered and ungrieved except by her alone, and that, she believed deep in the nucleus of her heart, was not good enough.

Locks clicked open and the door swung wide and Josie was in Sage's arms before she could blink.

"I knew you'd come back," Josie said.

"Of course I was coming back." Sage hugged Josie.

"That's what everybody says," Carl said, "but sometimes they don't come back."

"I promised I would." She ushered Josie inside and wheeled her bike through the doorway. Carl shut and locked the door behind her.

"How's Ula?" Sage asked Carl as she leaned her bike against the workbench.

"Sleeping. You get 'em?" Carl asked.

"The antibiotics? No. The hospital burned to the ground. The whole town. Everything." Sage touched Ula's forehead. "Where's Isaac?"

"Asleep in that plane over there," Carl said, pointing. "We gave him some cookies, and found a blanket for him, and so he just laid down and went to sleep."

"Well, since we missed breakfast, how about I make some lunch?"

Carl and Josie looked at each other.

"What?" Sage lifted the sleeping bag covering Ula so she could examine the bandages and splint. Ula whimpered in her sleep.

"We were hungry," Carl said, then started to cry. Josie stared at the concrete floor.

Sage turned, saw Carl's crushed face, the tears on his cheeks. "Oh, honey, what's the matter?"

"We ate all the food!" Carl was sobbing now. "We couldn't help it!"

Sage pulled Carl into her arms. He crumpled against her. "You couldn't have eaten all the food."

Carl led her to the scattered pile of belongings she'd dumped from her pack and panniers before leaving. Wrappers littered the floor. Sage crouched and poked through the pile. None of the cans had been opened; the instant rice packets were untouched, save one; the noodle soups, the same; there were a couple of packets of hot chocolate left (Sage had thought she'd used them all in the barn last night); all they had eaten was the fresh stuff—the last apple, some carrots—the last few granola bars, a half-bag of stale cookies, and a foil pouch of spaghetti sauce, which, apparently, they had licked clean.

"It's okay," she told them. "I want you to know that we all share here; this isn't just *my* food. We're like a family now."

"But I already have a family," Josie said.

Sage's heart sank with sudden dread. "Where, honey?"

"In Heaven," Josie said with such matter-of-factness that tears welled in Sage's eyes.

Sage spent the afternoon working on the airplanes, all the while wondering if she were wasting her time. The Skyhawk hadn't been flown in years, and appeared rather to be someone's project as opposed to a means of transportation, which is probably why it had been left unlocked. The Skylane was in pretty decent shape, while the Piper had one damaged tire. Both planes were locked up tight, but she was finally able to jimmy a door open on the Skylane. However, she had to break a window in the Piper—which had proved to be much more difficult than she had anticipated—and, as she'd feared, the Piper had a newer anti-theft datapad ignition.

The Skylane was older than she'd first guessed, so she was able to pry the ignition apart and disengage the datapad, and because the batteries were dead the lock-down didn't initiate. She rewired the ignition, as Quinn had shown her, in case, he'd said with a straight face, there was a malfunction in the datapad—and Cessnas were notorious for them—and the plane wouldn't start.

Everything seemed to be in order. Now she simply needed to know if the damn thing worked. The Skylane was equipped with standard solar rechargers, so all she had to do was push the plane out under the open sky and hope enough sunlight chewed through the smoke to recharge the batteries. Sage wasn't thrilled about parking the plane outside the hanger on the tarmac, sitting there like a homing beacon with its gleaming white paintjob. Wild dogs were one thing, wild hominids were quite another.

By early evening Ula had became feverish. Sage fed her more acetaminophen.

Isaac kept his distance. He didn't seem to want to trust Sage. She was worried about getting him into the plane—should the damn thing actually work—and keeping him there once he realized he was trapped. She'd have preferred kiddie impact-seats for both Ula and Isaac, but they'd take up far too much room, even if she could scrounge up a couple. She'd need to adjust the harnesses to hold them in place.

After boiling up some instant udon noodle soup for dinner, Sage spent the evening jerry-rigging the harnesses for Ula and Isaac. As the light failed she got the kids to help her roll the plane back into the hanger, where she continued to work by flashlight. The kids took turns helping Sage as best they could—holding the flashlight, or handing her tools—which was mostly a way for Sage to spend time with them one on one.

It was Carl who helped her bolt the last belt back into the wall, and Sage took the opportunity, as they knelt on the back seats, to tell him about her concern for Isaac.

"I won't leave him behind," Carl said, furrowing his brow.

"God, Carl! No. Why do you think we're moving these harnesses?"

He got suddenly quiet, and she realized she'd hurt his feelings somehow. She touched him on the arm, the hair there dark and soft. "Look, I just wanted to explain that I needed your help in convincing him to get into the plane and to stay there once he's inside. And even to help hold him there, if it comes down to that."

"Is it really gonna work?" he asked.

"Unless there's something wrong with it that I can't see—all the hoses are in good shape, electrical checks out, we scrounged up almost a full tank of fuel. I think we're good to go."

"When?"

"How does tomorrow sound?"

He shrugged.

"Do you think we should just stay here?" she asked, unsure if she wanted to hear his answer.

"No," he said slowly. "Ula needs a doctor; we need more food."

She handed him the crescent wrench. He tightened the bolt a final turn.

"Where did you live before Josie's house?"

"Wherever. My real dad, he was a pilot, he got killed when I was a baby. In . . . Sareeya?"

"Syria?"

"Uh-huh. Syria. I got a new Dad when I was four and we moved to Danville cause he worked on the Wall there. He did computer stuff."

"How old are you now?"

"Ten and three-quarters."

"What happened to your mom and your new dad?"

He turned to sit in the seat, eyes on his bare feet.

"You don't have to tell me if you don't want to."

He looked over at her. He scuffed his feet against the floor of the compartment. "My Mom said she was going to have a baby. Next thing we knew it was twins. In my dad's family—my new dad—there's lots of twins. Then the Lucy virus happened. Well, you saw Ula and Isaac. They were so small when they were born. They looked like little monkeys, not like real babies at all." He scratched his nose. "People from the hospital wanted to take them away, said they needed to be in . . . "

"Quarantine?"

"Yeah. My dad snuck my mom and the twins out of the hospital. We went to a cabin at this lake where we went fishing sometimes. He hid us there. That's when he went to get Ripper, and didn't come back."

"I'm so sorry, Carl."

"Yeah, me, too."

"What happened to your mom?"

"She got appendix-citis. We lived in the cabin a whole winter after Dad never come back. She said she had to go to the hospital. She put me in charge of the twins. She had another attack while we were walking to town. It just never stopped. It spread all over her stomach. I ran all the way into town to get help, but nobody would help. Finally someone called 911. But I wasn't fast enough and she was dead when we got back there in the ambulance."

"That's awful, Carl." Sage's heart was melting for him.

He sighed and shrugged. "We got sent to a camp full of kids. It *was* awful. I wanted to run away but I couldn't without Ula and Isaac. I was in charge. The food got real bad. Mr. Thornton, he always had a sleep between two and three in the morning—he'd put his feet up on the table and snore. I went and got Ula and Isaac. They were so asleep I had to carry them both. They woke up when the rain hit them, though, but they stayed quiet, just like I told them to. I carried them over the fence one at a time, and we ran into the woods. We walked for a long, long time. I don't know if they ever did come after us. We ate stuff from people's gardens, and just kept walking. Figured we'd go back to Danville. I wanted to find my dad. And besides, I knew all the places around there. I figured we'd be okay."

"You did good."

"It makes you awfully tired being in charge all the time, especially when the twins can't talk. Sometimes I'm not sure they even know what I'm saying to them. It was better when I found Josie. She helped me a lot."

"And you've helped her, I'm sure," Sage said. "Hey, I think I saw a couple packs of hot chocolate. You think Isaac would want some?"

"I bet he would," Carl said with a nod.

CHAPTER 20

Mr. Kratky stopped them in the yard beside the Quonset hut where Roy had said they kept the female lucy slaves. Two Rottweilers barked at them from a pen near a shed. One of the armed men taped Ronnie's hands behind her back, then threw her face-down on the ground and knelt on her back and legs, grinding her face into the dirt and chicken shit that littered the yard. She grunted with the pain, terrified, expecting the worst, eyes clamped shut, teeth gritted. She felt hands pulling something metallic around her throat, which was then clamped tight at the back of her neck, almost choking her. They flipped her over onto her back, and pinned her shoulders and legs, her taped hands jammed under her buttocks, while they undid her flak vest, her belt, and pulled off her boots and socks. Then they hauled her to her feet and let her go.

Kratky was still smiling. He stepped toward her, so close his hot breath bathed her face with an acrid garlic stench. He reached for the front her shirt. She jerked away from him; an electric shock jolted through her neck, rocketing down her body into the ground through the soles of her bare feet. She staggered, eyes blurring.

He simply waited.

Her head finally cleared.

He reached for her shirt.

She pulled away again and the pain drove her to her knees. Her head swam and her nose dripped snot. The blur abated. She pushed herself to her feet.

He reached for her uniform shirt a third time.

She held still and let him undo the buttons. He peeled the shirt and vest back over her shoulders and all the way down to the tape around her wrists. Then he slipped a knife from his belt.

Ronnie felt sick to her stomach. Her knees began to shake.

With lazy flicking movements, he tapped the tip of the blade against the center of her chest. Her heart monitor suddenly popped on, beeping her heart's frantic rhythm in her ear. He ran the flat side of the blade against her skin, up under the center of her bra. With a flick of the wrist, he cut her bra open. His men all laughed. The heart monitor died, and the sudden absence of its tone in her ear made her think her heart, too, had died, or suddenly cooled its molten self into steel.

"Tits," he whispered, loud enough for all of them to hear, "go *au natural* here." He flicked one of her nipples with a finger, and she started.

They laughed again.

One by one each of them were collared. They beat Kevin with their fists in between shocks. They stripped Janice to the waist and shocked her half a dozen times. Then they lined the three of them against the front of the Quonset hut while they beat and shocked each of the Gardener boys into unconsciousness. Ronnie made herself watch, absorbing each blow and shock, feeding the molten anger bubbling and popping underneath her fear. Finally, Kratky's neanderthals separated the women from the men, cut the tape from their hands and shoved Ronnie and Janice inside the Quonset hut.

The stench and heat hit Ronnie like another fist. Shapes moved in the dim interior. An opening high up in the far wall, covered with a metal grate provided the only light. Through the opening Ronnie could see clouds of smoke, eerily under lit in bloody reds and angry oranges by the Silverton fire just beyond the ridge. The Quonset hut looked to be about twenty meters long by ten meters wide, with a dirt floor, sleeping mats, buckets for toilets, and several long tables with benches. An open gang shower in the far corner seemed to be their only amenity.

Ronnie hugged her arms across her breasts and rubbed her wrists. Her eyes slowly adjusted as the shapes moved toward them. She counted fifteen or so young women and girls, from late mid-stage to full end-stage of devolution. Several made grunting noises. The younger ones held back, hiding behind the legs and backsides of the older ones. A few were dressed in ragged shorts, or had pulled simple wraps of torn cloth around their hips, but most of them were completely naked. Except for the metal shock collars.

Ronnie felt sick to her stomach. Janice, standing beside her, was trembling. "Promise me," she whispered, "that we'll kill every single one of those motherfuckers out there."

"Promise," Ronnie whispered back. "Hey," she said to the group as a whole, holding her hands in front of her, palms forward. "I'm Ronnie, and this is Janice."

A small woman in her mid-twenties slipped out of the group. Her hair was matted into lumpy dreads, her left eye swollen shut and purplish, and the left side of her jaw bruised and scraped. Hair covered her upper body, except for her small breasts, but it didn't cover the scars on her arms and shoulders. She wore khaki shorts and nothing else.

She jutted her jaw at Ronnie, worked her mouth as if her jaw muscles were stiff. Words, sounding like sandpaper on wood, tumbled out. "I'm Sachi. You're hurt."

Tears ran down Ronnie's cheeks. She shook her head.

Sachi cleared her throat. "You're bleeding." She reached up to touch the side of Ronnie's face with her long fingers.

Ronnie winced. Sachi's fingers came away wet with fresh blood.

Sachi nodded toward the shower at the back of the Quonset hut. "Have to be careful. About infection."

"How many of you are there?" Ronnie said as she followed Sachi past the long tables.

"Seven . . . teen, now. And twelve males. In the little barn."

Janice scurried to catch up to Ronnie.

"How long have you been here?" Ronnie asked.

Sachi shrugged. "Over one winter. Others longer. You can ask them. Not many speak anymore, but most understand. Some can sign."

"Sign?"

"American Sign Language. Some learned in school."

Sachi sat Ronnie on the end of a bench, then sent a young one scampering to retrieve a bucket of water. Ronnie continued to ask and answer questions as Sachi cleaned her wound. According to Sachi, the farm had been running for almost two years. Many of the younger ones had been captured in whole packs, groups of runaways and orphans squatting together in cabins up in the bush, and really, according to Sachi, unable to fend for themselves. They were baited with food, sometimes trapped with nets like animals, then thrown into a truck and driven here, where they were stripped and collared, fed and made to work in the gardens, or to tend the livestock, or clean and cook in the houses.

The collars would automatically shock anyone who ventured too close to the perimeter fence, or to areas of the farm that were out-of-bounds. Also, once locked inside the Quonset hut at night, you got shocked if you tried to go beyond the sleeping area. During the day, if someone misbehaved and an owner shocked them by remote, everyone got shocked at the same time.

"So, you will not disobey," Sachi said. The warning in her voice was clear. "Understood?"

Janice sputtered, but Ronnie held up her hand. She needed Sachi's trust. "We won't disobey."

"But we can't stay here!" Janice hissed through gritted teeth.

Ronnie gave her a hard look.

"You will not disobey," Sachi repeated. "Or *we* will punish you."

It was a tried-and-true boot camp method of control. One soldier disobeys, all soldiers get punished. They end up policing themselves. Extremely effective. And since Sachi appeared to be the Alpha female here, Ronnie would do as Sachi said. She wasn't interested in being throttled in her sleep by these women simply because they were afraid she'd bring hellfire and brimstone down upon them. But neither was she interested in being kept here to live like a slave until . . . well, until tomorrow when the Silverton fire—the literal fire and brimstone—swept down into this valley and swallowed this farm whole.

When Ronnie was sure Janice had given up protesting, she prodded Sachi with more questions.

It seemed that four families owned the farm, or maybe three and a set of grandparents, Sachi wasn't sure. But what was clear was the men ruled the workers with terrible force. The women in the families either didn't know about, or turned a blind eye to, the abuses: beatings for not working, or for disobeying orders, or for trying to run away. In addition, rape occurred regularly, at least one of the six male owners pulling a female aside, or into a shed, or taking her away at night. Worse yet, when one of the females came into heat—"Their words, not mine," Sachi added—they'd force a breeding with one of the male workers, collar-shocking either or both of them until they copulated. From what Sachi could see, the owners wanted as many of the women pregnant as possible. It seemed they were intent on breeding a large stable of devolved slaves.

"Don't any of these neanderthals have kids?" Janice asked, incensed. "Where are *their* children? Aren't they devolving, too?"

Sachi pushed up one eyebrow. "If they have children, we have never seen them."

A bell rang outside the Quonset hut, an old-fashioned iron farm bell. The crowd of faces surrounding them scurried away. Water flowed into basins as several children began to wash themselves. Others took turns urinating in metal buckets. The rest were scrambling onto their sleeping mats, crawling underneath their blankets. Hiding, it seemed.

"Do what you need to do"—she waved a hand at the water—"but by second bell be in your bed. They check. And hope they don't take you."

Dismayed, Ronnie looked around at the children hiding under their blankets. Yet she knew if she tried to stop the owners from taking one of the girls, he'd shock them all, and Sachi would know she'd lied about not disobeying. "Those bastards," she muttered.

Janice grabbed at her arm. "We can't stay here," she whispered into Ronnie's ear, her voice thin with fear.

"I know," Ronnie whispered back.

"We have to get out of here!"

"*I know*!" Irritation enflamed Ronnie's voice.

The second bell sounded.

"Shit!"

"Quick, find a bed."

"This is fucking insane," Janice muttered. "I can't believe this is happening."

They found several old blue insulates, dirty and stained, curled up near one of the walls. Sachi tossed them each a wool blanket, which stank.

Ronnie threw her mat on the dirt, crawled onto it, and pulled the blanket up around her shoulders. The stench nauseated her. She turned on her side to watch the front door.

"What are we going to do?" Janice hissed at her from her mat.

Someone several mats away growled at them.

Boots crunched on gravel outside the Quonset hut. The door unlatched with clang and swung open. Outside it was twilight. Cool air flushed across the floor. A head popped in, covered with a baseball cap, and a flashlight stabbed the growing dark. The door clanged shut again. Male voices arguing outside, moving away.

An audible sigh rose from the dirt floor of the Quonset hut. The interior was still hot from the day, and the stink of urine and feces from the buckets mingled with the stench of sweat and fear. Ronnie sat up and looked around. Many of the younger ones had pulled their mats alongside each other and lay huddled together.

"We need to leave," Ronnie whispered to Sachi.

"You will not disobey."

She pointed at the grated window at the end of the Quonset hut. "See that light out there?" Sachi made no move to look. Ronnie pressed her: "That's a forest fire. It's burning out of control and it's coming this way. It could be here by morning, or it could be here in a few days, depending on the wind—either way, it's going to burn this place to the ground. And all of us in here unless we leave."

"We made a break. For the fire. Mister says we are safe."

Janice guffawed. "Safe?"

Ronnie squeezed the back of her neck to relieve the throbbing tension knotted there, her massaging fingers hampered by the metal collar. "First, we have to get rid of these goddamn things." She fiddled and pulled and twisted, and only ended up cutting one of her fingers. As she sucked the laceration, she briefly considered throwing herself on the perimeter line and shocking herself until the batteries in the collar died. Well, she assumed there were batteries in the box at her throat, but maybe she was wrong and the collars were powered by some external source. No, she doubted that, they had probably simply adapted shock-collars originally used for dogs, like Roy said, those anti-bark collars or—

Perimeter fencing. The transmitters were buried, she realized, and had to be plugged into an electrical source in order to work. She threw off her blanket.

"Don't disobey," Sachi hissed.

"Need to pee," Ronnie said, and made her way over to a bucket, where she dropped her uniform pants and squatted. Her stomach growled at her. If she had a shovel, she could dig until she found the buried line, then simply sever it. But they still wouldn't be able to leave, since the only door was padlocked, which worried Ronnie in a sickening way: this metal hut would turn into an oversized oven when the firestorm blew through here, roasting them alive like Holocaust victims. She shuddered at the thought.

The sweet stink of pot smoke wheedled into the hut through the open window, followed by the gravelly sounds of male voices, boots scuffing dirt. Ronnie pulled up her pants and darted to her mat.She propped herself up on an elbow, straining to hear what they were saying, but she could only hear the rumble and cadence of anger and hushed argument.

Suddenly, with a change in wind direction, words blew in through the window, clear and harsh, the hushed tones amplified by the hard inner surface of the Quonset hut.

"Don't do this, Davy." A young male voice.

"He promised us." The voice of the younger Kratky. "I'm sick of fuckin' monkey girls, man."

"Doesn't matter. You know what he's like if you piss him off. He'd beat the living crap outta you."

"He won't know. It's not like *she's* gonna tell." Coarse laughter.

"She's not going to be easy."

Grunt. "That's just it. He should have put her in her place right from the start. Those bitches are only trouble if you don't do them right off. She's gonna give us trouble. I know it. She needs to be *orientated*."

Nervous laughter from the younger male.

"I can handle this. You just go back to bed."

"No. I'll watch your back. Watch out for the old man."

Their voices moved away from the window.

Ronnie trembled. Cold sweat made her shiver. Were they talking about her, or someone else? She pulled the stinking blanket up over her head and watched the door through a gap she made for air.

The quiet clatter of the padlock being opened. Her heart hammered like an automatic weapon.

The door hinges creaked and someone slipped inside. Ronnie stared into the growing dark. She heard keys rattle, like the clatter of tiny bones, then the unmistakable pumping action of a shotgun. Her blood froze. One of the children whimpered. From under her blanket she watched Davy Kratky walk into the sleeping area, placing his boots carefully and quietly. He used the shotgun to ease the blanket off one of the young women, then moved on, stopping at the foot of Janice's matt. Ronnie heard her gasp.

He reached with the barrel of the gun and dragged the blanket off Janice's face. Gave an annoyed grunt. Then he turned toward Ronnie.

"Are you looking for me, asshole?" she said, easing herself into a sitting position.

"Shut up, bitch," he hissed as he waved the shotgun at her. "Get up."

Ronnie stood. He was only about ten centimeters taller, but was thick like his old man, yet still probably didn't weigh more than ninety kilos, ninety-five at the most. He prodded her with the shotgun. "Keep quiet, and don't do anything stupid," he whispered, "or I'll shock the whole lot of them until they piss themselves." He waved the remote at her for effect.

Remote, shotgun, keys. She glanced at his belt, noting that there was knife or a utility tool in a leather pouch on his right side. He was right-handed then. Pot smoke reeked from his clothes, so he probably carried a lighter or matches in one of his pockets. Hell, his feet didn't look very big for such a tall guy, so those boots might even fit her, given her huge coyote feet, as Matt called them. The echo of his name in her mind stung her. She swatted it away. Needed to focus.

"Move!" He shoved her forward with the barrel of the shotgun.

Out the door—Ronnie noted to herself that he must have turned off the perimeter transmitters to get her out of the sleeping area without shocking her—and across the yard, avoiding the gravel path. The cool night air smelled fresh after the cloying stench of the women's quarters. She glanced around for the younger male, but didn't see him anywhere. Maybe he'd gone back into one of the houses. She could only hope. Or maybe he was waiting for her wherever this neanderthal was taking her. She shuddered.

Ronnie studied their route—past the two penned up Rottweilers who had barked at them earlier—to a small wooden shed. He pushed her down a set of concrete stairs she almost didn't see in the dark, which led underneath the shed. She stumbled into a rough plank door at the bottom of the steps, with a tiny rectangular window embedded in it.

"Open it."

She released the latch and pushed the door open. Dank, cool air rushed at her, the smell of dirt and mold. A light bulb flashed on, blinding her. She heard the door close. They were in a long, narrow root cellar, with concrete walls and a dirt floor and a single bare bulb. No second male, unless he'd come in behind them. Big wooden bins lined one wall and deep shelves with rows and rows of home-canned goods in half-liter and liter jars lined two other walls. The dirt under Ronnie's bare feet felt as cold as steel.

She crossed her arms over her breasts and turned to face the man with the gun.

"Don't," he said with a snarl, and jabbed her in the shoulder blade to keep her facing away from him. She stared at the jars of canned goods along the wall, scanned the dirt looking for a weapon, anything she might be able use against him.

"Drop your pants. Nice and slow. And the panties."

She did as she was told. She could hear only the breathing of one person, harsh and short, like he'd run up a hill or, better, was nervous and twitchy.

"Not all the way off. That's far enough. Now get down on your hands and knees."

The pants at her calves encumbered her, trapping her legs. The barrel of the shotgun nuzzled against the back of her head, its underside resting on her spine. He knelt on her pants, pinning her legs to the dirt floor. She was shivering with cold, and her terror only made her tremble harder.

He unfastened his belt, his zipper.

She gritted her teeth. "How come you picked such a romantic spot?" She wriggled her fingers in the dirt, searching for something, anything she could use, a rusty nail, a piece of glass, a sharp stone.

"Shut up!"

"What's the matter? Tired of fucking sheep, dirtbag?"

The shotgun barrel slammed into the side of her head, splitting her right ear and knocking her over onto her side. She thought she might throw up, but she struggled back up onto her hands and knees.

He kicked her hard in the ribs. Kicked her again.

"Do as you're fucking told, and shut up."

She struggled for air, retching. She climbed back onto her hands and knees. He was afraid—she could smell it on him—afraid of losing control of her, afraid of getting caught, afraid of not finishing what he'd started.

And, afraid of her. He just didn't know it yet.

"Baaaa!" she said and wriggled her ass. "Baaaa! C'mon, sheepfucker, what are you—"

He hit her with the stock of the gun in the back of the head. Then, as she rolled onto her back, he hit her in the face, breaking her nose. She cried out in pain, fiery static exploding through her head. Then he leaned over and punched her, again and again, in the eye, the mouth, the side of her face. She tasted blood and knew right then that she would win. Something had twisted and broken off inside her, fallen away. In the span of nanosecond all the anger that had been pacing around inside her like a demon sealed in a cave with a rock, all that rage, all that ugliness she'd tried to bury deeper than anything else in her life, it erupted, vaporizing her fear in a torrent of roaring hellfire.

She spun, twisted, and fell on him like an atomic bomb.

He'd been dead for several minutes before she stopped hitting him. Every time a jar broke against his face, she had simply grabbed another one. Ronnie crab-crawled to the other side of the cellar and threw up. She had trouble breathing through her broken nose. Blood filled her right eye, which had almost swollen shut already. Her head pounded, her hands were cut. Shattered glass littered the floor, along with the contents of canned tomatoes and peaches and pears. She was sticky from jams and canning syrup and blood.

She pulled off his boots and his belt, retrieved her own pants. His boots, sloppy and worn, were a couple of sizes too big, but far superior to bare feet. She searched him, retrieving his utility tool, a pack of matches, some dope and papers, his ring of keys, and the remote. She opened the utility tool and cut off her shock collar.

Then she switched to the knife blade and sliced him open, first from his sternum to his pubic bone, and then from left to right, like a baked potato. She carved out his liver to feed to the dogs. Dug her hands inside him and splattered his intestines all over the bins of potatoes and carrots. Pried out his eyes, set them on a shelf. Sliced off his penis, placed it between the eyes so it looked like they were its lost balls. Just in case the younger male came looking for his missing buddy, just so he'd know what he was up against.

She wiped as much gore and syrup off her arms and chest with the little cobweb-infested curtains someone had hung over the tiny window in the door. She gathered up the shotgun and his liver and crept out of the root cellar into the night.

CHAPTER 21

Sage stretched out as best she could across the backseat of the Skylane in the absolute dark of the hanger with Ula in her arms, trying to get comfortable, her swollen belly making things awkward in the cramped space. She'd given up her thermarest to Carl and Josie and they snuggled together on it in her sleeping bag as best they could. Isaac continued to hole up in his nest in the old Skyhawk. Ula felt feverish to the touch and squirmed a lot in Sage's arms. Sage stroked her hair, watched frown lines form between thick brows. Her cheek was red and swollen around the cut, her thin lips drawn. Sage felt for the pulse in Ula's wrist to make sure the splint still wasn't too tight, then lifted the damp cloth off Ula's forehead, turned it over to the cool side and replaced it.

She wondered what life was like for Ula. Perhaps not that much different from any other four-year-old, playing, exploring the world, working out relationships. Seeing how the world works and how she fits into the world. Pretty much the same as any other kid. Except for that non-acquisition of language problem. Spoken language, anyway. Maybe sign language would bridge that development. *Hmmm.* Sage shifted again, trying to take some pressure off her lower back.

Chimps learn sign language readily, and even engage in very human behaviors—mixing themselves a drink, watching TV, dressing themselves—when they are raised as if they were human children. In the wild, chimps are ready toolmakers and tool-users. Young chimps learn these behaviors by modeling, watching the adults and copying. The adults do not teach the youngsters. Perhaps that is the quantum gap between non-human primates and human primates: human adults teach their children, they pass on their knowledge and experience and skills. Somewhere along the evolutionary path, a proto-human mother knowingly demonstrated, taught, showed her child *how* to do something.

That's the key to Ula and Isaac's future, Sage realized. In fact, that's the key to the future they would all inhabit. As long as there are adults around with enough smarts to pass on their knowledge, maybe the devolving human race would still have half a chance.

Ula whimpered. Sage turned the damp cloth over to the cool side once again. She sighed, fatigue spreading a slow ache through her body.

The Skylane's batteries had only charged to half in the weak sunlight. They'd roll the plane outside at first light, get the embedded wing-panels exposed to the sunlight as early as possible. She'd been very tempted to try to fire up the engine on half-charge in order to keep from having to wait through the long night just to see if the damn thing would work. But if she drained the battery by starting it and there was a short somewhere, the first firing might be her only chance and she didn't want to waste it with darkness at hand. Besides, it wouldn't take that long to fly to New Denver once she got the plane into the air—an hour, maybe a bit longer.

It was almost over, yet she hardly dared to hope.

Sage wiped the sweat out of her eyes as she ran the path she'd pounded in the snow along the inside of the camp's perimeter fence, her breath easy in the December chill.

Once she had banished God to the "No Longer Used" shelf in her mind, she came to realize that life without Him engendered a kind of simplicity of thought and action. Without God, the consequences for her choices were immediate and obvious. If she stood up against one of the camp's power mongers, she got beaten; if she minded her P's and Q's, letting meanness run riot around her, people mostly left her alone. On her stronger days, she took the beatings; on her less strong days, she kept her mouth shut. Either way, it seemed all the fear she'd held in her heart her whole life had vanished with Maddie's last breath. God's presence had muddied her life, pressuring her toward indecision and fear, leading her to let others decide what was right or best for her. She already felt like an outsider in the Baptist Church where Quinn had taken her because she refused to denounce the theory of evolution (she was a librarian, a keeper of the tree of knowledge, so to speak, and would not deny access to any branch of that tree); and because she spoke out against spanking as a necessary and biblically-endorsed tool for the raising of children; and finally, because of their intolerance towards followers of other faiths. The onslaught of shoulds and should-nots was morally over-stimulating, like the barrage of city lights and the roar of traffic after a weekend away camping. She had lived a modestly well-to-do life that the church told her was given to her by God, while at the same time instructing her that she didn't deserve such blessing and needed to seek forgiveness for sins she did not feel she had committed, and then commit herself to acts of charity and generosity, little of which—as far as she could see—had anything to do with relieving the burden of the poor and the suffering in the world.

It was when she'd taken her children out of the church that she and Quinn had had their worst fight. He hadn't wanted to upset his parents; moreover, he argued, if they didn't learn right from wrong, where will they end up? That's *our* job, she'd thrown back at him, not the church's—*we* teach them right and wrong. *That's what parents do, teach their kids how to live in the world.*

She hit the halfway mark of her run. Snow had begun to fall again. Her feet were wet, her fingers numb. Nothing was going to stop her from running, though, nothing.

If there was no God-given order, then one had to create order for oneself. That is what Sage did, created an order of life and meaning for herself: she ate as well as she could; she exercised daily; she read whatever books she could get her hands on; she spoke out for what seemed fair and against what seemed mean-spirited and unkind and ignorant. She worked hard without much complaint.

She ran the perimeter fence and she waited.

The world outside the FEMA camp devolved into a kind of half-hearted chaos. There weren't really enough able-bodied people left alive to foment much unrest and disaster, and they were generally too busy trying to make the best of what little they had left in goods and time to cause much trouble. The devolving ones who had not been isolated in the camps roamed the countryside in packs, hunting for food, taking what they needed by force, and moving on.

Modernity collapsed in on itself without the human infrastructure to maintain it. Electricity sputtered like a candle flame and died out; manufacturing, like a combustion engine drained of its oil, simply seized up; hospitals sat like monstrous abandoned cars, stripped and crumbling under the merciless weather. Only the military seemed to maintain some cohesion, but even then there were limits to its reach and power, limits set by the soldiers themselves. Local warlords rose and fell, more often than not struck down by complications of the Lucy Syndrome than by their enemies. At least according to the thin Spokane newspaper, laser-printed on the backside of used letter-sized paper, that got smuggled into camp every few weeks, a welcome look at life, even if grim, beyond the fence now that there was seldom television reception or enough electricity to power the TV. The solars were saved for necessities.

It was mid January, a year and a half after Maddie's death. The National Guardsmen, who had resolutely kept peace in the camp since the Riot that hellish summer, had just as resolutely dismissed all requests for any kind of party, fearing that revelry might unleash the anger and violence that had fuelled the Riot. Many of the Guardsmen had moved their families into the camp, abandoning their homes to the packs and warlords, and turning the camp into a fortress, a safe haven against the smoldering outside world, and had no desire to allow any kind of activity that might threaten the surety of their overlord position, and as such, the safety of their own families.

One Saturday, however, when the winter temperatures had dropped suddenly, moonshine appeared out of thin air and got passed hand-to-hand, while wine-bottles of yeasty beer sprouted up like something straight out of a loaves-and-fishes bible story. Sage got herself rather drunk, picked one of the Guardsmen whom she had come to believe was an honorable man, a man whose company she had enjoyed over the past few months despite his overseer role, and seduced him in the same school portable where her daughter had died. It was the kind of feverish love-making that engenders release and a tenderness born of the knowledge that it will never be repeated. After his shift, he went back to his private barrack, to his devolving wife, whom he loved with a kind of fierce protectiveness that Sage admired.

Sage became pregnant, and began to feel that the part of her that had been blasted away when Maddie died was filling itself in with granulated scar tissue, tough and ragged, but healing none-the-less.

"When are we going to start the plane?" Carl asked over a breakfast of tasteless instant oatmeal.

"Soon," Sage said.

"Today?"

"If the battery charges to full."

"Is it going to work?"

"I hope so, Carl, honey."

"I never been in a plane before," he said. He looked at Josie. "Is it gonna be scary?"

Sage shook her head. "No. It's going to be lots of fun. Everything on the ground, all the houses and the cars and the trees, all look like little, tiny toys."

Carl grinned.

They spent the morning loading what they could into the Skylane, Sage doing a lot of guesswork about weight and fuel consumption. Ula was awake and whiny, crying if Sage put her down, but far too heavy to carry all the time. Isaac had come over for breakfast, and then wandered about just inside the hanger opening, refusing to be drawn into their activity, shaking his head and slapping the wall of the hanger whenever Carl tried coaxing him.

"What's the matter with you?" Carl hollered at Isaac as he rolled up the thermarest the way Sage had shown him. "You're coming whether you like it or not."

"Let him be, Carl," Sage said. "He'll come when he's ready."

"What if he's not ready when we are?"

"Then, you're right, he's coming whether he likes it or not. Sometimes we all have to have other people make choices for us when we can't. Like when we're sick, or too young to make a good choice (like Isaac), or when we can't think straight. We have to trust that those people are making the best choices for us."

"It's the best choice if Isaac comes with us," Carl pronounced, nodding his head with authority.

"I agree," Sage said, handing him an unopened package of batteries she'd found in the workbench cupboards.

Only two-thirds full. Sage studied the sky. There was no doubt that the smoke was thicker and heavier than yesterday, the sun a barely-smoldering ember.

As Sage heated water for another lunch of udon noodle soup, her stove sputtered and died, the last of the fuel gone. The water hadn't even boiled. She tried to hide her dismay by digging through the food supply in her pack. One can of (cold) ravioli, a thin can of lemon and pepper kippers (which she couldn't imagine any of the kids liking), more soup noodles. Cold ravioli it was, then.

"Okay, Carl, I don't want to wait any longer." It was already mid-afternoon and the batteries had barely scratched past the three-quarters mark. The running motor would bump the batteries up to full while they flew.

Besides, she'd been having cramps down low in her belly all day, which she hoped was just cramping and not premature labor. The baby wasn't due for another month, and she really didn't want to have him or her in an empty airplane hanger in Grand Forks if she could avoid it. "We need to catch Isaac," she said to Carl, "and get him strapped down in the plane before I start up the motor. I don't want to waste fuel idling while we chase him all over the place."

Carl nodded. "He bites, you know."

"I heard."

"He's gonna be mad for tricking him."

"You're right, he is. But he can't stay here, can he? These are the choices you sometimes have to make. Doing what's right, or best, even if someone doesn't like you, or gets mad at you."

Carl cocked his head to one side, looked at her. "I know. You told me already."

"I'm going to close the hanger door now. Josie, you're okay there with Ula?" Sage cranked the door down until it latched shut. She stood beside Carl in the shadow-light of the dim hanger. He had the blanket tucked under one arm.

"All right," she said. "Let's get this over with."

It ended up being much easier than she had anticipated. Isaac simply trapped himself in the back seat of the Skyhawk. He fought and screamed and cried and tried to bite, but once Carl had him pinned under the blanket he simply gave up. Sage carried him out to the Skylane and Carl helped her strap him into his harness. She taped all the buckles, though, just to make sure the little yahoo didn't get himself loose while they were in the air.

They crawled around into the front seats and Sage fiddled with the ignition wires, then hit the starter. The motor gave two valiant whines, sputtered, stopped. Sage tried again. This time the engine fired up, full and throaty. She let out a whoop and Carl bounced in the seat beside her. Josie ran from her post at the corner of the hanger, with Ula in her arms.

Sage climbed down out of the cockpit, elation crackling through her body like electricity. Suddenly she could taste the end of her journey: the home where she spent her teenage years, her parents, her goal for these last terrifying weeks was only a short flight away. "All aboard!" she called out, trying to ignore the cramping in her belly and thighs.

CHAPTER 22

Ronnie fed Davy's liver to the dogs. They seemed very appreciative. While they ate and snarled at one other, Ronnie moved around the compound. She determined which building the men slept in, snooped through several outbuildings, finding, much to her satisfaction, two jerry cans of gasoline, several pairs of tin snips, and an old plaid jacket hanging on a nail. Her favorite building, though, was the one that housed the generator.

Ronnie ran back to the Quonset hut, let herself inside, and gave Janice two pair of tin snips. "I want every single collar off. Then take them out and around to the back of the hut. I'll meet you there."

At the men's barn she unlocked the door and let herself in. A long, log building with a low ceiling and a dirt floor. Probably an early animal shed, she thought. Eyes stared at her from under blankets. Kevin snored in the corner nearest the door. She shook him awake.

He grunted and started.

She shushed him. Several of the boys made whimpering noises. Ronnie put a set of tin snips into Kevin's hand. "Get the collars off as fast as you can, even if you have to sit on them to do it. Nobody gets left behind. Not even the Gardener boys. Then meet me behind the Quonset hut."

He scrambled off his mat. "Oh my God, what did they do to you?" he said.

She touched her swollen eye. What could she say to him, or to anyone else, for that matter? That Davy'd tried to rape her, so she beat him into oblivion, and then—yet she felt no remorse, no guilt or shame. She knew only that no one would understand. She wasn't sure she understood—she'd let the demon out of its cave and suddenly, finally, she felt whole for the first time in her life. That's what scared her.

She turned from Kevin and let herself back out into the night. She ran to the generator shed, closed herself in, and flicked on the overhead light. The roar of the diesel motor deafened her as she searched for the kill switch. *There*. The silence, sudden and complete, was downright lovely, but it would be the silence that would wake Kratky, she was sure. However, she couldn't risk any electronic surprises, like alarms or motion-detector lights, when they ran for it, so the electricity had to go.

Convincing the younger ones that it was all right to leave their barracks had taken longer than Ronnie expected. The dogs had started barking, having finished their snack. Finally, everyone was accounted for, blankets wrapped around their shoulders against the cool night air, younger ones huddled together. Ronnie led them past the house compound to the front gate, then out onto the gravel driveway which meandered across the thirty-meter-wide firebreak, then disappeared into the forest, descending steeply through two long switchbacks until it met Stellars Jay Road. Ronnie urged them on ahead, with instructions to keep going until they hit the highway, then head north to Silverton. She'd catch up.

Sachi nodded and swung one of the smallest girls up onto her back. Kevin held the hands of two of the devolved boys.

"What are you going to do?" Janice grabbed Ronnie's arm, her hand sticking to the smear of blood drying there, blood that hadn't come off with the tiny curtains.

"I can't let them come after us. They're too heavily armed. They'd slaughter us."

"They're not even going to know we're gone until first light—even if they bother coming after us."

"Oh, they'll come after us, all right."

Janice gave her a look that said maybe she didn't want to know. "I'll go with you."

"No, I'm the only one with boots—you'll just slow me down. What I really need is for you to get everybody as far away from here as you can. And as fast as you can."

"What are you planning to do, Ronnie?" There was worry in Janice's voice, and a new wariness, as if Janice didn't trust that Ronnie was making the best decision here. Not that it mattered. No one was going to stop her.

"What I promised, that's what I'm going to do." She pushed the shotgun she'd taken from the younger Kratky into Janice's hands, then gave Kevin a little shove. "Just go," she said, more to Janice, though, than to him. "Go!"

He turned and waved at the others to follow him, mincing a little on the gravel in his bare feet. Janice gave her a hard look, then followed Kevin, scooping up the slowest of the children with one arm and swinging her up onto her back.

Ronnie made sure they were well on their way down Stellars Jay Road before she sprinted back up the long driveway to the edge of the firebreak, where she paused. In the distance beyond the farm, the fire crested the ridge. New spot fires flared up further down into the valley. It wouldn't be long now. The wind, blowing from the direction of the fire across the farm toward her, carried the sounds of the dogs' barking and the thick stench of fresh smoke. The houses, both still dark, showed no signs of movement within.

She absently wiped blood from the end of her nose, sending pain shooting up into her forehead. For a second she thought she might pass out. When the pain finally passed, she bolted up the last few meters of gravel driveway and slipped through the gate, then made her way to the fence near the closest house where she retrieved the jerry cans she'd hidden. Up and over the fence, down into the yard, crouching among the daylilies, listening. No point getting her head blown off now through a simple lack of caution. She could barely see out of her injured eye, so she kept cocking her head like a dog to listen. The sound of floorboards creaking in the upstairs of the closest house leaked through an open window. As quietly as she could, she doused the front porch with several big splashes of gasoline, making sure she got enough on the door and the wicker furniture against the cedar-sided wall. She stood back and tossed a match. Flames whooshed into existence as if summoned directly from hell. The sudden heat and light drove her backwards.

She scurried to the back of the house, splashed gas on the back steps and set those on fire. By the time she'd made it to the second house, she heard shouts from the upstairs of the first house. She set both entrances to the second house on fire then emptied the last dribbles from the second jerry can on the truck parked next to the second house, and lit that on fire as well.

Then she ran for her life across the firebreak, the oversized boots of the young man she'd beaten to death and butchered slowing her down only a little.

They made good time despite contending with bare feet on a gravel road. The children ran like straight-legged chimps, eyes wide with fear, whimpering or shrieking, demanding with slapping hands to be carried on the backs of the adults or adolescents. The boy Ronnie carried buried his face into her hair as she ran, holding tightly onto the plaid jacket she'd taken from the tool shed.

Stopping to rest, they deked off the road and out of sight into the yard of an abandoned house and threw themselves down on the dried up lawn. First light softened the night with a quiet gray, mostly reflected off the smoke hanging thick among the trees. Ronnie let herself into the empty house, hoping it still had running gravity-fed water so they could all drink something. But the taps offered only cold air. The small wood-frame house reeked of mouse shit and a pack rat. As she headed back outside, a cracked wall-mirror in the entryway stopped her in her tracks. The unfastened plaid jacket hung open, and smeared blood crusted her naked torso and arms; her hands, cut and swollen, hung heavily at her sides; her face was beyond recognition, her broken, twisted nose, her left eye swollen shut, the whole left side of her face swollen and bruised, and her ear was torn across the top and puffed out like a mushroom. The cut high on her cheekbone from the gunstock yesterday pouted two thin lips and oozed an ugly slimy substance.

Ronnie let herself back out, wishing she hadn't looked in the mirror. Somehow seeing how beat up she looked made the pain worse.

The group huddled together like a pack of animals on the dead grass. Kevin was inspecting the bottoms of his feet. Sachi cuddled the little girl she'd been carrying, who couldn't have been much over six years old.

"We need to get going," Ronnie said.

Kevin groaned, but climbed to his feet. "How much further?"

She shrugged. "Another couple of klicks to the highway, two or three into Silverton."

They slowed to a funereal pace. The gravel road had taken its toll on everybody's feet, even the workers from the farm who spent their whole time there barefoot, but walking in the ditch was worse—broken glass, cans, rocks—and walking through the woods at the edge of the road, with dried brush, conifer cones, fallen trees, made that route just as difficult and dangerous.

Ronnie wasn't sure how much time they had before Kratky came after them. Once they got the generator going and could pump water, they could fight the house fires. That would take up a decent chunk of time, she hoped. Then they'd find Davy spread all over the root cellar because by then the younger male would have confessed about Davy's disobedience in order to explain his absence. Finding Davy, she was sure, would hurl Kratky out of the farm after them, after *her*, and he would come after her with every molecule of raw inhuman violence he could muster, and of course, with all the firepower he had available.

She hoped they'd lose most of their weapons in the house fires, but somehow she doubted that, and she knew if they caught up with them, what they'd do to her would be worse than anything she could even imagine. She'd tasted the flavor of her own brutality, inhaled some of its range and depth—not the playtime fantasies of a few days ago, but the blood-and-death reality engineered by her own hands, her own mind——and still she was startled and stunned by it, her soul shaken out of kilter. Although she had been trained to fight force with force if need be, she had believed herself a compassionate person, with a heart for justice and rightness. And now she had become—what?—a murderer, a butcher, a monster of some unconscionably twisted kind?

The highway, with its wrinkled pavement and weed-riven cracks, was a welcome sight. The smoke was thick now, the air filled with falling ash, and even though it was certainly morning, the light remained as gray and muted as perpetual twilight. Ronnie didn't want to stop, even though several of the children were crying, and Kevin and the middle Gardner boy, Willis, both looked as though they were about to drop dead. She badgered them on, jogging ahead through the smoke, her head throbbing and her breath coming in harsh gulps, the boy on her back as heavy as the world. They couldn't stop now, she told them, they were so close. Just beyond that rock outcropping they'd be able to see Silverton, she said.

Her big boots slapped the pavement. As she rounded the outcropping she hit a wall of smoke. Fire licked the highway on her right, hot and raging. The boy on her back shrieked and buried his face against her jacket. She staggered away from the flames to the far side of the highway, stumbled to a halt, both eyes stinging. She squinted through the smoke. Silverton—what little she could see of it—was a burned-out shell of a town, smoldering and black.

"No!" she said out loud.

Did that mean New Denver was gone, too? Matt and all the others evacuated? Had they left her behind? Or worse, had they been caught in the fire?

"No!" she shouted, at the sky, at the fire, at the decimated town below. "*Goddammit*!"

She heard gasps behind her. She swung the little boy around to carry him in front of her so she could shield him from the heat. She pushed on, past the burning trees, charging downhill toward Silverton.

Spot fires erupted on the left side of the highway, the side that fell away to the lake below. She spun about to see how close the others were following, but they'd turned back, the pavement too hot for their already tortured bare feet.

She ran back up the highway, coughing, lungs searing. "We have to go over the bank, down to the water," she yelled above the roar of the fire.

"It's too steep," Janice yelled back. "Besides, there's nothing left," she added, jerking her chin at Silverton.

"We have to go south, to Winlaw," Kevin said.

"That's over twenty kilometers. No food or water. And who knows how close Kratky is behind us. Besides, we'll never outrun the fire if it keeps coming this way."

Sachi pushed between them. "These kids can't go much further. I say we go down to the lake."

A gust of wind hurled flames across the highway, igniting the crown of a massive fir tree.

"Let's just go, then!" Kevin shouted as he clambered over the bank and disappeared.

CHAPTER 23

The clanging of the church bell wrenched Alex up out of a dream: Gemma's head snapping back, blood spattering up the kitchen wall. The darkness outside Irene's window glowed a feverish orange. He could taste smoke.

Irene flung the comforter back.

Alex fumbled into his clothes.

Sirens joined the church bells.

He hobbled down the stairs, legs and back still stiff and sore. Irene appeared, dressed in her crumpled uniform from the day before. She had a bulging pack on her back. Alex wrestled into his socks and boots, grabbed his daypack, and lumbered out the front door behind Irene. The whole sky was on fire west and south of town. Ash and embers rained on them as they ran.

The bay door was already open, and the ambulance was rolling out into the driveway. Nathan was belting himself into the driver's seat. Alex climbed into the back, while Irene swung up into the attendant's seat, stuffing her pack between the seats.

"Stopped by the church," Nathan said, breathless. His hands were trembling as they gripped the steering wheel. "The fire's jumped both breaks, and is going in all directions at once, making its own wind. We're evacuating. But a couple of guys on the north break got hurt. They're coming down the hill and we're supposed to meet them at the bridge over Silverton Creek."

Alex's mind spun. "The fire's heading south, too?"

"Yeah," Nathan said as he roared up the street toward the church where everyone was mustering.

"Slow down," Irene told him. "Let's get there in one piece, okay?"

Nathan nodded, eased up on the accelerator.

Marika was waiting for Alex in the church parking lot, leaning against the side of Mickey's truck, when the ambulance pulled in. Darcy Khaira was standing on the top of one of the fire trucks, yelling for quiet. The church bells stopped.

"We have to get home," Marika said to Alex as he climbed out of the ambulance. "We have to warn everybody."

Darcy was swearing now. "Goddammit, people! Shut up!"

The crowd quieted.

"I want you to listen very carefully. We're going to evacuate—"

A wave of muttering and shouts rose from the crowd.

He held up his hands. "Quiet! Listen. Everyone will have thirty minutes, then we leave. No questions. We've done everything we could. The fire has a mind of its own now and there's no stopping it. We'll evacuate to the north: the highway east to Kaslo is impassable; Silverton is completely engaged and the bulk of the fire seems to be heading south, toward Winlaw."

Alex's heart stumbled. Marika muttered something but he didn't catch it.

"That's it. Thirty minutes and we meet back here as planned. Grab your emergency packs and if you have a functioning vehicle, great. Just remember, though, we may end up on foot if there's too much debris on the highway."

Irene grabbed Alex's arm. "I've gotta go. We're meeting the crew at the bridge. Darcy say's they'll be down in about ten minutes." She kissed him, touched his face, and was gone, calling for Nathan.

"The fire's heading south," Marika said. She swiped at a piece of ash that landed on her cheek.

"Christ," Alex muttered. "Silverton's completely engaged. We won't get through."

"Irene's going there in the ambulance."

"Yeah, but only as far as the bridge."

"It's not going to cost us anything to go look," Marika argued.

"Maybe we should just help out here, help get everyone out safely."

"And what, not warn our families? Not warn our community? Unless Mickey miraculously put out the fire at the bottom of the valley in the past twenty-four hours, Winlaw is going to get caught between two goddamn firestorms."

Alex threw his daypack into the back seat. "You driving?"

"You're the 911 junkie. You better drive."

"What about Yuri?"

"Yeah, what about him?" She made a face. "He's being evacuated with the other patients."

Alex eased Mickey's pickup through the knot of people and vehicles and bicycles unraveling in the church parking lot, then headed south down the highway toward Silverton. The smoke was as thick as fog in the headlights, the southern sky a violent red. Flames chewed the mountainside.

"Jesus, you leave home for one day and the whole damn world goes for a dump," Marika said. "They're going to lose everything," she added so quietly Alex almost didn't hear her.

The truck climbed to the top of the bluff between New Denver and Silverton. Through the smoke and flying ash, it looked as though every single building downtown was on fire.

"Jesus," Alex breathed. "We can't get through that."

"Well, let's at least go as far as the bridge."

He geared the transmission down and crawled down the highway to the outskirts of town. Several houses there were on fire, their asphalt shingle roofs having succumbed to the assault of flying embers. Nathan had pulled the ambulance well off the road by the creek, and he and Irene were busy dealing with patients and the exhausted people who had brought them down off the mountainside.

"The main street's pretty wide," Marika said.

"Jesus, Marika, I can feel the heat from here."

"And it's not very long."

"If we lose the tires—"

"Well?"

"Christ. Roll up your window."

Alex floored the accelerator. Out of the corner of his eye he could see Irene stop what she was doing and turn toward the truck. The truck picked up speed as it roared over the bridge. Alex could feel the temperature in the cab climb. He shifted into third, driving the engine hard. Marika touched the passenger window, pulled her hand back. Alex kept his eyes on his destination: the expanse of highway just south of town with green, vibrant cedars and hemlocks and Douglas firs on either side.

Flaming debris crashed on the road beside the truck.

Then they were through, roaring down the highway between cool, green trees, rocketing south toward Winlaw.

A chill gray light leached through the smoke. Alex drove the truck hard, banging over the cracks and weeds. Cool air rushed through the open windows.

"I see you took my advice," Marika said.

Alex frowned. "What?"

"Alex has a girlfriend, Alex has a girlfriend."

He blushed.

"Oh my God, you're blushing!"

"Girl, mind your own business," he said.

"Hey, if I'd minded my own business, you wouldn't be in the position of needing to blush, now would you." She was grinning at him. "Did you have fun?"

The truck sputtered and lurched, then lost power. Alex's eyes shot to the fuel gauge. "Oh, for the love of God." The accelerator didn't respond. The truck sputtered again and died. Alex eased it to a stop. "I don't believe it. We're out of diesel."

"I was hoping it'd take us all the way," Marika said. "I couldn't find any fuel anywhere yesterday."

"I guess we'll have to walk."

"It's not like I was sitting around with my thumb up my butt—"

"It's okay," he said.

"—even the hybrids were dying. With so much smoke the solars weren't recharging them, so they were eating up all their fuel."

Alex shoved his door open. "I just don't really feel like walking all the way to Winlaw."

Marika's face brightened. "How about just to Enterprise Creek?" she said. "There were half-a-dozen abandoned vehicles there, remember. One of them is bound to work."

"And how far is that? Ten klicks?"

Marika shrugged.

Alex dragged his daypack off the back seat and wrestled his arms through the straps.

"So?" Marika said as she pulled on her pack. "Did you have fun?"

"You don't give up, do you?"

"You thought I might? You don't know me very well, then, do you?"

They hiked in silence. Alex's back ached and he was hungry. The morning brightened about as much as it was going to. His mind wallowed in a static of dread and exhaustion and fear. He hadn't slept much in the past twenty-four hours, and the deprivation was catching up with him.

"Alex?"

He grunted in response.

"There's something I need to talk to you about. I didn't come on this trip just to get shot at, and stay up all night firefighting, and drive through a burning town—as fun as all that's been."

He laughed a tired laugh.

"I wanted to talk to you alone, without Bill around." She was quiet for a moment. "We've been friends a long time, you and me."

"Just spit it out, girl."

"I'm pregnant."

That stopped him. "You're kidding!"

She stared at the ground.

"You're *not* kidding. Well, are you happy about it?"

"I don't know." She started walking again. "I don't know if I can stand to go through what I went through with Colin. And yet . . . to have another chance . . . but, on the other hand, it probably won't be a human baby anyway."

"What are you talking about? Devolved babies are human."

"Yeah, yeah, I've heard all the rhetoric, Alex. But they're not human; they're proto-human, pre-human, whatever . . . hell, for all we know, they might even be a completely different sub-species."

Anger unfurled in Alex. "They're *human*!"

Marika stopped and faced him, tears on her cheeks. "My Darlene is not human!" she shouted at him. "Not anymore."

"Don't cross that line," he warned.

"Why can't you just accept the fact—"

"Humans have rights; animals don't."

"I didn't say Darlene was an animal."

"What is she, then?"

"I don't know."

"How can you say that?" he shouted at her. "She's your daughter!"

"Just because you've been running around with your head up your ass doesn't mean the rest of us haven't been paying attention. Have you *looked* at Gemma lately?"

"Goddamn you!" Grief and rage howled through Alex.

"Well, have you? I don't know if I can bring another child into *this* world. What kind of life can I offer it?"

Everything he'd tried to keep from feeling, everything he'd buried under work and busyness, erupted and roiled and spewed. He was on his knees on the pavement howling like an injured dog, tears pouring down his face. He rocked and howled, buffeted by grief and frustration.

Marika dumped her pack and fell to her knees and hugged him. "Alex, what's the matter?" She held him as he cried.

He needed to tell someone. Marika would understand. She would listen. *Gemma asked me to kill her when she's no longer human,* he tried to say, but the words caught in his throat like bits of bone.

"What is it?" Marika breathed as she stroked the back of his head. "You can tell me."

"I can't," he choked. *I'm her father. I have to do what's best for her, and maybe that's what's best.*

She wiped his face with the back of her hand. "C'mon, hon," she said. "Get up. Let's keep walking." She took his hand, helped him to his feet. After retrieving her pack, she slipped her arm through his, and they began to walk. "I told you my secret; you tell me yours."

He felt empty, scoured out. A single sob escaped him as he scrubbed at the tears on his face. Marika's arm felt warm against his, anchoring him, while a kind of numbness spread through him, as if his insides had been scrubbed with a topical analgesic.

He sniffed, wiped his nose on the sleeve of his T-shirt, as he tried to pour himself into Marika's life, Marika's problem: "I take it Bill doesn't know."

She shook her head.

"I won't tell him."

"I know."

"What are you going to do?" he asked. *What are* you *going to do?* he could hear Marika's voice echoing back. He sobbed again.

"Talk to me, Alex."

I'm going to kill my daughter. That's what I'm going to do. That's what I promised, and nothing can save me from that promise.

"Are you going to keep this baby?" he said instead.

She kicked a stone off the road. "I don't know. I really don't know."

CHAPTER 23

All but one of the vehicles abandoned at the slide at Enterprise Creek had their keys. Most of them actually started. Only one, though, had a decent amount of fuel left, a tiny hybrid commuter. Alex directed Marika along the path they'd widened with a chainsaw the morning before to get Mickey's truck across the slide. He rolled several rocks out of the way of the low-riding car, bent back branches. Finally, Marika clunked the car down off the dirt onto the pavement and Alex squeezed himself into the passenger seat with a sigh.

She drove carefully through the thick smoke that seemed to follow them down the valley from the Silverton fire, trying to avoid the worst of the potholes and frost heaves. Alex shivered in the chilled air, the feeble sun unable to penetrate, to warm the morning, leaving the sky a dusky gray with an ominous dirty-orange glow where the sun should have been. He didn't want to turn the heater on and burn up valuable fuel.

As first the lake then the abandoned homesteads and empty houses fell behind them, the smoke remained almost impenetrable, like an autumn river fog, except for the ash that streaked the windshield. They drove mostly in silence. The numbness that had followed the eruption of grief and anger earlier continued to spread through Alex. He felt calm, detached, as if nothing much mattered anymore, leaving him wondering distractedly if he had given up hope, if he had lost any faith he might have had that, as Irene had said, things were going to be okay. He didn't bother to pull out his journal. There seemed no point. Who would read about his life anyway, or Gemma's? Who would care? Who would be left to care?

As they approached Winlaw Alex could see a different glow against the belly of the smoke, seemingly not very far south of the village. He wondered how close the southern fires had come. Had it only been forty-eight hours since Mickey had warned him that he didn't think they'd be able to contain those fires? That the overnight lightning strikes had thrown up new fires behind their hard-won firebreaks?

Marika dropped Alex off at the fire hall. He needed to give report, and Marika didn't want to wait around, especially when they saw the bay doors were wide open and Mickey Evdikimoff was sitting in the empty bay staffing the Ops table.

"I'll borrow a bike," Alex reassured her.

"If you're not there by lunchtime, I'll send Bill down here in this little shitbox to come get you."

He nodded as he slammed the passenger door and she zipped around him back out onto the road.

Mickey wandered out into the parking lot, a radio in hand. His face looked substantially more haggard than when Alex had last seen him, and he had that peculiar gray color to his skin that cardiac patients sometimes get. And drinkers. In addition, there was no denying the devolution: the jaw-forward tilt of his head, narrowing of his chest, protrusion of his brow ridge.

"Hey, Mick," Alex said.

"What's going on, Al?" He glanced up the highway in the direction Alex and Marika had come. "Where's Yuri?" There was dread in his tone.

"He got shot, Mick," Alex said, but held up a hand: "Don't worry, he's on the mend, but he lost a chunk of his liver and a whack of blood."

"Christ." Mickey suddenly looked like he needed to sit down. "What the hell happened?"

Alex led him back into the bay, waited until he sat in the chair behind the Ops table, and then told him about the shooting and the subsequent operation at the school. About the murders, the kidnapped girl. The fire.

"Great," Mickey said. "That's just fucking great." He slipped his Nitro out of his shirt pocket, shot some under his tongue.

Alex didn't say anything.

"I send him away and he just about gets himself killed. Plus, now we got nowhere to go, not if they can't get a handle on the Silverton fire."

"They were evacuating New Denver when we left. Fire's heading this way."

"There may be twenty klicks between us and them," Mickey said, "but that's twenty klicks of the driest goddamn forest I've ever seen. We're already in deep enough shit, and I was really hoping—" He let out a long breath. "Since you left that goddamn fire is now barely ten kilometers outside of town, and it's coming at us like a fucking train." His face blanched and he clenched his teeth.

"Jesus, Mickey."

"My goddamn heart. It's driving me crazy. Won't let me get any work done."

"Has June given you anything besides the Nitro?"

"There's nothing to give."

Alex dragged a chair over to the side of the table and dropped into it.

"I pulled everybody off the fire," Mickey said. "I'm just letting it burn. I got them putting together a backburn just south of Lebahdo Flats. It's the only thing we can do. People are pretty mad 'cause I'm going to burn their houses. Al, I don't know what else to do. If it keeps burning the way it's been, it'll be on top of us day after tomorrow. Or sooner. But if the backburn turns on us . . . well . . . "

"What about the Silverton fire?"

Mickey shrugged. "If it keeps coming this way, we're going to have to do the same thing. Set up a backburn and get down on our goddamn knees and pray." Mickey pulled off his ball cap and scratched his scalp.

"When's the backburn?"

"They'll light it as soon as they're ready. Sometime this afternoon, probably, depending on the wind. I've got everybody on a one-hour evacuation notice, although now I'm not sure where the hell we're going to evacuate to."

"What about east? Try to cross over the mountains to Kootenay Lake and Nelson? The fire has already been through Nelson."

"On foot? Plus, we got a number of sightings of new fires to the east, between us and Kootenay Lake. We could end up trapped."

"We could end up trapped if we go west, too," Alex said, "and find out there's fires all through the Selkirks."

"I wish Yuri were here."

"Yeah, I bet you do."

"He's okay, though?"

"Marika saw him this morning. Said he was okay, that he was being evacuated with the other patients."

Tell Mickey that I forgive him. Alex grunted inwardly. Yuri can tell Mickey himself.

It was well after lunchtime when Alex rode June's bike across the bridge over the Slocan River, past his and Gemma's house high up on the bluff, and pedaled easily up the back road toward Marika and Bill's place. Bill never did show up in the commuter car to give him a lift, so he went to find June at the school-slash-hospital to borrow her bike. She was quite disappointed to see him returning empty-handed, so he ended up repeating the story of Yuri's shooting, and the murders, and the out-of-control fire in Silverton.

The smoke abraded his throat and sinuses as he rode so he tried to keep his pace slow, his breathing easy. A hot, dry wind swirled around him, rustling the parched weeds together at the side of the road, sandpaper on stone. Wind was bad. Any wind. Unless it brought a Noah's flood of rain with it.

His legs burned from pedaling. He was so tired. And numb. He wished he were back in Irene's bed, lost in the all-consuming tangle of her arms and legs, after-sex sleep numbing his worried brain.

Finally, when he turned into Marika and Bill's driveway, his legs were so tired that he got off June's bike and pushed it up the gravel driveway. Hot wind tormented the fruit trees. The little commuter car he and Marika had come down from New Denver in was parked behind his pickup. He leaned the bike against the wall of the house and threw open the door that entered into the basement.

"Hello!" he called as he shrugged out of his pack. He pulled off his boots and felt his way up the dark stairs into the kitchen. "Marika? Gemma?" The kitchen was empty. Wind blew in the open window beside the table. Dirty dishes spilled over the counters and into the kitchen sink. The woodstove was cold.

"Bill?" He headed down the hallway to the bedrooms. The door to Darlene's bedroom stood open. He glanced inside: the room had been torn apart, fist-sized holes in the gyproc, closet doorframe pulled right out of the wall, bed and dresser overturned, clothes scattered and shredded.

"Marika?" he called as he threw open the door to her and Bill's room. Their bed was unmade, clothes were strewn everywhere, but Alex knew that wasn't unusual for them. He pushed open the door to Colin's room, where Gemma would have slept. The bed had been made and her pack lay on it, its contents in neat piles on the duvet. Typical Gemma.

A door banged open. "Dad?" Gemma's thick voice called up the stairs. She was out of breath. He could hear her limping up the stairs, the distinct crack, crack of her wooden cane on the risers.

He hurried into the kitchen, relief sweeping through him. Coyote, her coat dusty and full of twigs and seedpods, burst up the stairs ahead of Gemma, almost knocking Alex over. He wrestled with her, trying to pet her head, but she wriggled and squirmed, so excited to see him. Then Gemma appeared. Alex opened his arms and she almost jumped into them. He hugged her hard. She smelled of sweat and smoke and dirty hair. "Hey, missy!"

She was crying.

"Hey," he said again, softer, as he loosened his grip so he could look at her. Her T-shirt was dark with sweat. Dirt was smeared over one cheek, and her lip was cut and swollen, her left eye puffy and purple. His heart surged in his chest. "Jesus, Gemma, what happened?" Images seared through his mind, fist to face, rough hands pulling at her clothes, at her arms, binding her to a post, hard hands pulling her legs apart—he swallowed.

"It's Darlene!" she cried, her voice a howl. "We tried to stop her, but she was too strong, too fast." A sob leapt out of her throat. "She's gone!" She pulled away, dropped her cane and pack onto the floor. She was sobbing. "And we can't find her."

"Gone?"

Gemma threw herself into a chair at the kitchen table, ground her knuckles into her eyes. "A pack has been hanging around, calling to her. She knows them, some of them anyway, from school. She's crazy to get away: she's come into season.

"She was different than last time I visited, you could see it in her eyes. Like she wasn't Darlene anymore, like she'd gone crazy, or—" Gemma frowned "—feral, that's the word. Like a wild animal. She was so frustrated and angry, and scared of what was happening to her.

"I went in to see her first thing this morning, bring her some tea and biscuits with jam. She was waiting for me. Scared the bejesus out of me, coming at me like that, all fists and feet. I tried to grab her . . . but she got me good." Gemma touched her cracked lip with the back of her hand. "She jumped on Bill, mostly just trying to get past him. He was coming down the hallway to see what all the racket was about. She really beat on him, though. I think she broke his arm, but he won't let anybody look at it. You know Bill."

Alex sat across the table from Gemma.

"And then she was gone. We looked for her all day today. Calling. Hiking all the old logging roads. Smoke's so thick now, it's hard to breathe. Or to see very far."

"And Marika and Bill are still out there?"

She nodded. "Dad, it's all my fault. I thought things were going so well, that she trusted me." Gemma scrubbed at her eyes again. "I didn't shut the door fast enough."

"It's not your fault, missy. Like you said, she was waiting for you."

Gemma pulled off her boots and socks, sniffed at her shirt, made a face, then curled her hands into fists and pushed up from the table with her knuckles. "Gotta get out of these clothes," she said and headed for her room, bare feet slapping the tired linoleum.

Alex watched her go, walking stooped and limping, muttering to herself, her hair a mass of snarls down her back.

She turned a little, as if to say something to him, but then simply continued through the doorway, awkwardly shoving her dirty hair up off her face with a long, thin hand.

CHAPTER 24

Ronnie leapt right behind Kevin. The boy clinging to her back shrieked with fear. The others followed. They raced the fire downhill, the roar and the heat snapping at their heels. A tree exploded right beside Ronnie, raining flame and burning limbs down on her. It was as if Hell itself chased them.

Fiery air scorched her lungs. Brush tore at her uniform pants and the oversized boots threatened to send her headlong down the bank.

Many of the children screeched and shrieked. Ronnie glanced back at the wall of flames falling on them from the road above. Kevin hugged a child in each arm and carried one on his back. His feet, cut and bleeding, flew over the rocks and detritus. Janice was right behind him, a sickening burn blistering on her right arm, her bare feet bleeding as well. She, too, carried a child on her back, with another in her arms. Ronnie couldn't see Sachi anywhere. Nor any of the Gardener brothers. She stopped, her breath hissing in and out of her lungs. Maybe they hadn't made it across the highway before the trees started candling.

A flaming branch slammed to the ground beside her. She jumped sideways, almost stumbling. The boy shrieked again and hugged her neck even harder.

There! Through the trees to the south, Sachi and two children, all three Gardner brothers, as well as several of the older kids and the rest of the children.

Ronnie plunged back down the embankment.

At the bottom Kevin stumbled across the rocky shore and splashed out into the lake. Ronnie followed him, wading out until the icy water was chest deep, trying to put as much distance between her and the flames as she could. "Keep going!" she shouted. The others waded in after her, shrieking and screaming. Pretty soon the air would be supercharged with heat, deadly on the lungs. They had to get further away from shore, preferably without anyone drowning.

Ronnie scanned the rocky shoreline for a boat, an old canoe, a plastic drum, anything they could load the children into or onto and get further away from the fire. Ronnie wracked her brain. She was pretty sure the old Millstone place had a boat sitting on the beach—but, it'd been there for years, so it probably wouldn't even float, and besides, it was half a kilometer further down the lake.

"Is anyone missing?" she shouted above the roar of the fire. "Sachi!" Sachi was wading out into the deeper water, yelling at the Gardeners to pick up some of the other children, to help them, for God's sake. "Sachi, is this everyone? Did we lose anybody?"

Sachi spun in the water, pointing and mouthing names. "I don't see Caleb. Caleb!"

The boy on Ronnie's back pulled his face out of her hair, made a hooting noise.

"Is this him, Sachi?"

Sachi let out a long breath. "I didn't see him there." She was nodding. "That's everybody. You got everybody out, Ronnie!"

Ronnie's legs started to burn in the glacier-fed water. She knew they couldn't stay in here very long without risking hypothermia, especially the small children.

Kevin was yelling at her, waving his free arm. He started pointing north, up the lake just beyond the bluff that separated Silverton from New Denver. She squinted with her good eye.

"Boats!" he yelled and started waving his arm and shouting. Janice joined in.

"Let's keep everyone together," Ronnie said over her shoulder. "Roy, Willis, c'mon. Levi, put that kid up on your shoulders, get her right out of the water. Good."

It looked as if a fleet of small boats had taken to the water, a convoy of canoes and kayaks and aluminum fishing boats. The roar of an outboard motor revving up thundered above the howl of the fire as one of the larger boats spun in their direction.

Ronnie felt suddenly sick, seeing the RCMP decal on the side of the powerboat as it rushed closer. She knew then why there were so many boats on the lake and it made her want to cry with frustration.

Janice splashed up beside her. "Please tell me—" But the roar of the motor drowned out her words.

The boat's driver was Darcy Khaira and although Ronnie was glad to be rescued, she knew he came laden with bad news. Two other boats pulled up behind the RCMP powerboat to help pull them from the water. Ronnie waded over to the RCMP boat to push Caleb into the arms of Irene Rilkoff.

"We were bugging out in the middle of the night, planning to head north, but fire came in from that direction as well," Darcy was saying to Kevin as he pulled him aboard. "So we took to the water and spent the rest of the night on the far shore and watched her burn. Not a fucking thing we could do—" The rest of his words were drowned out by children shrieking with fear as they were pulled from the backs of the older kids who had carried them.

Ronnie hauled herself up the ladder at the back of the RCMP boat and stood on the swaying deck and shivered. Water drained from her clothes. She fastened the plaid jacket shut and wrapped her arms over her chest to try to trap what was left of her body's heat. She was exhausted—her headache roared, and her nose hurt like hell—but she made her way to the wheel and grabbed Darcy's arm.

"Is Matt okay?" she said, her throat tight.

"Yeah, he's all right, Ronnie. We got everybody got out. But we thought we'd lost you and Janice and Kevin, couldn't get you on the radio, then the wind came up and the fire blew down on us like a fucking hurricane from hell, and all we could do was get everybody out onto the lake." He shrugged, licked his lips. His cheeks were blistered and red, his eyebrows had been singed off. "Didn't save much. Nobody did. Some of the animals; lots of them we just let go and hoped for the best. It all happened way too fucking fast." He turned away from her then, but she grabbed his arm again.

"What about Chris? The guy I locked up in the cells at the station?"

Darcy's eyes widened. He shook his head. She let him be.

Caleb tried to scrabble up her leg, wanting to get into the safety of her arms again, a grin of fear splitting his face. She hauled him up, cuddled his hairy little body against her chest, then settled on the deck against the side of the boat.

Jesus, she thought, that poor bastard burned to death, locked behind bars and concrete walls, nobody remembering he was even there.

Darcy swung the boat around, speeding away from the flames. The two other boats followed.

The boy whimpered. She stroked his head.

But Matt was okay. It hadn't sunk in yet. She hadn't realized how afraid she'd been, seeing the fire and Silverton completely gutted. But the house would be gone. All her photos, her diaries, her mother's treasured crystal goblets; all Matt's hunting and fishing gear, his guns, his drawings—that drawing he'd done of her she loved so much, when she'd posed nude for him on a deserted beach up the lake five years ago. Their house, their home, with its bright wooden floors, warm kitchen, their expansive upstairs bedroom with a view of the lake and the Valhalla Mountains right from the bed. All the memories of their life together, soaked into the wood and drywall and carpet of that house. And not only that: all their winter's supply of food and firewood gone. Gardens and fruit trees decimated. And the livestock. Ronnie shuddered. She didn't want to think about that, animals tucked away all over town, caught between the fire and the water, some probably still trapped in pens or coops or hutches when the humans fled.

Just like Chris.

Caleb snuggled in tighter, burying his head against her neck.

As the RCMP powerboat rounded the point, Ronnie wrestled to her feet. The scene stunned her. The town still smoldered, puking dense smoke into the air, but here and there a building still stood, peculiarly untouched by the flames. Most buildings, though, had burned away right to their foundations because the heat had been so intense. Almost all the trees were gone, save for one here, one there, just like those houses, mysteriously untouched.

The flotilla of New Denverites had been heading back across the lake to the town to see if it was safe enough to enter when Ronnie and the others had been spotted. They wanted to salvage what they could, if anything, from the skeletons of their homes.

They beached their boats on the rocky shore below what had been the Centennial campground and wandered, shell-shocked, up through the smoldering town.

Darcy eased the RCMP boat as close to shore as he could, then threw out the anchor. The adults slipped overboard, helped the children out, and waded to shore. The smoke was so thick Ronnie found it difficult to catch her breath as she waded through the icy water.

Matt ran across the beach, stumbling on the rocks, his heavy firefighter boots tripping him up. He splashed out to her, threw his arms around her and the boy she was carrying. He was weeping, pressing his face into her cheek as he held her and hugged her. She hugged him back, squeezing the thick turn-out coat as hard as she could.

He pulled away, then, and held her at arms' length to look at her. "I was sure you were gone," he said quietly as he scrubbed at the tears on his face. His face, like Darcy's, was blistered and red. A dirty bandage was taped on his neck just below his ear. He reached his hand out to the injured side of Ronnie's face, but instead let his hand fall onto Caleb's head and ruffled his dirty hair. The boy scrunched harder into Ronnie's shoulder. "Who is this?"

She shook her head, tears dropping from her eyes, and fought back the anguish that threatened to overflow. "Caleb," she said, and just then he began to cry. He was probably hungry and tired, she thought, and afraid. She considered his face, wet with tears, one hand rubbing his eyes, snot leaking from his flat nose, and she realized that he'd probably been through more trauma in his seven or eight short years than she'd endured her whole life.

She took a deep breath, shifted him over onto her other hip. Matt reached out, then, touched her cheek, and she winged. She'd been locking herself away from him for so long she didn't know how to talk to him, how to open herself up and hemorrhage emotions in front of him. How could she tell him about what had happened? How could she tell him what she had done? Worse yet, how could she admit that she didn't care, that she didn't feel remorse, that, in fact, she had been delighted to smash that prick's face into hamburger? And that she'd do it again in a millisecond. For Matt. For Caleb. For Sachi. For the sheer helluvit. Because the bastard deserved it. Because she enjoyed it.

She studied Matt's blistered face, his mary-jane green eyes, cracked lips. The man she'd spent the past decade of her life with, who loved her without really knowing who, or what, she was. How could she tell him how powerful it made her feel to pound that man's life right out of his flesh, how she became an animal, a predator ripping apart its prey, how, in the universe of that root cellar, she was a fucking *god*? And how, out here on this beach with him, with the others, she was a mere human, bound by the mores of compassion and kindness, duty and honor, respect and love? And how she was afraid it would never be enough anymore.

They piled back into the boats, taking what few belongings and animals they'd evacuated with, and set off down the lake to the head of the Slocan River, the fire raging at them from the shoreline. They were hoping to beat the fire to Winlaw, hoping to find the little village still thriving and not scourged by fire and abandoned, and hoping the people there would be willing to welcome them and provide them with food and clothing and shelter.

Ronnie found out from Sachi that Caleb could still talk when he'd been brought to the farm by Chris and Don almost a year ago. He'd come from a home way on the outskirts of Silverton; his parents had died and he'd been living with his older sister in their house until Don and Chris showed up, raping his sister while he buried his face in his arms and screamed until they beat him, then they took them both away in a truck and sold them to Kratky. His sister had died during the winter, pneumonia probably.

All this had been going on and Ronnie, whose job it was to protect the citizens of her jurisdiction, hadn't known. She'd failed somehow, thrashing about in the muck of her marriage and busying herself with the daily inanities of small-town police work, to look more carefully at exactly *how* the world around her had been coming undone. She, like most, generally attributed every disturbance, every disappearance, to the catastrophic fallout from the Lucy virus. The influenza pandemic had been bad enough, and the Lucy virus simply made matters ten times worse, but the societal dislocation which resulted from people simply not being there to do their jobs—be they doctors or electricians, garbage-collectors or politicians, researchers or bank tellers—was the biggest killer. People fell through all kinds of meter-wide cracks. People like Caleb and his sister, like Sachi and all the others. This was no longer the small world it used to be prior to the virus; the world now was as big and as wild as it had been ten centuries before. Twenty centuries. And just as dangerous. Perhaps even more so.

Ronnie huddled in the bottom of the RCMP boat, Caleb sleeping against her chest, while Matt sat beside her, his knees drawn to his chest, forehead on is knees, his dirty hair littered with the ash falling from the metal-gray sky. The sun, a smudge of filthy orange, glowed feebly overhead. The boat barely moved, staying back with the slowest of the paddlers, while Darcy, who was at the wheel, squinted through the smoke. Her stomach rumbled. She hadn't eaten since lunch the day before, but it didn't seem to matter.

Something had changed in her. It was as if she had awakened after a long and troubled sleep. She had let her life tread water, staying afloat but going nowhere, thinking drowning was her only certain future. The warmth of Caleb breathing against her chest told her she should not have given up trying to get pregnant. She had given up on herself, and on Matt, without realizing she'd done so. And it wasn't as if having a baby had been her *raison d'être* but it seemed that she'd used the miscarriages build a steel cage around her heart. There was no steel cage there now, and yet the tenderness she felt for Matt was not the tenderness she used to feel. It had changed, evolved, shocked into clear relief by the demon she'd set free. She'd muted her inner vision just as the smoke muted the sun. It was as if she'd been sealed away in that cave with the demon. It had been so damn dark in there for so long she'd forgotten how to feel alive, forgotten how to love, how to *be in* love; forgotten how to hate, how to fight; forgotten what it felt like to laugh, to lust after a particular familiar body, comfortable and safe. She shook her head at herself. *What a fool*, she thought. She'd wasted all those years.

Caleb whimpered in his sleep, struggled against her. She stroked his hair and rocked him ever so slightly.

It was the demon who had melted the cage she'd erected around her heart this time, who set her heart free to murder and mutilate. Her heart and the demon had become one, writhing ecstatically in bloodlust, slathering after the primacy of predator over prey.

There is no demon, she told herself. *This is who you are, who you have always been, who you have tried for so long not to be.*

Kratky was coming after her. She could feel it in the core of her gut. He was going to hunt her down and kill her, of that she was certain. But she was like iron ore, heated and pounded until the slag had been driven out of her, until she'd become steel, gleaming and hard and unafraid.

CHAPTER 25

Alex dished up scrambled eggs, with fried potatoes and cooked carrots, and slid the plate in front of Marika. The kitchen was scorching hot now. Bill had gone downstairs for the beer Alex had brought earlier. Gemma was still in the bathroom washing up. They had come down off the mountainside for food, and to load up with water.

Marika hunched over her tea, eyes dark, rubbing a hand through her sweat-soaked hair. "I can't believe she's gone." She was barely audible over the crackle of the fire in the stove. She picked up her fork, moved the eggs around on her plate. "When I found out I was pregnant with Colin, I was so afraid. Even though Darlene was fine at the time, I was still afraid. I'd seen what so many of my friends were going through, and I didn't know if I could stand it. But we wanted another baby. It just seemed right. A new little life, full of hope and love and promise." She stopped moving her fork, lost now in the memory. She smiled, but only for a moment.

Bill thumped up the stairs with the six-pack of Mickey's home-brew in hand.

"He was gone from day one, not a typical lucy baby, but his face wasn't really a baby's face. And yet, he had Bill's eyes, my mouth, my hair." She sighed.

Bill stood frozen in the doorway.

"But Darlene . . . I couldn't help hoping, I just couldn't. Then the signs began to show. She began devolving, and all that fear I'd been stomping down underneath the hope got loose. I knew, in the end, that I'd lose her, too. I just didn't think it would be like this. Her alive and out there with a pack, but as unreachable as if she were dead."Marika took a breath. She put a forkful of food in her mouth, talked around it. "Thought maybe we'd be lucky, and she'd devolve more slowly, you know, like Gemma. I envied you that, Alex. Then I thought maybe Darlene didn't get exposed, that somehow she'd been skipped over." She scrubbed a hand through her hair again.

Alex poured himself some tea and sat in the chair opposite her. "Eat," he said.

She shook her head. Tears splashed onto the table. "I shouldn't have gotten pregnant," she whispered.

"C'mon, Marika," Bill said, "don't do this. We'll go back out as soon as we get some food into us." He set the beer on the counter.

"I shouldn't have gotten pregnant."

"Honey, we'll find her; we'll bring her home." He pulled out the chair beside her, twined his fingers in the close-cropped hair at the back of her head.

She half-turned in her chair to look at him. "No, Bill, I'm pregnant *now*!"

Bill's mouth opened and closed.

"I don't know if I can do this," Marika said.

Bill took one of her hands in his. "Someday this has all got to end. The virus will wear out, or people will develop immunity, or somebody will find a cure—" Marika was shaking her head, but Bill pushed on "—and babies will be born who will live and grow up, and things will be like they were before." He squeezed her hand.

She looked at him. "I don't believe that anymore," she said. She took back her hand, pushed away from the table. "It's not going to happen. We're going to lose this baby, too. Just like Colin, and . . . and Darlene. All the babies are lost, Bill; all the children are gone." She stood up, hands hanging limp at her sides. "I'm going back out there to find her."

Bill stared after Marika, his arms propped on the table, hands opening and closing, grasping nothing. Alex watched him in the reflection in the window. Blue-gray smoke hung outside the window like fog.

"Pregnant," Bill said, as if sounding out the word.

"You didn't know?"

He let out a long breath, shook his head. "She's been shutting me out these last few months. I knew she wasn't feeling well . . . " Resentment flashed through his voice. "Sometimes I'd catch her sitting here at the table crying, and when I'd ask her what was wrong, she'd just say, Nothing. Always *Nothing*. I knew something was wrong—it was so goddamn obvious—but I figured it was just losing Colin, and then Darlene, watching her go downhill like that, trying to deal with her day after day, all that stress." He stood, got two bottles of beer off the counter, set one in front of Alex. "I tried to get her to go see you or Willow or even Gemma, thought maybe she might talk to one of you if she wouldn't talk to me." He sat back down, took a long pull on his beer. "Jesus, Alex. Darlene was such a funny kid when she was little. Everything she did made me laugh. This past year, though . . . she's devolved so fast." He was quiet for a long moment. "She's not the same kid, Alex. She's not my Darlene. If she didn't have Marika's red hair, I wouldn't know her." He stared out the window. "I miss *my* Darlene," he said quietly.

"C'mon, Bill, she's still the same kid—"

"I don't know, Al. She doesn't even seem human anymore."

Gemma scuffed into the kitchen in her old fuzzy pink slippers, wearing a clean T-shirt and trousers, her head wrapped in a towel. "I'm shedding like a damn dog," she said. "It's disgusting." She sat in a chair near the window, towel-drying her hair. "Who's not human anymore?" she added with a sidelong glance at Alex.

"Hey, Gem, you want a beer?" Bill asked as he got up to retrieve her a beer. "We're celebrating. Marika's pregnant."

She looked from Bill to Alex and back again.

"Who's not human anymore?" she repeated.

"Marika's pregnant!" Bill announced again, his voice as false as the grin on his face. He handed Gemma a beer.

"I know." She pulled off the cap, took a swallow. "She told me."

Bill stiffened. "Oh," was all he said.

Alex winced at that.

Gemma moved onto the floor beside the stove, so that she could scratch Coyote's big head with one hand while she dried her hair with the other. She set the bottle of beer on the floor beside her.

Bill uncapped himself a second beer, dropped back into a chair.

"Who's not human anymore?" Gemma said a third time.

Alex held up his hands. "Let it go, missy. Now's not the time."

"When *is* the time, Dad?"

Bill took another long drink. "We weren't planning to have another kid," he said. "Hell, nobody is these days. It just happens."

"It doesn't *just happen*," Gemma said.

Alex threw her a sharp look.

"Dammit, Bill," she continued, ignoring Alex, "you guys weren't using protection. What did you expect?"

He seemed to choke a little, then said, almost inaudibly, "We ran out."

Gemma opened her mouth, as if to retort, but Alex glared at her. "That's enough," he said.

"No, no," Bill said, "it's okay, Alex. What does it matter?" He shrugged. "Things were so hard last winter with Colin gone, looking after Darlene, having all those problems with the electricity, no job, no money, the government—" he took a breath "There was that week there, in April, when the weather was so nice." Tears dropped down his face. "It's like we fell in love again." He wiped at his face. "And now she's pregnant, and it's just going to start all over again, being afraid, knowing what's coming, trying to steel yourself against it, trying not to love the little kid—"

Alex reached across the table, put his hand on Bill's arm. "Go on, Bill," he said. "Go be with Marika. Gemma and I'll clean up here. Then we'll head right out; we'll go look for Darlene."

Bill wiped his face with his shirtsleeve. "Yeah," he said and pushed his chair from the table. He sounded defeated. "Yeah. We'll find her, right?"

He stood, took his beer bottle off the table, turned and thumped slowly down the stairs.

Alex rubbed his face with his hands. Bitterness filled his mouth like ashes. "C'mon," he said, "give me a hand here." He gathered up the dishes.

Gemma clapped her hands lightly for him. A tired joke.

"Very funny," he said, but he gave her a little bow anyway, like he always did, while sadness blew through him. "I'll wash, if you dry," he choked out.

His thighs burned from the climbing; he was soaked with sweat and his left ankle ached from twisting it when he had slipped off a fallen log. In the distance he could hear Bill's voice, calling Darlene, and then Marika's. Gemma, cane in hand, scrambled up an old deer trail ahead of him. He called to her to slow down, to wait up. She seemed tireless, as if in her element, moving easily through the bush in the smoke-filled heat, while he stumbled and tripped over rocks and ran into heavy, crisp branches.

"You're out of shape, Dad," she said as she crouched on a flat-topped stump.

He ignored this. "We're not going to find her, are we?" he asked as he tried to catch his breath.

She shook her head. "She's like an animal now. Her and the rest of the pack could be sitting in the bush a meter away and we'd never know it." She wiped sweat from her brow ridge with the back of a hand. "She couldn't stand being locked up. She'd just say *'Out, out'* over and over again. She'd even say it when we were outside in that goddamn zoo-cage Bill built: she'd climb the chain link, and just say *'Out, out'* under her breath." Gemma shrugged. "I don't know, Dad. It's like she didn't even have much of a memory of her life anymore. She still recognized us—could even say 'mom,' 'dad,' 'Gem-ma'—but it was if everything else was lost to her. Forgotten. I'd try to get her to talk, or we'd play recognition games, but she seemed unable to participate, or maybe she was just so uninterested in her surroundings that it didn't matter. She got frustrated really easily. It's as if she's forgotten that she grew up in a house, eating at a table, having birthday parties and Christmas and going to school . . . "

They'd searched all afternoon, mostly in silence, climbing up and across the ridge in the heat. Alex looked up at Gemma crouched on the stump. Her lips tightened on the right side of her mouth: she was close to crying. A lump rose in Alex's own throat.

"What's going to happen to her, Dad?" Gemma said quietly. "Now that she's out here, what kind of life is she going to have? She's coming into heat, like a dog, and some older kid'll be more than happy to knock her up. She'll get pregnant, have a baby. Maybe she'll live, maybe she won't; maybe the baby'll live, maybe it won't. Then what? Gather food? Maybe hunt if they know how. Live in caves or abandoned barns. Get burned alive if the fire comes this far, or freeze to death in the middle of the winter. She's just a kid!

"What kind of life is that? Is that what it all comes down to: eating, shitting, fucking, having babies, and then dying? Is that all there is? Is that all there's *going* to be?"

Alex's heart ached for her, crouching on the stump above him, her arms flailing as her gravelly voice rose. She was trying not to cry, scrunching her face against the tears.

"Maybe sometimes that's enough," he said. "Maybe sometimes that's all we need." But he didn't believe it himself.

"That's bullshit, Dad!" she shouted, suddenly standing on the stump to tower above him. "That's absolute *bullshit*, and you know it! Maybe that'd be good enough for you, but it's sure as hell not good enough for me. I want books and movies and talking for hours on the phone; I want running water and electricity and a heated bed; I want friends and lovers and maybe even kids one day, kids who go to school and who grow up to be kind, compassionate, *human* adults; I want *normal*. I want to *be* normal." She gulped air.

Alex wanted to hold her, stroke her hair as if she were eight years old again and still believed he really could make it all right, that he had the power just because he was her dad. He bit back his own tears.

"I don't want my life to come down to *that*," she choked out.

Sadness coursed through him, as thick and as harsh as the smoke wending through the trees. And then above him, above Marika's voice—tired and devoid of hope, calling out Darlene's name again and again—above the trees, above the ridge, above the smoke, came the whining growl of a small airplane motor.

Gemma looked up, suddenly still. Alex's heart stopped: silhouetted against the snarling gray sky Gemma was an icon of a proto-human, head tipped back, square jaw jutting forward, gawking with curiosity at the inscrutable heavens.

Then she lost her balance, and, arms flailing, fell off the stump.

A gargled cry. Coyote bounded over to investigate. Alex scrambled up the slope. Gemma was on her knees beside a fallen log, her good hand impaled on a thin broken branch sticking up from the trunk, the ragged point sticking ten centimeters up through the back of her hand.

"Shit!"

With a howl she wrenched her hand up and away, then sat hugging it against her chest.

Alex struggled out of his daypack, grabbed his water bottle. "Can you move your fingers?" He dropped to his knees beside her.

"It hurts too much," she muttered through clenched teeth.

"Let me see it."

Gemma slowly unfurled her hand. The wound in her palm was jammed full of bits of bark that had come off the branch. It bled, but not enough. "I have to clean it," Alex said. Her eyes were scrunched shut. Coyote was licking her ear and the side of her face. Gemma shrugged her off.

Alex helped Gemma stand, then got her to sit on the stump she'd fallen from. "Keep the hand lower, I want it to bleed. That'll help keep all that crap out." He splashed water over the wound, pulled it open, trying to get the water to flow through to the other side to flush out as much debris as possible.

"Jesus, Dad, that hurts!"

"Sorry, missy. Punctures are a bitch to clean, and with all those tendons and small bones in there you could end up having a helluva time if it gets infected."

"I know, I know."

"We should go to the hospital. June can freeze it and clean it out properly."

Gemma was nodding, her face pale.

"I'll wrap it up, then we'll hike down to Marika and Bill's and take that little car."

She jutted her jaw at the sky. "So, was that what I thought it was?" she asked as he rummaged through his pack for the first aid kit.

CHAPTER 26

Sage realized she hadn't expected the plane to start up so easily. The engine sounded fine, the batteries were almost charged to capacity. She flicked through the radio channels. Nothing but static.

Ula woke only briefly while Sage buckled her into the harness beside Isaac, who had settled into sulking and whimpering. Sage helped Carl into the back seat beside Ula, and got Josie settled in the front seat. Then she strapped herself into the pilot's seat, struggling a little to latch the buckle under her bulging belly, pulled her door shut, and went through her checklists.

"Ready?" she yelled above the noise of the engine, and without waiting for a reply taxied the Skylane across the bumpy tarmac and out onto the runway. The absence of radio chatter was unsettling, and she caught herself before doing an automatic check-in with the abandoned Grand Forks tower.

As she lined up on the runway, her heart pounded so hard in her chest she thought she could hear it above the engine. It wasn't because she was afraid of the takeoff or the flight itself, rather it was the exhilaration of doing something familiar, something she hadn't realized she loved because flying had always been Quinn's thing, and his childlike excitement seemed to outshine any simple delight she had taken in the flights he'd overseen. Or maybe she loved it because flying and Quinn were synonymous, and as she pulled back on the throttle and rushed the Cessna down the runway, Quinn was there, lifting the plane off the weed-ridden asphalt, pushing it above the trees, the skinny Kettle River, the highway, and up into the sky, that world without end.

The hum of the engine cradled her; she felt comforted. Sage had not felt this safe in a long time. Tears filled her eyes, blurring the gauges. She glanced around the cabin. Josie had her face pressed against the window beside her. She turned just then, saw Sage watching her, and gave her a big grin. In the mirror she could see Carl, eyes wide, face the color of bone, staring straight ahead, avoiding the scenery out the window at his shoulder. Isaac sat motionless, eyes scrunched tight, fists over his ears, while Ula simply slept.

Sage followed the highway east. The smoke was high and thin enough not to impair her vision significantly. The landscape unfolded below, and she had that familiar sensation that she was looking down upon a miniature world: tiny trees, tiny buildings, tiny roads. It's what Maddie had liked the most about flying, that up in a plane they were like giants staring down upon the land, or like God. Jovan had liked the plane itself, and the sensation of freefall when he and Quinn would try to make pens and action figures float momentarily in the cab by doing sudden descents, which had never been Sage's favorite airborne activity. She was surprised by how much of the landscape lay untouched by fire. She'd had this belief that fire had swept across the land more or less like something apocalyptic; in truth, though, the fire swirled and blew this way or that, missing houses, leaving a copse of trees untouched in a sea of black, turning back on itself, or suddenly charging one way or the other. The pattern of damage seemed erratic, a kind of madness. And outside the burning touch of the fire lay hectare after hectare of green, thriving wildness.

It made her think of the Lucy virus, how it seemed that the population of the whole country was being consumed, that contracting the virus and devolving or developing virus-induced complications was inevitable. But maybe it would turn out not to be so. Perhaps the virus blew here and there like a firestorm, infecting much of what lay in its path, yet leaving others virtually untouched. Infected but unaffected. Unless there was a built-in dormancy, like HIV, like a fire smoldering under the duff all through the long winter simply waiting for the right conditions in which to erupt into flame. If that were the case, then at least maybe there was time. Maybe she had time to find her parents, maybe even to raise this baby she carried, perhaps even to see Carl and Josie and Isaac and Ula all into adulthood.

Time.

The True Gorilla had not been caught as far as Sage knew. At least nothing had been announced publicly before the media fell off the air, and even, while it still ran, the Homeland Security public information channel offered nothing concrete. Mostly *via negativa* pronouncements: the True Gorilla was not from Syria, as originally thought; he (or *she*, one top-level spokesperson had insisted) was not an American citizen; and the rumors about the True Gorilla having a connection with the Brazilian eco-terrorists who were claiming responsibility were unfounded. There had only been one *via positiva* statement, and as far as Sage knew it had only been said once: the initial science behind the Lucy virus had been constructed in the US. *End of statement.*

Christina Lake lay green and bright to their left, much smaller than Sage remembered, with wide, rocky beaches falling away from the cottages and cabins that still rimmed the lake, all mercifully untouched by the fire. People in gardens, waving, running out onto the rocky shoreline or up onto the highway, as if they'd never seen a plane before. Or as if Sage's little plane represented something hopeful, good news maybe that life beyond the interior of the province was perhaps returning to normal. She waved her wings back at them.

Now came the long climb, pushing the plane up into the mountains to crest Paulson Pass. She took the plane up through the layers of smoke trapped in the valley, up into the shockingly clear, sunny skies, all the more surprising after weeks and weeks of smoldering gray. Josie gasped, squinting her eyes at the brightness. Sage darkened down the windshield a few degrees with several taps of a finger.

She especially loved this part of flying: climbing above the gray, the clouds, the fog, the beaten down mundanity of ant-like life stuck to the planet surface, climbing into endless brightness, and clarity, and hope. *No matter how crappy a day you had on the tarmac of life*, Quinn would say, *up here, darlin', it's all sunshine and roses.*

The fires had been busy in the mountains, undoubtedly helped along by lightening and various human-related factors. In several places, Sage had to carve wide detours up and away from the highway because a massive burn ate up both sides of the road, throwing heavy smoke and ash into the air. The plane was buffeted and bumped by turbulence caused by the fires, even at the distance she was trying to maintain, as the fire created its own wind, its own roaring maelstrom. Carl cried out behind her as the plane pitched and dropped.

"It's okay," she told Carl. "It's just a little windy. We'll be okay."

The cramping was getting worse. And now Sage had to pee again. Momentarily she considered cutting northeast across the Selkirk Mountains, beelining for New Denver, but she knew that would be foolish. If anything happened to the plane and she needed to land she'd want a nice open strip of highway in front of her, not the rocks and trees and near vertical slopes of a mountain range.

Two attempts to escape left Sage frustrated and despairing. Her belly was getting bigger and she had no intention of birthing this child behind a five-meter high fence topped with razor wire. Yet time was running out. After her second attempt, the Guardsmen punished her whole barrack with shit chores for a week. Sage endured a lot of abuse. At one point she thought she might have lost the baby. There had been blood when she peed, but during the night when she felt the baby move again, she wept with relief, the blood probably from the punches to her kidneys.

She wasn't sure why they hadn't just let her go. Maybe there was security in numbers: if all the inmates left, the Guardsmen and their families would be alone in the camp, easier targets for outside interests. Maybe it was simply about maintaining the status quo, holding onto what little power they still had. She couldn't figure it out.

Smoke had hung over the camp most of the summer, the Guardsmen assuring them that it was blowing in from fires in Idaho and Canada, that they had nothing to worry about. The smoke got worse. Then, one week in July there was a lot of lightning—no rain, but the underbelly of the clouds lit up with frenzied slashes and sweeping blankets of whiteness, followed quickly by thunder so loud it seemed apocalyptic.

When word hit the camp that most of Spokane was burning out of control, the Guardsmen started to look especially nervous. Then, when flames swallowed up Booth Hill to the southwest of the camp, panic poured through the barracks. The campers weren't about to be roasted alive, they said to each other, so they gathered *en masse*, demanding to know what was going to be done if the fire—

The riot weapons were brought out. The people were told that everything was under control.

The fire stalked closer. Ash fell from the sky, which glowed an ugly, angry orange at night, and if you climbed up on the roof of the school portable you could see whole subdivisions burning this side of Booth Hill.

Days passed. The Guardsmen asked for volunteers who would be willing to fight the fires closest to the camp, with a clear caveat that anyone who tried to run would be shot, no ifs, ands or buts.

Sage volunteered.

Over the summit, which burned as if it were the entryway into Hell, and down the other side, following the winding road into Castlegar. Delight filled Sage: this was so much faster than walking. In no time at all they'll be flying over New Denver, maybe even landing right on Main Street—if memory served, it would be long enough, but she couldn't recall if the trees hung too far over the road to make a safe land. Well, if that wouldn't work, there was always the arrow-straight chunk of highway through Silverton. She realized then that she was grinning.

As she dropped down over Castlegar, she could see right away that the destruction from the fires had been extensive, and many of the larger buildings still smoldered. Briefly she considered landing at the Castlegar Airport just to climb down onto the tarmac and pee, but decided in the end she could wait. She was so close to home. She followed the highway that paralleled the Kootenay River now, towards Nelson. Fires burned on both the south and north sides of the river. Sage pushed the plane higher to avoid the worst of the smoke and the winds. The closer she got to the junction where she would follow Highway 6 to the north into Slocan Valley, the worse the fires got: bigger, hotter, fresher, as if she were suddenly catching up to the front line of the maelstrom. As she made the turn northward, she drove the plane higher, leaving the highway buried under layers of heavy smoke, and using the familiar ridges that bordered the Slocan Valley to guide her. From this vantage she could see that the whole valley was smothered in smoke. The largest fire appeared to be ten or so kilometers south of where she thought the village of Winlaw lay.

The plane bumped and twisted.

"I don't like that," Carl said.

"Sorry, honey. I'll go a little higher, see if that helps."

"Sage, I gotta go pee," Josie said.

Sage grunted. "You're not the only one. It won't be long, now: we don't have very far to go now."

Sage ran, as best a woman seven months pregnant can run. It was the end of the day. They'd been digging out hotspots, tromping through the woods, shovels over their shoulders, for three twelve-hour days, heading back to camp each night at dusk to eat and wash up and fall onto their cots. Sage had hung back, towards the end of the line of campers heading to the trucks. The Guardsman, *her* Guardsman, the father of the child she carried, was bringing up the rear with another Guardsman, a stocky, perpetually angry woman. Sage stopped to squat, wedging herself between some brush and a tree about ten meters off the trail. She didn't drop her pants.

"Hey!" the female Guardsman called out. "Hurry up!"

"I've got the runs," Sage called back, throwing a bite of irritation into her voice. "Gimme a minute, will you?"

The woman grunted and turned away.

He was listening as his co-worker chatted at him, but he watched Sage over her shoulder as she squatted behind the brush. He caught her eye.

Sage gritted her teeth. *He knows*, she thought, frustration cutting through her.

Then he turned his back on her.

She ran. Back towards the fire, twisting through the trees, smoke choking her, until the air grew hot and dense and flames sprouted out of the ground around her. She stopped, then, to look back, hands on her hips, chest heaving. Over the crackling of the fire she could hear shouting. She turned and ran again, hands supporting her belly. Gunfire cracked through the air, but it was in the wrong direction, far off to one side, east of her. She headed deeper into the fire, all the while angling west, away from the trucks, away from the camp, away from everything that had happened to her over the past four years.

She ran until she threw up, splattering the remnants of her sack lunch on the charred duff, then she wiped her mouth with the back of her hand and started running again. She'd trained for this run, this race, since Maddie's death, pounding a narrow rut into the soil along the inside of the perimeter fence at the FEMA camp.

Following the edge of the fire, she found a dirt road that took her past several burned out farms, then into what was left of a small spread-out town, with its gutted stores, smoldering vehicles, crumbling foundations where family homes used to stand. Her destination was north—north-northeast really—but it would behoove her to lose herself in the burned out sections of the countryside, even if it took her off her course. Less chance of predators, especially the human kind, even though it meant less chance of food and decent shelter, too. After escaping the episodic savagery of life in the FEMA camp, Sage had no desire to experience more of the same now that she was free.

Free.

She didn't feel free, however. Mind you, she didn't feel trapped anymore either. Exposed, vulnerable, terrified, but not trapped. Exhilarated, though. Definitely exhilarated.

It was getting prematurely dark, the pall of smoke scrubbing out the last of the weak orange daylight. She was hungry and thirsty, and feeling sick to her stomach from the cloying stench of the smoke and ash. She needed shelter for the night: no point running around in the dark and twisting an ankle or getting impaled by a pointy branch. But she was hard pressed not to keep running. She wanted so badly to put as much distance between her and the camp as was humanly possible, in case they bothered to come looking for her.

They won't, she told herself.

And she imagined *him*, her Guardsman, putting up some kind of mock chase, shooting wildly into the woods, telling the others he thinks he might have wounded her but didn't want to waste any more time, especially with night on the way and the others needing to get back to camp. Besides, she imagined him telling his chubby counterpart, how would she survive anyway, what with being pregnant and the fires and all those gangs out there?

Aye, there's the rub.

Sage hugged the Skylane as close to the mountains as she felt was safe. As the tree-topped Selkirks morphed into the mighty Valhallas, with their stark glaciers and raw rocky peaks, she knew Slocan Lake was underneath the shroud of smoke at the foot of those mountains. And halfway up the lake would be New Denver.

Above the smoke, hugging the peaks, clouds roiled, as thick and dark as the mountains. Lightning snapped.

She eased the plane out into the center of the valley, away from the storm, wishing the Skylane had one of those topographic programs that the new Cessnas came with to show her the lay of the land below the smoke. And without even basic e-scroll maps she'd have to rely on her memory as she began her descent.

"It might get a bit rough again," she warned the children.

"I have to go pee bad," Josie said.

The plane pitched and dropped. Visibility vanished in the smoke. Lightning arced against the mountains. Sage lightened the windshield again, but it didn't help. Then suddenly they were through the worst of the smoke, maybe only thirty meters off the water. All she saw on the eastern shore across the lake from the Valhallas were flames, roaring and raging, the whole mountainside an inferno, bits of blacktop highway here and there shining through the fire.

Sage tried to orient herself on the lake. Was she too far north? Had she already passed Silverton and New Denver? Or were they ahead, protected from the clutches of this fire by a wide, tidy firebreak? She willed the plane to go faster.

There.

Sage's heart fell like a stone, and for a moment she thought she might be sick. New Denver and Silverton, both, were smoldering ruins, the fire having spread out and away from the towns like a bomb blast.

"That's not it, is it?" Carl asked. "That's not where we're going, right?"

CHAPTER 28

Ronnie woke with a start as the bottom of the boat scraped gravel. Caleb whimpered in his sleep, burying his face deeper into the jacket she wore. She'd dreamed of fire, of it chasing her like a raging giant, trying to strike her down for the evil thing she'd done, hurling exploding flame at her as she ran, a fire-giant whose face swirled and changed and she gasped in recognition at each new face.

She shook herself awake, blinking her one good eye at the dull daylight, but couldn't remember whose faces the fire-giant had worn. Kratky's, she assumed, the old man chasing her down for butchering his son. But that didn't feel right. It had never been his face. She struggled to her feet, shifting Caleb to her other hip. Every muscle screeched at her: she could barely pull herself upright. Now that she was safe and the running was over and the adrenalin and endorphins had leached away, her body had started to seize up. Her eye was swollen shut and her broken nose throbbed.

But her headache was gone.

Matt was slumped on the bottom of the boat in his firefighting gear, asleep. Darcy was still at the wheel, taking up the rear of the rag-tag flotilla floating downriver. Caleb was awake now, rubbing his nose with the back of his hand, and whimpering. He laid his head on her shoulder. She rubbed his back.

The patrol boat putted alongside a long aluminum row-boat, which Nathan was handling. Thea Hlookoff lay across one of the bench seats with her head in her mother's lap. On the other bench seat was that Yuri guy, who had been shot the day before. He laid there, eyes closed, with his head on a life jacket and his boots propped up on the gunnels. Lindsey, the vet, slept with her shoulder nestled into a soot-smeared backpack.

"Hey," Yuri said to her, shielding his eyes with a thick hand.

"Hey yourself," she said back.

"Looks like you've got a friend for life," he added, nodding at Caleb.

"Looks that way," she said. "How're you doing?"

"Getting better every minute," he said. "Thanks for asking, Officer."

Ronnie winced. She'd arrested Yuri after he'd killed that kid, driving drunk.

The boat scraped gravel again, stuck momentarily, then drifted free. Matt woke and struggled to his feet while shedding his turnout coat. He squinted. "Where are we?"

Ronnie glanced over her shoulder at his familiar face: several days' growth of beard, green eyes, dark hair stuck to the sides of his head. The tenderness she'd felt earlier, when he'd run out to her on the beach, amplified.

Matt put a hand on her hip, nuzzled into her neck, brushing his cracked lips on the skin there. He ruffled Caleb's hair.

For too long all she'd had was her anger, decked out in the accessories of resentment and self-righteousness and bitterness. She didn't know what to feel now. Tenderness swelled, grew, pulsed with life. She didn't understand what the demon had done to her heart. Ripped it open, for good and bad.

Maybe killing, Ronnie thought, *and being killed, is simply a normal part of the human experience, arbitrary stops on the continuum of what could be. Chimpanzees killed other chimpanzees whom they thought might be a threat to their territory, their family—hunted them down and slaughtered them, beating them into oblivion with rocks and sticks and fists. Chimpanzees intermingled with baboons, young chimps playing with young baboons, then suddenly a chimpanzee grabs an infant baboon, slams it's head against the ground despite the protestations of the mother, and climbs up a tree to eat it for lunch. Humans have engaged in killing for all of known history, perhaps as much as, or even more than, not-killing: war, genocide, fratricide , homicide, infanticide, patricide, matricide, euthanasia, abortion, ethnic cleansing, capital punishment . . .*

She leaned into Matt.

Why is some killing wrong and other killing not? Why is killing abhorrent to some, but a pleasure to others? Why is killing a pet dog considered socially depraved, while killing and eating a cow is not?

Maybe humans, as a species, are not meant to be moral creatures. Ronnie considered that for a moment. *Maybe humans are too confused by life's choices. Vice is as rampant as virtue, if not more so, at least it looks like that in her line of work. Everyone has done something to someone they regret, are ashamed of, wish they hadn't done. Everyone has a dirty little secret. Mores are just rules brainwashed into a population by the powers that be so that they no longer look like rules but like right and wrong instead.*

What are you, then, she wondered, *if you do what everyone else abhors, and you enjoy doing it? Are you a monster, or simply a person for whom the powers that hold sway in other people's hearts hold no sway in your own?* If Ronnie remembered correctly, the God of the Bible was quite a killer. *Maybe, then, to kill is really what it means to be made in the image of God.*

It was late afternoon when the first of the boats beached on the rocky shore next to Winlaw Bridge and the occupants stumbled up the bank, stiff and bone-tired.

Ronnie thought she heard the tinny growl of a small airplane motor, high above the smoke. She tilted her head back. Looking up into all that bone-colored gloom, though, made her dizzy.

Everyone moved around Ronnie, dreamlike, landing the boats, getting onto shore. No one seemed to take notice of the sound of the airplane.

Maybe she had imagined it. She stumbled after them, her body clumsy and leaden, Caleb still clinging to her neck, while she watched herself dispassionately, as if from above, maybe from the airplane she'd heard. Matt fussed over her.

She plodded across the road and over the baked soccer field to the elementary school with the rest of them, barely able to carry Caleb, her arms were so tired. People rushed out of the school. There was shouting and hugging and tears.

Ronnie was led inside the school. People talked at her, their voices buzzing, a layer of white noise. She had no idea what they were saying. Someone tried to draw Caleb out of her arms. He refused. She bathed him herself, at a low steel sink in a classroom, cool water splashing on the carpet as he stood in the sink, shivering ever so slightly, the thick fur on his bone-thin body bleeding dirt and soot down the drain. She toweled him dry as best as she could, then, when someone suddenly appeared with bowls of food. She sat on the floor, her back against a wall, and watched him shovel boiled potatoes in his mouth with his fingers and crunch on raw carrots.

After Caleb had eaten he crawled up onto Ronnie's lap like an oversized kitten and went to sleep.

The room was filled with the mingled stench of cooked food, dirty bodies, and bleach. Ronnie simply sat there, her back against the wall, with Caleb's warm body smelling of soap and damp hair nestled against her belly. People were eating, bathing various children and themselves, talking to each other, having their injuries attended to by clean, brightly scrubbed strangers. Ronnie had never been this tired before.

Next to one of the three beds in the room sat a man with a stained black baseball cap and thick glasses that bumped up against his brow ridge. He looked like an older, heavier version of Yuri Evdikimoff. Ronnie realized then that the man was Mickey, Yuri's brother, the fire chief who owned the garage in Winlaw. He didn't look well: his skin was pale with a grayish tone to it, almost smoke-colored.

A woman crouched beside her. Ronnie tipped her face up and let it be cleaned, wincing as the dried blood was peeled away, the wound freshened and stitched shut. The woman injected something into her upper arm. There was more pain as her split ear was cleaned. The woman excused herself, returned with clean cloths, a razor. She shaved a clump of hair from the back of Ronnie's scalp, then scrubbed and stitched.

"You're not hurt anywhere else?"

Ronnie shook her head.

"Hold still. Use your words."

"No." Ronnie said. "I'm not hurt anywhere else."

When she had finished stitching the laceration at the back of Ronnie's head, she straightened Ronnie's broken nose, pain exploding fireworks between her eyes.

Someone touched Ronnie's shoulder, startling her awake. Caleb squirmed a little. It was Matt, crouching beside her and looking freshly scrubbed and shaved. "How are you doing, honey?"

She worked up a smile for him.

"Sorry I woke you. I'm going out with a crew right now. Just wanted you to know. Fire chief wants to do a backburn to try to block the fire coming down from Silverton, and needs extra hands. They've backburned the fire to the south and it's doing well, but just about everybody who's available is tied up down there."

"It's okay," she managed. "You don't have to explain."

He ran his tongue over his cracked lip, nodded once. "Okay. See you later." He bent over, kissed her on the mouth. She kissed him back, that comforting sensation of wanting him rising like Christ from the dead.

He pushed to his feet and was gone.

She should get up and wash herself, she thought. She knew she stank: she could smell the sweat and smoke and blood. Besides, her scalp itched maddeningly. A screeching hot bath in a big tub with water jets, that's what she had in mind as she struggled stiffly to her feet, although she assumed a sponge bath at a classroom sink was all she was going to achieve. Caleb clung to her like Velcro.

She sought out the woman who had stitched her cuts, and was directed to the teachers' staff room where there were showers, but probably a line-up to use them, she was warned, and she could count on there not being any hot water left—the solars can't keep up—and, by the way, don't get those stitches wet.

Alex Gauthier stepped through one of the doorways just as Ronnie was about to leave—the paramedic whose brains she had come so very close to blowing all over the side of the truck—with a young woman, quite devolved, under tow. Her right hand was bandaged and she walked with a strange limp, as if the left side of her body wasn't cooperating with the right side. He didn't seem to recognize Ronnie, perhaps too intent on getting the young woman attended to, or perhaps because the swelling to Ronnie's face, and her lack of uniform, made her unrecognizable. Just another human casualty.

She wriggled Caleb over onto her other hip and headed down the school hall. *Time is the true God*, Ronnie mused, the thought lancing through her fatigue-fugued mind like a bullet. *Of all the forces in the universe, Time alone kills with utter certainty.*

Caleb bawled at first when she wouldn't let him in the shower with her. The moment he heard the water explode from the showerhead and pummel the acrylic floor, though, he backed away to huddle in a corner, tears streaking his face. There had been no line-up. She'd carried Caleb through the staff room, nodding at people she knew, their faces scarred and grief-burdened.

She dried herself with somebody's wet bath towel, steering clear of the stitches in the back of her head, which she hadn't been particularly successful, or vigilant, in keeping dry. Bruises had flowered over much of her upper body, an ugly cottage-garden of green and yellow and purple. Her legs fared only somewhat better. Her hands bled fresh blood from the thin lines of glass-cuts that criss-crossed like Clematis vines. She tied the towel over her breasts, crouched while Caleb clambered up onto her back, scrawny arms tight around her throat, and went in search of fresh clothes.

The staff room was strangely empty.

Out in the hallway, back down near the classroom where she'd washed Caleb earlier, was where she heard her name being called. It was *his* voice, Kratky's, calling to her to come out, come out and play. The sneer was unmistakable.

Caleb began to shake, and Ronnie could feel hot urine seep through the towel against her back. *You poor kid*, she thought.

He had hostages, Kratky announced, and she had one minute to appear or he'd kill the first one.

She swung Caleb to the floor, found him a cupboard to hide in, and for the first time he let go of her willingly.

A feeling sparked in her. She thought at first it might be fear. She reached for it. It wasn't fear. Or anger, her old friend. Aha. There it was. *Anticipation:* the shivering pleasure of good things to come.

CHAPTER 29

Sage couldn't believe it.

She circled the plane over the twin towns, stunned at the sight below, the smoldering ruins, deserted streets, vehicles littered like corpses. She gunned the plane north. *Maybe they'd evacuated to Nakusp before the fire hit the town*, she thought, afraid to weight the words with too much hope.

The cramps were getting worse. And she was feeling nauseous.

She flew to the north end of the lake then wrestled the plane up and over the fire that sprawled and meandered all the way to Summit Lake. Lightning cracked, and wind pounded the tiny airplane. Thunder rumbled over the whine of the motor. From there to Nakusp was nothing but charred landscape. Sage's hope perished as Arrow Lake came into view: Nakusp looked the sad sister of New Denver and Silverton, burned out, cold, a wasteland.

"Is this it?" Carl asked, disappointment evident in his voice.

"No, honey, New Denver was back there. This is Nakusp."

"Oh."

As she banked over the town a second time, her water broke, gushing warm liquid through her trousers and into the seat. "Dammit, dammit, dammit," she muttered. She looked for a safe stretch of road on which to put down.

"What's that smell?" Josie asked.

She ignored this. "I'm going to land and we'll all go pee and have a snack and then I'll decide what to do." Jovan and Maddie had both been long, horrible births, but Linus had come quickly, as if in a rush. Sage didn't want to be in the air if this baby, like Linus, decided to make a quick getaway from her womb.

Landings were harder than they looked, and the wind roaring in off Arrow Lake wasn't helping her keep the nose aligned. Rain whipped the windshield. In addition, she was trying to land on a road, not a level, smooth, tenderly maintained airport runway. She was coming in a bit fast, so she turned the nose slightly, creating drag. Just above the pavement she straightened her approach. They bounced once, then touched again, solidly. Sage hit the flaps.

She worked up a smile for Josie as she taxied to an intersection and turned the plane around, ready for a quick take-off if needed. Disappointment flushed through her like a bad fever. "Stay close," she admonished. "And keep a sharp lookout."

Josie gave a single nod.

"What about Isaac?" Carl asked. "He probably has to pee, too."

"Too bad. He'll have to pee where he's sitting."

"Boy," Carl said, "I sure hope he doesn't poo. That'd really stink things up in here."

Sage couldn't help but laugh as she heaved herself out of the plane and helped the older kids to climb down. They dashed off to the side of the road. Rain, something she hadn't felt in months, lashed at her skin and clothes. She checked on Ula, who was still quite hot to the touch. "What am I going to do?" she muttered to Ula and Isaac. Isaac hooted his annoyance at her, fiddled with the tape on the buckles of his harness.

She climbed down, surveyed where she'd landed on the wide truck route that bypassed Nakusp proper, and, satisfied that she hadn't seen any untoward movement, found herself a half-burned fencepost she could hold onto and squatted as best she could to pee. Cold rain dribbled down her neck.

They couldn't stay here. She had to get back into the airplane. If something happened during delivery, she couldn't leave these kids in this wasteland all alone to fend for themselves. It wouldn't be fair.

This baby was on its way, almost four weeks early, whether she was ready for it or not.

Sage walked from first light until dark through the burned-out forest along the roadside, stopping only to scavenge for food and useful artifacts. She wasted several hours her third day of freedom hiding inside a skinny culvert littered with glass and dirt and animal turds after she almost stumbled through a camp inhabited by a gang of devolving youths. Then she had to sneak away into the dark, spending a sleepless night huddled up in the skeleton branches of an oak tree.

She tried to be more careful after that. But as the days and kilometers blurred one into the other, she knew she wasn't getting enough to eat. Or even enough water. It was hunger, and the fear that she might be undernourishing the baby she carried, that motivated her to steal food from the second camp she came across. She waited a whole day, fighting her hunger, planning her timing, scouting out her access and egress points, ensuring she knew how many members the pack maintained and when they were in and out of camp. She should have waited a second day, but her hunger won out.

Her late-night theft was successful, her stealth sure, but she was greedy and took too much. She had thought herself safely gone, four hours steady walk, when she stopped. She'd eaten as she walked, a mistake she realized when a few hours later from the vantage of rise in the landscape she caught sight of the pack, seven strong, only four or five kilometers back and coming on hard.

She quickly sorted through the two bags of food. Tried to talk herself into parting with half, but hedged her bets on only a third of the contents, and threw the smaller bag down the trail behind her, watching its contents scatter like fallen treasure in the underbrush. Maybe it would be enough of a find to make them give up chase.

She used every trick she could remember from every movie she'd ever seen to try to lose them. She ran on the open pavement to hide her scent, for she was sure scent was partly how they'd trailed her, scurrying undercover when the exposure became too much to bear.

She darted across the road, through a burned-out farmyard, charred animal corpses bloating under fallen timbers in what was once a barn. She couldn't keep running. They had chased her the whole day. She had nothing left to give. She hadn't had enough food or water or sleep for days on end, and her back was killing her from running for too long with all this weight up front in her belly. She feared she was going to have to, at the worst, make a stand, or at the best, find somewhere to hide and hope they didn't find her.

Some choice, she thought with a grunt of panicked frustration as she studied the remnants of the collapsed farmhouse, arms akimbo, hands on her lower back for support, trying to catch her breath.

At the side of the basement foundation lay a pair of metal doors. One of those old coal shoots, or entry to a root cellar. She heaved on one of the doors. It swung upward and open with a screech of metal-on-metal. The stink of death and rotting potatoes mushroomed up the half-dozen concrete steps. In the dim interior Sage could see a man and a woman on the dirt floor, lying as if asleep. But she recognized corpses when she saw them and couldn't believe her good fortune.

They had probably hidden here when the fire went through, unable to run, and either the cellar air had heated up so much they broiled—a theory which, from the lack of damage to the bodies and the environs of the cellar, Sage discarded, although she was no forensics expert—or the fire had simply siphoned off all their oxygen, suffocating them.

After taking the man's pocket knife, and as they were only a few days dead, she hauled them both up the stairs, laid the woman on the door she hadn't opened and sat the man up against the frame in front of the open door. Then she closed it, locking herself up in the almost-dark with an old axe-handle shoved through the door handles as a makeshift lock, tied in place with some baling twine from a hook on the wall in the cellar.

She remained there two terrifying days, in the damp and the stink, heart leaping at every sound, eating the food she'd stolen, wishing she'd stolen a second bottle of Gatorade, and watching the light brighten and then dampen down into night through the gap between the two doors.

When she was sure the pack had given up its search, she rose up out of the root cellar, thanked the bloating couple, and headed north again. She was determined to have this baby in New Denver, in her parents' house if need be, and not here in this burned out wilderness that used to be central Washington.

Sage hurried the kids back into the plane.

"What's the matter?" Carl cried as he scrambled into his seat.

"My water broke," Sage explained as she lined up the nose of the plane and brought up the RPMs for take-off, "which means I'm going to have this baby really soon, and I don't want to have it in the plane."

"Where are we going, then?" Carl asked, frowning, rain dripping off his nose as he buckled himself into the back seat.

Isaac started to cry as Sage drove the plane forward. Ula woke up then, joining him with a miserable wail. The plane left the ground, climbing away from the trees, buffeted by the wind. Sage glanced at the fuel gauge. Slightly over half. They could make it all the way back to Christina Lake, to where the people had run out of their homes to wave at her as she flew over. But first: she retraced her route back to Slocan Lake, then, staying only thirty meters off the lake surface, raced past the remains of New Denver and Silverton, past the inferno eating up the mountainside, to the south end of the lake, to follow the Slocan River to the village of Winlaw.

If they hadn't gone north, Sage decided, maybe they'd gone south.

Isaac and Ula's crying almost overpowered the roar of the motor.

"Isaac!" Carl shouted. "Be quiet!"

Sage ignored him as she fought to keep the ride as smooth as possible despite the buffeting winds created by the titanic clash between the fire and the storm. She had outrun the rain, at least.

There: the mouth of the Slocan River, gaping lazily, and the village of

Slocan looking its usual abandoned self, its mill torched by eco-terrorists a decade before.

"Aren't we kinda low?" Carl asked.

"I want to stay underneath the thickest smoke, so we can see what's on the ground."

"Why?"

"I'm looking for people."

"Why? We don't need people."

"I might need help having this baby."

"I can help," Josie said.

"I will definitely use your help when the time comes, people or no people," Sage affirmed. She grimaced as a cramp tightened in her belly.

She swooped the plane through the curves of the river, flying over empty homes, abandoned farmsteads.

Ula had cried herself back to sleep. Isaac simply whimpered and sniveled, fists over his ears, eyes clamped shut.

"See that bridge up there?" Sage asked, pointing, but then shook her head at herself: Josie couldn't see over the control panel, and Carl was in the back seat. "Well, anyway, that's Winlaw Bridge."

The Skylane shot over the bridge and banked left.

"I see people!" Josie called out, her face pressed against the window.

A crowd had gathered in the parking lot of the elementary school. Sage let out a whoop, a heady gust of relief blowing through her, and buzzed the crowd, waggling her wings at them. She shot the Skylane south, heading for Lebahdo Flats. Her heart was pounding.

"We're leaving?" Josie was incredulous.

"No, honey, I just need a long strip of straight highway to land on, like in Nakusp, then I'll drive the airplane up the road and park it in the school parking lot right in front of all those people! How does that sound?"

"Yeah!" Carl said.

Well, she thought, Winlaw was the closest place to home she was going to find where there were still people. She felt like a comet knocked slightly off course, about to plunge into the sun, not into destruction but into a fiery hope: maybe her parents would be here, evacuated from New Denver, they themselves still hoping beyond hope for her return.

Sage grunted as another labor pain gripped her abdomen.

CHAPTER 30

Alex hugged Gemma against him with one arm as they stood outside in the school parking lot. He couldn't see Irene, she must be at the back of the crowd. The smoke irritated his eyes.

Men with guns had pounded into the school while Alex was hugging Irene hello. June had just unwrapped Gemma's hand to look at the puncture wound, which bled stigmata-like. There was shouting and shoving and then they were herded outside where an older man waited beside several trucks with a shotgun pressed against the jaw of one of the firefighters from New Denver, who looked to Alex like Ronnie Sapriken's husband. There were two other hostages, hands duct-taped behind their backs, another strip of tape over their mouths, guarded by a small greasy-looking man in his twenties. One was Nathan, his eyes wide with terror; the other was Darcy Khaira, who stared at the ground as if willing it to open up and swallow his captors.

Alex's own heart pounded with terror. Gemma clutched her bleeding hand against her chest and leaned into him. On Alex's other side, Mickey stood holding Yuri, who half-crouched, splinting his side with a crooked arm. Mickey himself was pale, Alex noted, and quite diaphoretic, his face twisted, not in fear but in pain.

Alex tried not to make eye contact with any of the armed men. They had told them that if anybody ran, or did anything else they didn't like, they'd shoot them down like dogs.

The leader wanted Ronnie Sapriken, shouting at the school building for her with a meanness and a violence in his voice that made Alex shudder. Ronnie's husband looked wild with terror, and was apt, Alex sensed, to do something stupid and heroic, and it would most certainly all go to shit from there.

The one minute the older man had given Ronnie to appear stretched painfully like skin over a swelling joint. Several people wept into the silence. Kids bawled. For a second Alex thought he could hear an airplane motor again.

"Maybe she didn't hear you," Yuri Evdikimoff said with a grunt.

"Shut the fuck up," the older man told him. "She'll definitely hear her beloved husband getting his head blown off. Then she'll come."

"What do you want her for anyway?" Yuri said.

"Be quiet! What are you doing?" Mickey hissed at him through clenched teeth.

"Listen to the man, dirtbag, or I'll kill you first."

A door opened, whacking back against a doorstop screwed into the concrete. Alex could feel fear hemorrhage through the crowd, which sliced itself apart to let Ronnie Sapriken through.

Her hands were bandaged and she wore a plaid jacket, buttoned up, her torn RCMP uniform pants, dirty and bloodstained, and work boots that looked too big for her feet. She walked straight at the leader, arms at her sides, until he threatened to kill her husband if she didn't stop where he told her to.

She stopped.

"Corporal Sapriken," he said with a nod, his eyes roiling black.

It took all Alex's willpower to keep his fear from moving his feet so that he could get Gemma out of here, get her somewhere safe.

"Mr. Kratky," she replied, "to what do I owe this honor?"

"Honor? Are you mad?" he said with a sneer.

She nodded ever so slightly. "Perhaps."

Alex was certain he could hear an airplane motor from upriver, to the north.

"Let all these people go, and you can have me," she said.

He shook his head. "You took *my* people, Corporal," he said, "so now your people are mine. Did you know, Matthew," he said to Ronnie's husband, his tone mocking and volatile, "that your lovely wife here murdered my son, cut him open like a hog, ripped out his innards, then carved out his eyes and hacked off his . . . member? And, as if that weren't enough of a horror, she set my home on fire, with me and my family inside. My dear wife and my youngest, darling daughter did not escape. She was three years old." He choked on his words, then. "And my dear friend here—" he nodded at the little man guarding Nathan and Darcy "—lost three of his children when she set fire to his home. He was forced to watch one of them die in his arms, burned so badly there was no chance of survival."

Ronnie Sapriken said nothing.

"Do you *know* your wife?" he continue, although his eyes never left Ronnie Sapriken's face. "Do you know what kind of a monster she is? You should. You're her husband, the man of the house, and it is your duty to *know* your wife. And to control her. But you failed, Matthew. And such failure must be punished."

A single heartbeat, then an explosion, and half of Matt Sapriken's face vanished. Blood and brain and bone splattered people on the edge of the crowd, who cringed and screamed and began to run.

Kratky let Matt's body crumple to the pavement.

Alex was stunned and deafened by the blast. He pulled Gemma hard against him, half-turning, instinctively shielding her. He saw it before he heard it then, the small airplane, shooting over the Winlaw Bridge only twenty or thirty meters off the ground, well below the ceiling of forest-fire smoke. The plane buzzed the crowd, waggling its wings, then shot south toward Lebahdo Flats.

Ronnie Sapriken moved.

Another explosion. Shots cracked through the air, people screamed and ran, bolting like rabbits flushed by dogs. Gemma sagged beside him, hauling Alex to the pavement with her weight. Blood bubbled from a hole in the side of her T-shirt half a hand-span above her right hip.

"Gemma!"

Someone fell over him, scrambling to get away.

CHAPTER 31

Ronnie knew from Kratky's voice when he called out to her that people would die. Vengeance has a hungry sound to it, like teeth on bone, and Ronnie's death alone wouldn't satisfy him, no matter how painful he might make it.

She quickly wrapped up her bleeding hands so they wouldn't be slippery with fresh blood, wrenched a thick metal shelf from the cupboard she'd hidden Caleb in and taped it over her torso as body armor. Then she dressed in the clothes she'd arrived in: heavy plaid jacket over the metal shelf, uniform pants, and dead Davy Kratky's boots. She took a scalpel out of a tray of liquid disinfectant sitting on a shelf with other surgical tools at the back of the classroom.

Outside the hot August air bled fear. Most of the crowd had their backs to her, while Kratky and his three neanderthals faced her direction. She saw Matt, then, duct tape over his mouth, hands behind his back, probably taped, and Kratky holding a twelve-gauge shotgun at his throat.

She avoided Matt's eyes.

Kratky's eyes, though, she sought. Bright as crushed glass they talked to her, telling her how much blood she was going to have to pay for what she'd done to him.

Ronnie had planned to skirt the edge of the crowd, not wanting to end up with a curtain of flesh behind her, but the crowd parted, forming a funnel of space that sucked her like a vortex toward Kratky.

She glimpsed a nanosecond of recognition in his eyes when he saw the boots she wore.

They exchanged words. He taunted Matt.

Behind Kratky, a small airplane darted from behind a bend in the river just beyond the bridge. Maybe it was the sudden epiphany of the airplane; maybe she'd misjudged Kratky's desire to inflict emotional pain on her; maybe she'd simply lost focus for a second, monkey mind playing tricks. The side of Matt's head evaporated, and Ronnie was shocked into immobility, cast outside of time.

The airplane flew overhead in utter silence, dipping its wings in a cartoonish greeting, then vanishing. Not even a whisper of a sound.

Then Ronnie found herself back in time, sound roaring in around her like a furnace. With a howl of rage, she lunged, the scalpel slipping easily between Kratky's fifth and sixth ribs. She twisted, feeling the blade slice through the tougher muscle of his heart. Exhilaration roared through her like a clean wind.

As Kratky fell, already dead, Ronnie wrenched the shotgun from his fingers and shot the closest neanderthal, blowing a hole in his belly the size of a soccer ball. She pumped Kratky's shotgun as she spun to locate her next target.

A shotgun blast slammed her in the chest, knocking her off her feet. It was Kratky's 'dear friend' who had shot her, and as he stepped toward her to finish her off, she shot the surprised look off his face.

Ronnie wrestled to her feet, trying to catch her breath, her chest burning with pain. She could see from where she stood, half crouching, that the fourth and final member of Kratky's party was being beaten senseless with the stock of his own hunting rifle. She crawled over to Matt, then backed away, wishing she hadn't looked, the image of him on the ground with half his head missing now branded on her mind.

Five other people lay injured or dying on the pavement. The young woman Alex Gauthier had brought into the school with the taped hand;

Mickey Evdikimoff; some fellow from Winlaw Ronnie didn't recognize had been shot in the leg; a little girl from Kratky's farm, the one Sachi had carried, was crying and covered in blood with a gunshot wound in her belly; and, finally, at the back of the crowd, Polly Sherstibitoff, one of the Dragon Ladies from New Denver, objecting loudly, saying that it was nothing, go help the others who really needed help.

All this pain and death was her doing, if not directly, most certainly indirectly. She stumbled toward the school, ripping open the shreds of her jacket and pulling off the metal shelf-cum-armor. Pinpricks of blood leached from her skin where several of the pellets had punched the metal into her flesh. The shelf clattered on the pavement.

She could feel the corrosive burning of remorse swirling in her chest, and she knew, then, the pleasure she felt slicing Kratky's heart open would soon be buried under an avalanche of loss and regret and guilt.

She had intended to leave Caleb behind, to walk to the highway that poured through the center of Winlaw, and start running south, hitting her easy stride, waiting for the endorphins to blunt the leading edge of whatever figurative instrument of psychological torture was hovering outside her heart. She'd follow the backburn until it met the fire, then out through the dead zone into the abyss of the world. There seemed to be no point in dragging Caleb along just so that he could become one more statistic on her list of collateral damage. But he squeezed out through the school door, naked and bawling, head snapping this way and that, until his eyes locked onto her and he came at her like a missile. She held his squirming body while she knelt in front of the school. He buried his face in her neck and she began to weep, great sobs lurching from her chest.

After a moment she convinced him to scoot around to her back, his arms at her throat, legs gripping her waist, and she headed for the highway, where she began to run, holding him with her arms behind her so he wouldn't bounce too much.

She ran past an airplane driving up the highway into Winlaw, piloted by a familiar looking woman, partially devolved. Kids' faces were plastered against the windows. They waved at her. She waved back but kept running.

Her whole life was an afterMatt now. *Careful what you wish for*, she told herself bitterly. She steered her thoughts away from Matt, from the surprising tenderness that had been raised from her dead heart, and from the shocking end of him, lifeless and mutilated, crumpled on the pavement like an unwanted—

Her fault. All her fault.

Despite the oversized boots, despite the weight of Caleb on her back, despite the complaints of her beaten-up body, she began to enjoy the easy, familiar fluidity of her pace, the smooth motion of her legs, boots hitting the pavement a comfortable eighty strides a minute.

She ran as she had always run, like an animal.

CHAPTER 32

Alex tore open Gemma's shirt, slapped his hand over the gunshot wound in her side.

Gemma's eyes opened. "It hurts, Dad," she said.

"You stay with me, missy," he said to her.

Someone appeared opposite him, crouching at Gemma's side. Irene. She raised her head, shouted, "We need help here!" but her voice was eaten up by the screams for help around them.

Gemma's mouth twisted with pain. "I didn't want it to be like this," she said.

Lindsey appeared beside Irene, kneeling. "Let's get her inside the school, Alex," she said, reaching underneath Gemma's back, roving her hands over her chest and side. "No exit wound," she said. Helping hands reached for Gemma's arms and legs, raising her off the pavement, carrying her through the chaotic crowd, into the school. Alex scrabbled to keep up, his hand sealed over the hole in Gemma's side, keeping her life inside her. Someone cradled her head.

In through the double doors, down the hallway.

They laid her on a table in the hospital room near the windows—Lindsey said the light was better there. She was listening to Gemma's chest with a stethoscope; Irene was getting a blood pressure; June pulled Alex's hand away, taped a dressing over the wound, and prepped to start an IV.

Gemma's chest heaved up and down with each breath. "Dad?" she said, reaching out her hand.

Alex shoved his way to her side.

A shudder of pain rippled through Gemma's body.

"No," Alex said, shaking his head. He reached in front of June and ripped the dressing off the wound, which burbled thick, dark blood.

Irene slapped her hand over the wound. Alex pushed her hand away.

"Hey, Irene," Gemma said. She smiled, then coughed and winged.

"Don't be scared, girl." Sudden tears streamed down Irene's face. "What are you doing, Alex?" she whispered through gritted teeth.

Lindsey scowled at him.

Irene reached up and stroked Gemma's hair.

Alex climbed up onto the table and lay with his daughter, his fingers stroking her cheek, feeling her breath on the palm of his hand. She lay on her back, her eyes open, as if staring through the ceiling, staring up into the sky, as if looking for meteors burning through the atmosphere. Alex's heart clenched with pain as he talked to her, whispering in her ear. "I'm here, missy. Try not to be afraid. I know you're not ready; I'm not ready. Lindsey could work on you. She's a veterinary surgeon, you know—that's funny, isn't it? She saved Yuri." He swallowed. "But then it would just be a matter of time, wouldn't it? You and me, just waiting it out." He rubbed his lips against her cheek. "I don't want to let you go, missy. You are my world. Don't be scared. I'm here."

"Alex." It was Irene. "Don't do this. At least let Lindsey try."

He shook his head without taking his eyes off Gemma.

He watched her chest rise and fall, rise and fall, until her breath no longer tickled the palm of his hand and her chest was finally still.

CHAPTER 33

He was numb, as if his heart were now a stone thing, fossilized by the last breaths his daughter took.He scuffled off the table and out of the way, Irene holding him up.

They laid the dead in an empty classroom so that family and friends might sit with them for a while, and to make room so that they could work on the injured. Tomorrow the bodies would be cleaned and dressed and buried. He sent Irene away, so that she might help with the wounded, and because he wanted to be alone with his daughter.

Alex sat on the floor with Gemma's head in his lap while her body slowly cooled, muscle and skin sagging as if already reaching for the earth. He stroked her hollowing cheeks, traced his finger along the line of her heavy brow ridge, down the bridge of her flat nose.

The room grew dim. Shadows moved about, ghost-like, lighting candles. People sprang into the light like epiphanies.

Yuri sat on a chair meant for a child, his brother's limp hand clenched in his. "He had a heart attack," Yuri said, wretchedness scarring his voice. "They said he was probably dead before he hit the ground, so I don't know if he heard me. I wanted him to know I forgave him, but I waited too long."

Alex swallowed, cleared his throat.

"I told him I'd never forgive him for sending me to jail, for calling that

Sapriken woman and telling her it was me who'd killed the boy. I told him I'd never forgive him, but I did. I forgave him a long time ago. I just never told him."

"He heard you," Alex said, his throat dry and clenched. "He would have heard you." He cleared his throat again.

Yuri's body trembled, his chest heaved. Sobs leapt from him as he pulled Mickey's hand to his mouth and kissed it.

"She asked me to kill her," Alex said, the words tumbling out of his mouth like a rockslide.

"What?" Yuri stared at him.

"She asked me to kill her when she wasn't human anymore."

Yuri shook his head. "*They* killed her, not you," he said.

"I told her I would do it for her. I promised." Alex couldn't keep the words inside him anymore. With all that grief, there was no room. He could no longer hold onto them: they spilled out of him, fell out, arcing away, bright stones of pain and release. "I let her die. Lindsey could have saved her, but I said, No. I let her die."

Yuri nodded, just a little, as if he understood.

It's over, Alex thought. *Everything she was afraid of becoming; everything I was afraid of having to do. It's all over.*

The candles burned lower. Alex slid himself out from under Gemma's head, his own body stiff and cold. He gently lowered her head to the carpet, kissed her cold forehead, then covered her up to her chin with a blanket someone had left for him, tucking it in around her as if she were eight years old and he was wishing her a goodnight.

He struggled to his feet. People avoided him in the hallway, as if the death he'd suffered was contagious. But before he made it to the door that would let him out into the night, someone took his arm, steered him around to the teachers' staff room.

"You need to eat," she said to him, her voice accented with that familiar Doukhobour Russian chop to it. He looked at her, suddenly seeing her, an older woman he didn't recognize, short and round with thinning hair, probably from New Denver. She had a bandage on her left hand with a space where her ring finger used to be. She saw him look at her hand as she filled him a plate from a central table bearing dishes of food, jugs of wine and cider, bowls of apples. "I lost a finger. They shot off my wedding ring. Nobody can find it. It is nothing. He's been dead twenty years. It was time the ring came off." She carried a plate over to the coffee table in front of the chair where he sat. "But you lost a daughter. That is something. Irene, the ambulance lady, she found her daughter, she came to her in an airplane. That, too, is something. And, her daughter, she is having a baby."

Alex stared up at her, not really understanding, the numbness like dense smoke swirling in his mind.

She retrieved cutlery for him, then poured him a tumbler of red wine. "Eat. Drink." She sat in the soft chair at a right angle to him as if to ensure he did as he was told. "It will be a while before the baby is born."

"Irene's daughter? Sage?"

The woman nodded. "She brought with her four children. Four! The littlest, she is sick, poor thing, attacked by a dog. She has a fever, but that woman, June—she's a nurse, you know, I went to school with her older brother—June says that the antibiotics she's giving her, they'll do the trick."

As she talked on, Alex stared at the plate in front of him, mashed potatoes with gravy, cooked green and yellow beans, sliced raw carrots, slabs of pale venison half drowned in more gravy. Dill pickles. His brain felt leaden. It couldn't keep up with what she was telling him.

"Sage?" he repeated.

She leaned over and pushed the plate closer to him. "Eat. You'll feel better."

Alex found Coyote wandering around outside the school. Seeing her there, without Gemma beside her, made him weep. He crawled into the little commuter car he and Marika had taken from Enterprise Creek, and convinced Coyote to jump into the passenger seat. He drove it home, up the steep driveway to his dark house. He dreaded going inside, but he couldn't stay at the school, there were too many people, too much talk, too much grief. He needed to be alone.

After letting himself inside, he groped his way around until he found the kitchen table and the candle and matches that always sat there. The inside of the house radiated Gemma-ness. His breath came in short, hard jerks. He hobbled around, lighting more candles, and collected his pack and sleeping bag and thermarest, his notebook and pen, a headlamp that still worked, then blew out the candles and almost ran out into the darkness as if escaping some lurking terror.

He shouldered his pack, switched on the headlamp, and headed up the trail behind the house, Coyote bounding ahead.

On the very crest of the ridge, at the edge of an old clearcut, Alex found himself above the smoke but below a night sky riddled with light. There was no moon, but the stars threw so much light he turned off the headlamp and continued along the trail until he came to a clearing, a place he and Gemma had hiked to often, that, in daylight, presented a stunning view south down the Slocan Valley. Wind blew from the north; clouds muddied the sky there.

He threw down his pack, rolled out his thermarest to let it inflate, dug out his sleeping bag and his notebook and pen. Coyote wandered about the clearing. The air was cold and hard, sharp with the promise of winter. Alex wriggled into his sleeping bag with his feet pointed northeast, and stared at the sky. Coyote eventually came back and lay with him.

Only two nights ago he had laid on his deck with Gemma to watch the first full night of the Perseids meteor shower. Only two nights ago. And now she was gone, her short life burned up and extinguished.

You are dead, he said to her in his mind because this was the time they'd agreed upon to say what needed to be said, *and I miss you so much already I don't know if I can stand it. I never wanted to let you go; I wanted you in my life forever.*

He scanned the sky. The Perseids usually lasted several days, sending hundreds of meteors to their bright deaths every night. He scratched Coyote's ears and waited.

There! And there!

Alex woke with a three-and-a-half-million year old face staring down at him. He started. The face jumped back, mouth wide in surprise. Alex squinted up at the cloud-packed sky, memory of last night sparking a fire-storm of loss that roared through his chest.

Coyote was barking playfully and jumping about.

The face reappeared, grinning this time. A finger poked his nose.

Alex realized, then, that knew that face.

Darlene scampered backwards, Coyote dancing around her. She stopped beside a thatch of thorny wild rose bushes. Alex rolled onto his side, partly to look at her, and partly to endure better the almost physical pain of loss that candled in his chest.

"Ah-lex," she said, jerking a finger at him.

"Darlene," he answered, pointing back at her.

"Gem-ma?"

His throat clenched so tight he couldn't speak. "Let's go home," he said when he could finally find words.

"Momma?"

"Yes."

"Hung-ree."

He rooted through the pockets on the side of his pack. Pulled out the survival kit he kept there and found two sad-looking energy bars, which he unwrapped. He gave the peanut butter one to Darlene, who snatched it from his fingers as if afraid he'd change his mind; he ate the other one while he pulled his gear together. He stuffed the damp unused notebook in the top of his pack.

"C'mon, Dar. Sage should have had that baby by now. Let's go see if it's a boy or a girl."

"Baby?"

"Uh-huh." He started down the trail, legs stiff and sore from the climb up, from half-carrying Yuri when he got shot, from sitting with Gemma's body late into the night. He didn't look back to see if Darlene followed but after a while he could hear the quiet *tup-tup* of her bare feet on the ground a couple of meters behind him.

He found Irene in the same room in the school where Gemma died. She took his hand in hers, touched his face, and smiled. "She was born about an hour ago," she whispered in his ear as she leaned against him.

The large, open room was crowded with people, talking about how well the backburn was working, about getting on with preparing for winter, about who was going to stay with whom and what houses were abandoned and therefore available for residency, about who was going to build the coffins and how soon they might be ready. Someone announced that it had started to rain. Somebody else asked if anyone had seen Ronnie Sapriken anywhere.

In the far corner of the room Alex recognized the woman from New Denver who had kindly but firmly ensured he'd eaten before escaping last night.

"So what are you going to name it, Sage?" Carl, one of the children Sage had brought with her, asked as he bounced on his elbows against the edge of the bed that sat near a wall in the corner of the room.

Sage, her face pale, dark moons under her eyes, cuddled the bundled newborn against her breast, where it suckled.

"*Her,*" Sage corrected. "She's a girl."

"Well, what are you going to name *her*, then?"

"I'm going to call her Lucy."

"*Lucy*? That's a dumb name," Carl said. "She's already a lucy. Look at her."

"Do you know what the name 'Lucy' means?" Sage asked Carl. He shook his head.

"Josie," Sage turned her attention to a ghostly white-haired girl, "tell him what it means, what I told you last night."

Josie, shy, seemed to have to wrestle the words until they came out. "Lucy means 'bringer of light.'"

"That's right. And that's why I want to call her 'Lucy,' because she'll bring light into this dark world of ours."

Irene held Alex, her touch cool and strong and sure. "Someday," she said to him, her voice a whisper, like soft rain on leaves, "someday it'll be okay. I promise."

Although sure of nothing but the loss he felt, as black and deep as the river of night sky he'd slept under, Alex nodded. Her words were tiny things, but because they were jagged with her own loss and love and hopefulness, they burned brightly through his dark sky, saving him, even if only for a moment.

ACKNOWLEDGEMENTS

I have been well-supported in my writing through the amazing community of writers in the Southeastern Region of the Federation of BC Writers, in particular, special thanks to Barb Turpin, who was there in the beginning; through the on-line SF Canada community; and through my teachers and mentors along the way. Specifically, thank you to Tom Wayman, Caroline Woodward, Verna Relkoff, Rita Moir, Sally McBride, and Dale L. Sproule. Thanks also to my BC Ambulance Service crewmates in Winlaw, Nelson, Winfield, and Kelowna for their support and interest.

In the work of researching and writing **Burning Stones** I owe debts of thanks to several people who patiently answered my questions: Deb Thomas for her help with library- and librarian-related information; Don Pedersen for everything about guns, hunting and all things lethal; Karen Leman and Sherry Antonishen for pointers about the art of running; Randy Harris, RPF, and Kristine Sacenieks, RPF, for everything about wildland fire behavior and firefighting; and, Corey Viala and Elizabeth Nunn, respectively, for their gracious hospitality while I was waiting for my transfer to the Okanagan (the final third of **Burning Stones** was written in their homes).

This novel wouldn't exist without the friendship and keen eye of Holly Phillips (acclaimed author of **In The Palace of Repose** and **The Burning Girl**), who has been my first and best reader since our Kootenay School of the Arts days, and who kindly told Sean Wallace about my novel.

continued

Sheri, Andrew, and Faye, thank you for your love, support, and encouragement; and, Mom and Dad, thank you for raising us in a house with a really big dictionary, and for making trips to the public library a regular part of our growing up.

Finally, I live the most extraordinary life with my partner, Christine, our two dogs, four cats, Amazing Live Sea Monkeys®, and numerous tropical fishes. Christine, thank you for your love, laughter, and everything.

Steven Mills
February 2006
www.stevenmills.com

Printed in the United States
62172LVS00002B/84